$HADOWORLD

Veil of Shadows

Ash was an orphaned street urchin who grew up in the gutters of a desolate medieval city; his bitter youth spent picking pockets and snatching trinkets from the wealthy to survive.

Over the years his art for stealth and sharpened skills had drawn the attention of the Thieves Guild who took him into their folds. Little did they know that the boy's tragic past would one day find itself woven within the treacherous schemes of a mysterious spider cult.

As of late, a series of chilling murders have befallen several nobles within the privileged upper districts. Their gruesome deaths had appeared to be centered upon an ancient skull, a cursed relic which had recently found its way into the hands of a rich collector. There were few who would trespass upon the strange realms of witchcraft and dark magic ...but a master thief does not fear those who dwell in darkness, for he is one with the shadows.

Titles by Michel Savage

Faerylands Series
The Grey Forest
Soulstorm Keep
Sorrowblade
Ivory

Shadoworld Series
Shadow of the Sun
Veil of Shadows
Shadows Gate

Outlaws of Europa
Rebels of Alpha Prime

Hellbot • Battle Planet

A Couple of Zeros

Forgotten Future

Broken Mirror

Project EVE

Witchwood

7

෯෨ඏ

Table of Contents

middle of the night while a pompous judge who was dictating my case had sentenced me to immediate execution; whereupon I was swiftly thrown back into my cell without being allowed a word in my own defense. My head was to be removed from my shoulders come dawn. There was someone behind this farce. Someone had it in for me ...I just wasn't sure as to who, but I was damn well going to find out if I could manage to weasel myself out of this situation. Within the gray and dismal city of Stilgrave, the shadows themselves have eyes; and the few moments of an inconspicuous street urchin whispering through my basement cell window was a way to pass words to the ears that needed to hear them.

The ragged smudged-face child melted back into the bustling crowd unnoticed. The juvenile was one of the countless orphans with hungry eyes and nimble fingers; skilled as pickpockets and shoplifters who traded stolen trinkets for food and shelter. Such adolescent miscreants were also valuable messengers who could travel like the wind through the labyrinth of broken alleys among the cobblestone streets. Many of these strays were couriers of gossip and information whose confidential services could be hired for the right price, and old man Beren was one of them.

Beren was my private fence for most of my ill-gotten gains who exchanged my contraband for coin, and from our dealings over the years the portly merchant owed me more than a few favors. Besides, without me around to line his pockets with stolen goods there would be a lot less jingle of silver in his pockets. Luckily, a fair majority of the citizens who dwelled within Stilgrave were religious zealots who were blinded by fearful superstitions hand-fed to them by the grace of the charlatan priests of their local order.

The horde of peasants eager to see blood that morning

The Headsman

I was still a little shaken, my close brush with death still lingered; feeling an odd mixture of adrenaline and anxiety which coiled itself into a sour knot in the pit of my stomach. I had recently spent the last few months holed up in the palace dungeon after being caught red-handed taking a private tour of the Lord's estate and pinching a few valuable trinkets during my moonlit walk of the grounds. It was supposed to be an easy job, to relieve his Eminence of a few small burdens among his glittering riches while he was busy out entertaining his guests in the courtyard as they enjoyed the festivities.

It was the Feast of the Autumn Solstice our lords and ladies were celebrating at the private gardens, however, there weren't supposed to be any guards patrolling the upper chambers. In hindsight, I should have listened to my gut instinct and faint suspicions that this had all been a setup. I had entered through the upper terrace to the bedchamber as silent as a shadow, and had been busily snatching up jewelry and other baubles scattered about as if they had been intentionally lain out on display, when the chamber door suddenly burst open. The two-score of guardsmen who cornered me was my first clue that this had been a trap, the second, was the mock trial of my trumped-up charges which followed.

Get caught in this city and a thief might get a lashing or a few days bound in the stocks on public display. If the victim of the heist was of the upper class and had any influence, the burglar could expect a branding by hot irons or lose a hand at worst. I knew better than to be surprised when I was dragged into an empty courtroom in the

SHADOWORLD – Veil of Shadows

The Grey Forest
P.O. Box 71494
Springfield, OR 97475

www.GreyForest.com

Cover art by Michel Savage

ISBN: 978-09719168-3-8

First Edition: March 2019

Printed in the United States of America

0 9 8 7 6 5 4 3 2 1

Shadoworld
VEIL OF SHADOWS

MICHEL SAVAGE

Dreams are but a shadow
of something real
ଯଓଗ

www.**GreyForest**.com

were cheering on, but their insults and jeers were dulled by the grinding pain of the iron shackles chaffing at my wrists. I was dragged from my cell and out into the chill of the morning air of the courtyard and thrown face down upon the hard wooden rack of the raised blade of the guillotine. With little formality, the lever was promptly pulled and the anchor pin released, but with a gasp of breath, a sudden silence fell over the crowd when the sharp blade seized-up within the rigging halfway towards its fateful journey towards my exposed neck. Like a rising ocean wave, the mutters and whispers of the miracle grew louder, that it was an act of their prophetic deity by which my life had been spared.

Behind the soiled mask of my burly executioner, I glimpsed the confused look in his red, blurry eyes. By the outcry of the crowd and their overwhelming rise of appealing voices, which demanded that I was to be set free while they praised their divine prophet. Taking the opportunity at hand, several hooded peasants suddenly vaulted themselves upon the deck, whereupon I was quickly unshackled and whisked away by disguised members of my guild and ushered beyond the hails of the crowd towards safety, but not before looking over my shoulder to see the stifled glare of a robed figure standing upon the overseer's balcony. He was a gaunt apparition of a man, who appeared to storm away in heated anger at the revelation that I had been spared.

The fazed, dreary eyes of my executioner that morning was no mere accident of fortune, for Beren had called upon the talents of a shapely tavern wench to keep the man up drinking spiked mead, among other sinful diversions throughout the previous eve, to guarantee that he overslept into the coming dawn; and as such, failing to make it to his post that morning to check that the rigging's were in proper order, per his duties. As I sat in my cell the evening prior,

I could overhear the prison guards who had gathered by torchlight to gawk and jeer at the spectacle of the drunken headsman, while he groaned like a goat during the pleasures of fornication as a well-endowed whore rode his naked torso in the hay of the horse stables, in full view for all to see.

While the guards were distracted, another member of the Thieves Guild snuck into the dark courtyard and set the blade of the guillotine in position before he jammed a solid granite pebble into the channel of the rail. As a finishing touch, he gently placed a handful of fine goose feathers upon the top edge of the steel plate, which were carefully held in place by several pinches of silver shavings.

As the stage for the spectacle was set, when the blade of the guillotine snagged in the rigging, those in the crowd close to the gallows gasped in awe as they witnessed the shimmering of silver glitter in the morning sun and a flutter of white dove feathers appeared, as if from thin air, to shower down upon the holy scene. In their awe, those devout to the Church witnessed that I must have been spared by the blessing of their gods. The rising babble of their righteous preaching were spewed towards the boggled guards, who themselves, were promptly overtaken by the fever of the chanting crowd and their demands to set me free. A young watchman hastily unlocked my shackles with shaky hands, and edged me off the steps of the worn platform to ease the tension of the howling mob who were keeping the anxious guards at bay. Though embraced by shock while a moment of relief escaped my lips, I didn't question the opportunity I was given and made my hasty escape from the gallows by the protective escort of the Guild.

* * *

"You dodged a close shave, Ash," Beren remarked as we sat in the backroom of his shop, "I hope you appreciate that

I had to barter an unpleasant deal with your Guild Master to orchestrate that little rescue from the gallows, and by the powers that be, I'm surprised it actually worked!"

"I would thank you, but I know you would only use it as leverage against me another day," I groaned while rubbing my sore and bleeding wrists as I wrapped them with brandy-soaked bandages.

"Hah, you're damn right I would," Beren chuckled, "and for this, I assume that we're all square?" The old merchant held out his hand for me to accept this deal. It took me a moment to contemplate how many favors he owed me that I would be relinquishing in this sudden gesture of good faith, but finally grasped his forearm, and him mine; which was the ungentlemanly, but customary handshake as a gesture of trust between men of dubious character like ourselves. There, in fact, is honor among thieves... but only as long as there was an advantage to be gained by it, of course.

"I don't get it, Beren, you could have just squared your debts by letting the blade fall across my neck; so why go through all the effort to save my sorry hide?" I asked with a glint of doubt flickering in my eyes. The truth was that Beren would have owed nothing to a dead man, so there must have been another motive behind his ambiguous act of generosity.

"Why so suspicious, Ash; we are friends, are we not?" Beren jeered with a fake smile, "And by no small measure you're also my best customer; so I think of looking after you as a wise investment," he admitted.

"*Humph*, well that makes much more sense than any sentimental drivel you can offer," I granted, "but as you can guess, I still have a little problem at the moment."

"Yes you do, old friend," Beren grinned as he took a shot of honeyed rum and leaned forward to speak to me in a whispered tone, "there is someone who wants you dead;

someone of influence who has apparently pulled a lot of strings to have you framed," he breathed with the stench of liquor wafting about him.

I contemplated his words and thought back at the list of suspects I had made while I was languishing in my cell. Someone had left me to rot, which caused me to ponder the question as to who that might be. I had apparently crossed someone powerful without knowing it and they had gone to great lengths to make me suffer. Was it because of something I had taken, or someone I had stolen from? The real question was; who was it that had ratted me out?

Compulsive liars and braggarts are a bad combination, but I was neither of those. Any dealings with Beren or the Thieves Guild were strictly confidential, so the only alternative was that there must be a mole within our trade who had set me up to take a fall. The only other alternative that might apply was far more disturbing ...that I was being stalked.

"Do you know who it was?" I asked Beren as I leaned away from his fetid breath.

"Not a clue," Beren snapped as he sat back to take another swig from his cup, "but I may know someone who does," he answered as I waited for him to refill his drink, "I'm not exactly *agreeable* with the upper class, as you can see," he noted to his unkempt figure and the dingy shop he called home, "nor am I exactly the kind of fine gentleman of persuasion who gets invited to their lavish soiree's and dinner parties," Beren gestured as if he was dancing in his chair while sloshing his rum about the floor in his antics, "however, I am acquainted with a certain individual within their circle who may be able to get you some of the answers you seek."

"And how is it that a lowly merchant of stolen goods in the back alleys of Stilgrave would have an acquaintance in high society?" I responded towards him with a sharp edge of skepticism in my tone.

"Ah, well now," Beren grinned as he put down his empty goblet only after realizing its spilled contents were now no longer within the cup, "not all of high society was high born. A few ...not many, but a few, are the worse swindlers and cheats you would ever cross, who could outshine any veteran of the Thieves Guild, mind you," he added with a drunken slur, "they are worse than any of us rogues who wander these filthy streets; because they don't steal to survive like you and I, and pretend to be someone they are not. There's not much honor in wearing a mask, but someone acting to be our betters, when they're absolutely *not*, is just downright sinister!" Beren spat at the distaste of those people who displayed such a counterfeit character.

In Beren's line of work, fake jewels and forgeries were a mockery of his trade, so I could see how he would detest phonies, especially so in the upper society of Stilgrave. They were a class of pompous aristocrats whose lavish estates were always warm in the winter and their tables lay heavy with exotic cuisine, while the destitute children on the streets shivered in the cold, wandering the dark alleys with empty stomachs and hunger in their eyes as they fought the rats for scraps of bread. The upper class was the detestable side of humanity, which is why I held no sympathy for stealing from those overburdened by their wealth. Beren had a point; with all their drama, and scheming, and backstabbing one another, the pretentious nobles were far worse than any feral rodent that ambled through the sewers. At least you could tell a gutter rat when you saw one, and you don't see rodents dressing up in jewels and finery, and pretending to be something else than what they are.

"So who is this contact, and what can they tell me?" I inquired to my old associate.

"Ah, well now, Ash, there's the crux. You see I need a

certain item to coax him into cooperating with the line of questioning I ...ah, I mean '*we*' will be applying; and I was hoping you would offer your talents of persuasion in this situation," Beren answered.

"So you want me to do you another favor and steal something for you?" I asked bluntly.

"Oh, no, no, not a favor per se ...think of it as a means to an end to secure the answers you seek," Beren added as if to somehow sway me from seeing straight through his transparent manipulation; but this was a glaring trait of his character I had become well accustomed too.

"Spit it out, Beren. You know I have no appreciation for suspense," I advised with a cold stare. I had suffered through a great deal of grief these past few moons and though patience was the virtue of any good thief, mine had been worn thin like the bruised skin around my wrists.

"There's a flashy lad up in the Ivory Quarter by the name of Vale, and word is that he has recently come into possession of a certain relic of immeasurable value," Beren advised, "and if by chance that relic should go missing, Vale could be swayed to do anything to get it back."

"A relic?" I asked with curiosity, for holy artifacts were the keepsakes of the Builders; a local religious order that followed the doctrine of their long-dead prophet they called 'the Architect'.

Such fanatics placated themselves to mummified bodies of their saints, as if their dried cadavers were something to be worshiped. Anyone with a mind of their own could see that the Priests of their Order were the worst kinds of crooks and scoundrels, and were the type of men who would steal both your will and your coin in exchange for empty promises of a lavish afterlife. It was the worst kind of con, to steal the hard-earned money from one's family as an act of faith merely to embroider their pale robes with golden threads. These pious clerics were skilled liars who offered extravagant pledges they knew they could never deliver.

Distasteful as it was, men like that were at least semi-predictable. It was the twisted minds of their followers who were the real cause of worry. Their disciples would do anything in the name of their prophet at the slightest whim of the priests; solely on the scant promise of a better life after death. For many peasants of the lower districts, anything was superior to the misery of their current existence, so they let the clerics of the Builders fool them into giving their pitiful lives an ounce of meaning for a hollow icon in return.

"Yes, this so-called relic is a strange thing. I was told it was a skull covered in ancient carvings found within the maze of tunnels beneath the minister's palace." Beren noted with a raised brow.

"That place is a stronghold, and one of the oldest structures in the city." My thoughts trailed off as I remembered the primeval stone that comprised of its sturdy foundations.

"Quite true, and word has it that the palace was built upon what turned out to be an ancient burial ground of a forgotten cult, one which had existed for many centuries here before the city was founded," Beren whispered as if the walls themselves were listening, "...they even say this skull has mystical powers, which is why Vale spent a pretty coin to secure it; being the collector that he is."

"But why bother with all the cloak and dagger when you can just buy the information from him for a sack of silver, and simply expose who put a target on my back?" I asked.

"To attain his current position among the upper class, Vale has made a few enemies along the way," Beren conceded, "and he knows he would never get the chance to spend his wealth if he ratted out the wrong people. However, this exotic artifact is something he's personally grown a bit fanatical about; and my guess is that it's the only thing that will sway him to risk his own neck to retain."

It sounded like a long shot, but I could trust that when Beren found a worthy mark he had usually done his homework first. I didn't look forward to scoping out the Ivory Quarter. It was a section of the city on the upper tiers constructed of alabaster, which is how it got its nickname. Although the high society of Stilgrave made it a place to build their manors and villas; it was also heavily guarded with the armories finest. The fancy tile roofs were difficult to run, and the abundant lamps made it problematic to find a friendly shadow for a thief to dwell; so members of the Thieves Guild usually avoided the area because of the inherent risks involved.

Beren gave me a map of the quarter and warned me that Vale was a cautious lad. Let alone, whoever had put a mark on my head was still out for me, so I would need a convincing disguise. My old friend had me covered on that one. In his basement storeroom he had a chest full of costumes from the theater; leftovers from plays long past; pawned to him by a traveling show which had fallen upon hard times.

To get close to Vale, I knew I would need to blend into the atmosphere of the upper class wandering the district. There was little chance I could pass myself off as a member of high society, and the thought of taking the role of a servant did not sit well with me. Beggars and vagrants who wandered into the upper quarters looking for handouts were given the stiff boot by the local guards. The security there was paid well to filter out the undesirables, which was the appeal of living there.

I determined that posing as a courier would be the best tactic, where a new face wouldn't fall under suspicion. However, my particular face was still being sought, and I couldn't wear my dark mask in the role I was about to play.

Beren had a solution to that problem and presented me with an odd array of fake beards and sideburns to choose from. With a touch of make-up powders and various pastes, I could look much different from my usually stern mug.

Rifling through his outfits, I came up with a costume I thought was appropriate until Beren stepped in and corrected my apparent lack of fashion. Adding in a flashy scarf and brooches with an oversized cap, I felt like a peacock in a hen house. The old shopkeeper made the point that the outfit was meant to blend in with the crowd, not for skulking in the shadows. At his demand, we practiced a few voice lessons until Beren was satisfied by adding in a sprinkle of flowery words into my vocabulary so that I could mingle into polite conversation when it was called for.

Vale was supposed to be attending a luncheon that day, which Beren described as nothing more than a glorified tea party where the locals could boast about themselves and catch up on the weekly gossip. With a messenger bag full of phony scrolls and letters slung across my shoulder, I was ready to start my task. Beren, being keen of eye, also told me to change my gait; and I had to keep reminding myself to correct my posture. Opening up a hidden door behind his storeroom shelves, Beren showed me a tunnel he used for transporting private shipments.

"What is this you've been hiding, old friend; a secret passage?" I asked with mild surprise, although I should have realized any shady merchant in his line of business would have alternative routes in and out of his shop.

"What?" He charged innocently, "It's an escape route under the city streets in case of an emergency, which just so happens to have a few extra exits to choose from. Just follow the green line attached to the wall and you'll find your way to the upper district," Beren pointed to the pine-colored cord where several bells were attached on his end, "and ah, as one friend to another, don't tell anyone about this tunnel, eh?" He offered with a hard smile while his eyes turned up towards a set of armed crossbows lining the ceiling above.

After the false wall closed behind me, my nocturnal eyes picked up several shafts of light cutting in from the streets above, which made navigating the passage possible without the need for a lamp. I observed several strung lengths of cord dyed in various colors lining the walls, all leading back to Beren's storeroom. Many of them had small bells attached to them as if to give the shopkeeper notice of a shipment approaching through the passage. Likely so that he could disarm the numerous booby-traps he had in place to protect this secret route from unwelcome guests.

Time dragged on while I cautiously made my way through the long tunnel until I crossed upon a ladder which led up to the surface. Lifting the hatch above, I found myself in an inconspicuous corner of a lavish garden at the edge of the Ivory Quarter; the entrance itself was cleverly hidden behind a row of cypress trees. Once above, I place the camouflaged lid back over the shaft and waited until I was sure there were no eyes turned my way before I stepped out from the garden wall.

Vale's apartment was at the back end of a manor, so I scurried off to find him; minding my step and posture as Beren had schooled me to carry myself in public. Personally, I felt naked without my dagger strapped to my chest, but Beren strongly advised against it. The guards that patrolled these streets for the elite were observant and could spot such hidden weapons and suspected prowlers. Many a burglar and pickpocket had been caught by the vigilant City Watch that roamed the upper district, and was avoided for the most part by us roguish types for that reason.

However, Beren did provide me with a few choice wires

for use as lockpicks which he had inconspicuously sewn into the hem of my vest; arranged in such a way to be easily used in an instant. This job was supposed to be a simple snatch and grab, and I would rather avoid any unpleasant violence lest it bring the city watch down upon my head. The chance of being exposed once again to my mysterious antagonist was too great if I came boots-to-boots with the guards, so I kept a wide berth from them as they strolled through the cobbled lanes.

I chose an elderly lady to approach as I was betting that her eyesight was dull from age; even though she was wearing an uncomfortably low cut blouse that flaunted her sagging breasts. Asking her for directions to the tea party where Vale was attending, she noted that she knew the collector himself, and invited me with a surprising pinch to my rear if I would join her to the brunch as her personal escort. Doing my best to stay in character, I politely declined as she flashed a well-practiced pout which only accented her wrinkled face as we parted ways. My plan was to search Vale's abode while he was busy at the luncheon, so as not to be disturbed while I was trespassing in his quarters.

With a courtly nod to the passing lords and ladies along the way, I hastened my course to the manor while cleverly avoiding the staff. With my hat low, I made my way through the sparse crowd while pretending to inspect the names scribbled on the counterfeit letters which I carried as props. After making my way to his front door, I found it securely locked. The entry was comprised of thick oak with gilded iron hinges, but its placement was far too conspicuous as it faced the open street. I pretended to knock on the door as a pair of city guards strolled by and glanced my way. A moment after they stepped out of sight I could feel the paste and makeup starting to drip down my face as it mixed with nervous sweat.

Picking the lock while exposed out here in the open would be too chancy, so I glanced up to see if there were any open windows within reach. With a spot of luck, I found a lush tree with limbs that stretched out to a small balcony around the side. Taking a moment to step back out on the street for lack of foot traffic, I took the opportunity to ditch my messenger bag behind a bush and climbed up the trunk like a skilled acrobat. The trade of a thief made one nimble when you are used to jumping from roof to roof and climbing through windows. I made short work of the sturdy limb and dropped down upon the narrow balcony attached to his suite.

The outer shutters were open, so I slipped into Vale's apartment without further delay. I had expected the lavish retreat of a playboy with candelabras and carved filigree, but what I discovered within confounded me. The darkened apartment was untidy and littered with strange and exotic items; few of which I could identify. Lying scattered about the tables were severed animal paws and several antiques of questionable quality.

There were various jars filled with a milky substance and aged wooden idols rife with cracks. Pinned upon the wall I found several sketches of a peculiar emblem that resembled the body of a spider. Surrounding its image were markings of some obscure language I could not decipher. A vast majority of the contents looked like random bits of junk collected from some lost expedition in the wilds. None of the larger items I saw lying around had any particular value that I could discern.

I was only here for the skull, but saw no harm in pinching a bauble or two that might be worth a silver coin. Sitting within the center of the table there was a space which had been cleared away from the other relics. Within this barren area sat a heavy black cloth covering something spherical under its veil. I dared to step forward to inspect what lay hidden beneath when I heard the latch on the door being turned; it took but an instant to dash into the dark shadow of a large wardrobe cabinet as I hid from sight. For a moment I had feared that a city guard had seen me leap onto the balcony and trespass within, but the visitor turned out to be the collector himself.

Beren had told me about this fellow, but his description of the lad was strangely off. Vale was finely dressed and carried himself well by his stride; however, he had a haunting face that appeared far older than the man was purported to be, which made me wonder at first if this was some other intruder who had found his way inside. After making his way up the stairs, the man removed his coat and set it upon the hanger in the study and made his way through the apartment as if he was familiar with the place. He then began muttering to himself like a madman about nameless liars who were out to get him and how he was going to exact his revenge.

I watched from the shadows as he approached the bundle at the center of the table beneath the black cloth, and stroked its top gently as though it were a lover's caress. Leaning forward and placing both hands upon the table he began to speak to the object softly; as though it were somehow listening to his every word. There were odd pauses in his speech, as though there was a missing part of his strange conversation I could not overhear. From where I stood, I could not discern his words precisely, but they contained a dark overtone of murder and retribution.

At first, this did not seem like the same person whom Beren had told me about; yet the description of him was more than just vaguely familiar. Suddenly, without warning, the man stood back and turned to remove some small item from a desk drawer and promptly stormed out of the room while snatching his coat along the way. A rattle of boots down the entry stair and the door slammed behind him; while a turn of its heavy lock confirmed this unusual character had possessed the key to the flat.

I quietly stepped from the shadows and made my way over to the table where Vale had stood a moment before, and with mild apprehension, I dared to peek beneath the ebony cloth lying before me.   My suspicions were confirmed as I glimpsed an intricately carved skull lying beneath its folds. It appeared ancient, yet the sparse light revealed its texture was not dry as one might expect, but appeared to have been oiled as though fresh from the grave. The rendered emblem of the spider displayed upon the walls was set upon its forehead in a patina of age-worn gold.

With but a moments' hesitation, I quickly bundled up the skull within the very cloth it had been covered with and hastily made my way to the open balcony. Standing in this study surrounded by these bizarre remnants made me feel a strange unease.   Even if there was anything of value in Vale's apartment, it wasn't worth lingering here any longer than needed. My gut feeling told me to leave.

I made my way to the window and climbed my way down the wall using the embellished stonework. I snatched up my courier bag and stuffed the skull inside, covering it from view with the letters and scrolls. Moments later, I started to feel hot and unsteady and could sense the makeup upon my face peeling away, so I hastened my stride at the risk of drawing attention to myself. I wasn't the superstitious type but what I had just witnessed made me feel oddly uncomfortable, and I wanted nothing more than to rid myself of this unnatural souvenir I had acquired from Vale's collection.

I stumbled into the gardens and cautiously made my way to the subterranean shaft.   Through the musky dark, it seemed as though it took forever to retrace my steps on the route through the tunnel while making sure to pull the green line that rung the bells, so that Beren would know I was on my way back. For some reason, I began to feel sick and dizzy as I slipped through the secret door back into Beren's storeroom. Dropping the bag from my shoulder, I grabbed for a pitcher of water to chill the sudden fever. Beren took the bag and peeked inside as a smug smile of satisfaction washed across his face.

"Well done, Ash. Hey, are you okay there, old pal?" He asked with a hint of concern as I was washing the mess of makeup and paste from my face, which had gone suddenly pale, and I was overcome by a bitterness rising in my throat as though I was about to vomit.

"I just need a moment," I breathed wearily, and took a seat on a chair, "...how old did you say this guy, Vale, is supposed to be?"

"Oh, maybe 30 or so, give or take a few years. He is quite a charmer I've heard, and not unpleasant to look at; so the ladies say," Beren confirmed.

"I think we crossed paths when he almost caught me in his suite, but the man I saw appeared as though he was nearly twice that age; with sunken eyes as if he had seen a ghost," I responded as I felt the smothering nausea begin to subside. I was wondering if it was the bad air in his study that I had reacted to; although I held an uneasy feeling that there was still something yet unexplained.

Beren reached into the bag to remove the black cloth and lifted out the skull with one hand to examine it in the light. Every inch of it was covered with ancient runes and designs woven around its cranium. There was something unsettling about its scent and the way its slick surface struck the light which I found deeply troubling. I couldn't hold down the feeling that this unholy artifact was something that belonged in a crypt and should have stayed buried in the dark.

Night Sparrow

Beren promptly placed the relic in an iron-bound chest, which he locked and hid out of sight.

"There, now we have leverage against Vale for the information you seek. When he becomes desperate after a day or two, I will have a message delivered to him outlining an ultimatum to cooperate should he wish to have his precious little artifact returned," Beren smiled, "In the meantime; you're welcome to use any of the outfits here to conceal your movements about the city until we find the individuals who are after you."

Beren's advice made sense. Whoever had me framed would be fuming that I had escaped the gallows and likely would have eyes on the streets to locate me and finish the job. I had a secret apartment on the lower end of the city which was held under an assumed name. My coming and goings were unpredictable since I rarely ever used the front door but instead chose to use the rooftops as my route of choice. I bade the old shopkeeper farewell as dusk approached and made my way out into the night wearing a loose black ensemble from Beren's collection of costumes.

Taking the time to scout out my main living quarters from a respectable distance before entering, I saw nothing that would raise my suspicions. I made my way across the rooftops to the chimney adjacent to the window and slid myself in from the concealed handles I had equipped under the awnings for that purpose. I had expected my dwelling to be in shambles if the perpetrators stalking me had found and searched my apartment, but it appeared that nothing had been touched. After staking out my flat and finding my applied tripwires by the doorway still intact, I felt a peace of mind that I was safe for the moment.

Most thieves tend to sleep during the day, but I found comfort in my own dusty bed after spending the last several months lying on the stone floors of the city dungeon. I awoke at dawn to the bitter stench of decaying produce emanating from my small pantry of supplies, which had been left to rot during my extended incarceration. With a grimace, I tossed the spoiled meats and assorted vegetables covered in various shades of mold out the window and took the time to tidy my apartment. Checking the hidden panel I had built into the wall, I found that the array of assorted tools of my trade I kept stashed there had been left untouched.

I was still missing a few key items which had been confiscated during my incarceration, so my next plan of action was to visit the Thieves Guild. Of course, the meeting place was changed every month to keep the local authorities off the scent of our whereabouts. Thus, I had to bump up an old acquaintance, one of which I recognized who had been present at the gallows to help me escape the guillotine that fateful day. I slinked out into the morning light to scan the local alleys for signs left by my fellow rogues; which were secret messages left in code which would only appear as indiscernible odd marks to the common man.

What I read upon these shadow marks led me to the steps of the Ailing Beggar Inn. The tavern itself was located on the east side of the lower quarter where the tramps and panhandlers were as common as cockroaches. There was always a hired muscle stationed at the door to keep out the coinless riffraff who frequently wandered these streets. The stench of sweat, ale, and spiced rum mixed heavily with the stale air; and within a few moments of scoping out the joint, I found who I was searching for.

The man looked as drunk as a fish in a pond, and the puddle of piss by his leg was a fair clue that this was indeed the person who I was looking for. With his battered hat flopped low off the table and a heavy pint in his swaying hands, I slid into the bench across from him and pulled down the scarf covering my face.

The man didn't react at first, almost as if he hadn't realized someone was sitting there before him, but I knew he was measuring me up while staying in character.

"Quite an act you have there, Dirk," I breathed to him.

"Ah, well it's convincing enough," Dirk whispered back under the dark canopy of his farmer's cap, "I thought the splash of urine was a smite clever, don't you think?"

"Anything to keep the guards away..." I responded while trying to crack a grin as the bitter fragrance of it wafted around us.

"When pretending to be drunk out of your gourd, you would be surprised what interesting rumors you can overhear in a place like this," he replied, "and you're welcome, by the way, for saving your neck the other day, Ash," he added.

"My fence told me you and the boys were well paid for your services, so don't go begging for gratitude," I noted, "besides, I need to find out who put me there in the first place, and I'm a little short on gear at the moment," I added with the clunk of a leather purse, fat with coin, onto the soiled wooden table. Dirk's hand reached for the purse but I snatched it back with the tether I had strapped to my wrist. Dirk gave a paltry sigh of grief and slowly withdrew his sticky fingers from the empty air where the pouch had lain a moment before.

"The guildhall has been relocated in the north district next to the Raging Stallion; look for the shadow marks on the 2nd floor. Meet me there tonight after sunset," he finished with a tip of his hat to the soiled table. I knew Dirk wouldn't get up and leave with me that moment and blow his cover, so I slid out the back alley and returned to my apartment long before the first light of dawn broke over the high walls of the mountain city.

Later that eve, I slid back into the shadows as the turquoise sky of dusk gave way to a blanket of stars. Over the smoky rooftops, I made my way to the north end of the city as the bright moon began to rise over the towering mountains. The Raging Stallion was a middle-class saloon and brothel most frequented by the city's guardsmen; making it a risky but interesting location to place the guildhall right under their noses, which the Ward would never suspect. A majority of the guards in this town were nothing more than a bunch of thugs and ruffians in polished boots and armor.

No matter how they were dressed, the sentries hired by the City Ward were merely goons who bore the badge of authority; a charge which they frequently abused upon the populace. Needless to say, the street soldiers were not loved and were merely puppets paid by the upper society to maintain separation between the classes. Most of them were but brutes and drunkards themselves, and they squandered their salaries on cheap rum and loose women on their time off, just like the strays in the lower districts. However, the murder of a guard would bring down the entire City Watch upon one's head, so members of the thieves guild always kept a respectable space from engaging with them.

The purpose of the Guild, itself, was to keep a measured pace of robberies within the city walls, so as not to have crime become so rampant that the city ward would militarize the town under the iron hand of law and order. Street swindlers and con men that became a little too conspicuous in their crimes were quickly dealt with by both the Watch and the Guild itself. It was a precarious game of cat-and-mouse where it only paid off if you kept your balance upon a narrow tightrope. The guild kept order within our own ranks, and men in our field kept the flow of money running from the excessively rich back into the hands of the poor. This was the cycle of life in the secluded domain of Stilgrave.

The city itself was located at the edge of a valley upon the climbing slopes of a vast mountain range that merged near a narrow fjord to the open sea. There were but a select few maritime ships that would visit this remote city, and even fewer dared the perilous journey during the bitter winter months. Every year a handful of unfortunate pilgrims and travelers wandered in, but few ever found their way out; for the teeth of its stone walls and hungry streets would consume them.

Those families with old money and wealth went to great lengths to keep their fortunes and influence; lest they too fade into the stagnant pool of starving vagrants which lined the city streets. It was an ugly reality, and it was the few skilled entrepreneurs like myself who weren't thus blessed as being highborn to silk sheets and a silver spoon, where the mere clink of a coin meant life. The Thieves Guild had access to an ensemble of specialized merchants and craftsmen who provided the gear and equipment for our nefarious trade. Such rogue smiths and shopkeepers valued our business; for as living in a city of desperation where a bag of silver was scarce, it mattered not to them where it came from.

Sneaking through the dark, I found the Raging Stallion saloon where several drunken soldiers were carousing outside in the street; the whitewashed facade of the tavern striking its harsh silhouette against the gray stone of the surrounding buildings. Dodging the guards to get there was more of a hassle than I had planned, for there were no connecting paths between the buildings; making for a great deal of effort on my part without the aid of rope and hook. During my arrest months before, most of my standard gear had been stripped; and now I was in a desperate need to replace them.

Viewing the cryptic sign of our guild scrawled upon the wall on the upper floor, I climbed my way inside the warehouse window. Following the symbols to the entry, while avoiding the corridors that were secretly marked as booby-trapped, upon which end left me standing before a blank wall. I stood there in the milky shadows next to a single candlelit lantern, and after a moment of silence, a single word was whispered through a barely visible crack in the wall.

"Password?" The voice inquired; but I didn't respond, "Last chance, what's the password?" the voice called again while the sharp bolt of a crossbow poked through a section of the wall; placing me square in its crosshairs. Again, I remained silent in the face of death.

After a brief pause, the bolt was retracted and the grinding of stone pulled away the facade to the secret door, allowing me entry within. The sentry with the crossbow nodded as I stepped into the inner warehouse, where a slew of guild members were working at various tables and craftsmen with booths lined with their crafted goods. There was no password of course; as such a ruse employed by the Guild sentry was merely used as the last ward to trick the unwary. Anyone who dared to make such a wild guess or questioned the guardian, would quickly find a sharpened bolt lodged in their throat to remind them of the value of silence.

I made my way down the stairway deep into the bowels of the building where the shopkeepers had made their entry beneath the city streets. Dirk stepped forward and greeted me in our common handshake of forearm to forearm. He was out of his transient costume and dressed in his usual attire; his goatee was trimmed and the man himself was not entirely uncomely to the ladies in his own fashion.

"Ah, my friend, now what can I do to assist you?" Dirk inquired while he held out his empty palm. With a smirk, he accepted the familiar bag of coin I had teased him with previously that morning. Weighing its contents with a few jostles of his hand, he turned and bade for me to follow him into a small corner of the market. There we met a bald and brutish man with a single glass monocle working at his station. Before him were lain out several blades upon an oil-stained mat.

"You need a real blade instead of this pig sticker," Dirk grinned as he nimbly slipped my back-up blade from my belt and stabbed it into the worn wooden counter before us; he then proceeded to hand me one of the shopkeeper's fine assortments. The weapon he chose was an unusual blade which was curved like a cat's claw. "See here, its sharp on both edges making it easy to slit a throat from behind or to gash open the belly of an assailant," Dirk stood back while slashing with the blade mid-air to act out his narrative.

"I try to avoid bloodshed if I can," I answered while snatching the blade from him with a quick swipe and gently placing it back upon the board. Intentional butchery of anyone was simply not my style.

"Okay, okay; then how about this little baby?" he added while taking up a strange blade attached to a horizontal handle. It was made to fit in one's grip, with a single long blade that protruded between the middle two fingers. "With this, you have both power and function," Dirk continued, "the serrated edge can cut ropes in an instant and its broad tip can easily penetrate the thickest armor."

It was an exotic blade with an interesting design but felt awkward and heavy in my hands. For me, a dagger was usually just a tool for prying open windows or hinges and anything else I needed in the field. Dirk had a personal fascination with assassinating the elite class, but his delusional attraction for such violence was kept at bay by the direct order of the guild. Regardless, he was quite deadly with a blade, and I respected his advice.

"I was thinking more along the lines of a blunt device for such instances; which would be fairly less ...*messy*," I suggested to him. Dirk took my reservation to heart and directed me over to another booth where a spindly old man worked with a cluster of intricate tools.

"Ah, then take a look at this," he motioned like a brothel pimp displaying his wenches. Dirk picked up a pair of thin leather bracers and showed their special functions, "See here on the left armguard is a retractable wire, which you grab the handle with your other hand and it serves as a concealed garrote," he pulled the double ring and a flexible two-foot metal wire extended from its cuff. Letting it go, the wire retracted on its own back into its spindle. That I liked, "And on the other arm guard you have a lead weight which attaches to the forearm here, tethered to a braided coil," and with a flick of his wrist a short flail dropped out into his empty hand and he spun it around with notable skill. I was impressed by how fast it was. The small mace was relatively non-lethal for knocking someone out, with its own capabilities to be fatal if called for in any given situation. With both devices conveniently attached to the forearm, it allowed for better mobility.

"Sold! Now show me a sample of ranged weapons," I demanded as I looked around the market.

At another booth, Dirk further presented me with a few new improvements to some current designs of throwing knives, but I found them awkward to aim; so I chose a few sharpened spikes instead since they were cheap and had a variety of alternate uses, such as wall anchors for climbing or setting up tripwires. Many members of the guild were fond of crossbows since they could easily penetrate armor, but I found them a tad bulky, somewhat heavy, and extremely slow to reload in a tight situation. More to my favor, we found a horseman's bow, which was short enough to strap onto my back along with a selection of arrowheads which could also serve a variety of useful functions in the field. While browsing, I grabbed a two-pronged climbing hook and rope which was designed to strap to the lower leg, and Dirk sold me on a pair of boot flaps lined with felt that where curiously fashioned to tug down and fold under the soles of the foot, which enabled one to walk silently on hard surfaces.

With what I had leftover in coin, I picked up some new threads and a studded coif and mantle; all in black of course so I could blend in with the shadows. Thieves like Dirk and his accomplices favored a fast hit and run when they pulled a job; but my own preference was to slip in and out like a ghost, taking a good haul without leaving a trace. It was the mark of a master thief who could do the impossible without being seen. My only stop left was to speak with the Guild Master, who had been informed of my current dilemma.

Koda was older than most of our members, but he was undeniably sharp of mind and skill for his age. He had survived where others had faltered, and escaped from dungeons and prison ships alike. He had been our guild master for the past decade and the other thieves respected his experience, and any fledglings who didn't, quickly learned from their lack of judgment.

We entered the lower chamber and asked for an audience with the sentry posted there, and were eventually granted passage to the inner sanctum. There we found Koda, sitting amongst the elders of the guild as they hovered over a map of the city. Upon it was traced every known route and doorway, like an intricately detailed architectural draft. This was the key map used to plan heists and other acts of larceny in the area and was utilized for choice placement of safe houses for those who needed temporary refuge.

"Greetings, Ash, we have been awaiting your arrival," Koda turned to meet me with his piercing eyes; his thick brow resting above the glare of his chiseled face.

"Koda," I nodded in reply. Guild members weren't exactly subservient to one another, but we had a set of rules we followed which separated us from the common rabble of the streets.

"Come with me, I would like a word with you..." the guild master motioned as I followed him to a private chamber beyond sight of the others. It was a cozy little room where a measure of privacy could be assured. Sitting down across from one another, I couldn't help but ask the one question that had been biting at me for the past several moons.

"Do you know who framed me?" I inquired with a hint of impatience.

"Right to the point; that's what I like about you, Ash," Koda responded as he pulled out a small leather scroll from the folds of his tunic. Unraveling it, revealed a strange set of markings tattooed into the skin.

"What is this?" I inquired, curious as to what it had to do with my situation. Koda handed it to me for my inspection. It was what he said next that made me instantly drop the roll of thin parchment onto the table.

"My sources tell me that hide you are holding, is human skin," he pointed towards the leather scroll, "written in a cryptic language lost to the past, from their analysis."

"Any idea what it says?" I asked, not wishing to touch the leather scroll and left it where it lay. Koda was not so squeamish and pulled it back to his side of the table.

"We're still not sure, but we came across this clue, so we've asked the rest of the guild if they recognize this symbol or might have seen it someplace by chance," Koda admitted as he displayed a small emblem of a spider set in a diamond-shaped border. I recognized it as a duplicate of the one I had found etched upon the brow of the skull and the several parchments displayed upon the walls within Vale's apartment.

"Hmm, interesting ...were there any leads?" I asked, turning the line of questioning away from me. I wanted more information as to what Beren had gotten me involved in before revealing my hand to Koda.

"Not as yet, but do keep your eye out for this insignia, and report back to me directly if you ever cross it," Koda ordered.

"But ...what exactly does this odd scroll have to do with my recent trip to the gallows?" I pressed.

"A particular fence of yours paid our Guild a generous fee to have you retrieved; an amount notably more so than what your life might be worth," he added as a slight insult, "but many within the guild know you possess a higher level of skill than most of these miscreants. Your fence, this Beren fellow, made it sound as if you were an invaluable asset to his business; so we took the job. Before receiving payment, we had one of our scouts follow him and he inadvertently dropped this particular item from his person at a remote location on the docks. For whom it was intended for, we don't know," Koda finished as he tapped his finger upon the etched skin.

"I've known Beren for many years and know he can be trusted," I relayed, "but I will pressure him for answers about this when the time is right," I nodded as Koda met my gesture.

"As to whom it was that framed you for that particular job in the upper district that fateful night, our conclusion was that it was clearly a setup. My sources tell me a group of guards were already stationed inside the mansion and were signaled to capture you. Perhaps you should be asking who baited you for that job, Ash; and maybe your answers lie there," Koda finished. With that, he got up after pushing the rolled leather scroll back across the worn table towards me. "You can hold onto that for now, and maybe someday it will shed some light on your predicament," he stated before leaving the private booth.

I sat there looking at the thin bound hide while remembering the details which had led to my capture several months ago. I had taken the time to scout out a planned party at the lord's manor for the Autumn Solstice, and kept a keen eye on the spending spree he had went on for one of his new courtesans, who was admittedly of a far higher quality than most girls within the city. I had gathered valuable information about the pair and their purchases through several street urchins and first-hand observations; so there was no reason for suspicion which would lead me back to Beren being involved. Perhaps this cryptic scroll was something he had acquired to target Vale for information, but right now I just didn't have all the pieces to the puzzle to make sense of it.

Strolling back into the thieves market, I was confronted by a woman with coal-black hair and striking green eyes. She looked me up and down as if to measure up my stature, while I saw Dirk standing behind her leaning against a post with an amused smirk smudged across his face.

"So, you're Ash?" she declared abruptly, "Koda sent me to keep an eye on you until we discover who it is that wants you dead."

"Koda ...sent *you*?" I stumbled on my words reaching for the logic in her statement. Females in our field were rare, but not unheard of, and I had only seen this girl once or twice in recent years. Thieves don't mix well socially, so I had never gotten her name.

"This is Nyx, the Night Sparrow," Dirk remarked from over her shoulder, "the guild master assigned her as your apprentice ...just until you settle your little problem," he finished with a shrug.

"I work alone, Miss," I breathed, not happy about Koda failing to mention this himself when he had the chance. Although, staying in hiding made life in Stilgrave notably more difficult if my movements were, in fact, being tracked at any given moment; which might well lead me to end up on the sullied floor of the gallows once again. If that happened, I could be assured that whoever had set me up wouldn't wait for the process of a public execution, and I would just wind up dead in my cell.

"I heard that you're one of the best; just let me know what you need me to do," Nyx uttered with a glare of confidence and a tilt of her head. As I tried to sidestep the female rogue, she shuffled herself back into my path. Clearly Nyx wasn't one who liked to be ignored.

"I can confirm she was appointed to keep an eye on you by the top dog, Ash; and I really don't think she'll take *no* for an answer," Dirk stepped forward with a friendly slap to my shoulder. With that said, Dirk disappeared into the bustle of the black market, leaving me with my new sidekick glaring at me with her emerald eyes.

The Dark Weavers

I got the impression I wasn't going to be able to shake Nyx for a while, so the following morning I sent her on an assignment to pick us up a variety of provisions from the central market. She didn't seem too happy about being sent on such a petty errand like some household servant, but Nyx finally accepted the situation that it was a risk for me to be seen in public for the moment until we resolved the identity of my mysterious antagonist. I was hesitant to reveal the location of my main flat to her, so I used a secondary residence which I infrequently used as a decoy. It was a decrepit shanty located on the east district which I employed as a personal safe house whenever the need arose.

"Your rations, your Lordship," Nyx stated with heavy sarcasm as she came through the door and plopped down several canvas bags full of meats and produce.

"And my change...?" I inquired as I held out my hand while looking through the bags. Nyx plopped a few silver coins into my palm, but my open hand remained in place with a look of expectation carved upon my face. Nyx just rolled her eyes with a grunt of annoyance and reached inside her vest to relinquish the rest of my funds she had been withholding. I didn't hold it against her for trying to shortchange me; a thief is a thief after all.

"Go ahead, put it all away in the pantry ...and ah, make us something to eat while you're at it," I motioned while I tucked the minted silver into my pouch.

"Am I your scullery maid or your apprentice?" Nyx barked back, seemingly offended by my remark.

"For the moment, both, and now you're *assisting* me by making a meal while I think about what I should do with you," I cracked back at her. The girl's hard glare met mine, but her attitude soon softened as she began to feel a tinge of hunger after she started stashing away the food. I had to admit that Nyx came across as a self-absorbed brat, but a quota of self-reliance was necessary for this line of work. I too was a lone wolf and didn't like being forced to mix company. If we were to be partners in the midterm, then I needed to know what her skill level was and what I could trust her with.

"How long have you been in the game?" I asked as I plopped down on a tapestry covered chair, the plume of dust that rose from my impact was evidence that it had been a long time since I had used the apartment.

"Robbery and pickpocketing was a way to put food in my belly when I was a kid," she noted while she paused to look at a pair of potatoes she held in her hands at that moment as though she was reliving a memory of the hardship she had endured in her childhood, "and have a distaste for serving others," she added while slamming the spuds into a bucket; though she continued with an evident change of tone as her voice softened ever so slightly, "so I figured I had a talent for it. If you haven't noticed, there are only a few, if not entirely demeaning jobs available for womenfolk in the city, so one day I figured; why not take what you need rather than be someone else's slave?"

I understood her rationale better than anyone. It was true that women in the city had few choices for a decent life in Stilgrave. Even the young and attractive girls were used up equally by the prowling lechers and noblemen with money in high society; and it was heart-wrenching to see them living the lavish life with their old and degenerate lovers one day, only to be seen in rags and covered in bruises on another from the forced abuse they endured. The homely girls were used as maids and servants if they were lucky enough to get a job in the upper district; but such positions frequently turned into bouts of indentured servitude. Those who were less than homely, found unappealing relations with the locals in the lower districts; which was a hard life that could only be escaped by selling their bodies in the local brothels.

Even that life had its risks and sapped them of their spirit for life. It was easy to see that the caked layers of make-up the prostitutes wore were merely an attempt to disguise the way they truly felt inside. It was a sad life for most, and any profit to be had was far outweighed by the amount of dignity leached from their soul. A man like me made a living from observation and I had a knack for reading situations. Like Nyx, I preferred to make my own way without living under somebody else's thumb.

"And what is your skillset? Lock picking, forced entry...?" I asked, when a small knife flashed through the air and embedded deeply into the backrest near my head, "...hmm, throwing daggers I see," I finished as I pulled the blade out of the chair where it had pierced the fabric; a mite unhappy about the hole it had left.

"I can hold my own in a fight," she bragged, "but acting the innocent bystander while swiping things without being noticed is one of my specialties."

"Good," I blurted back to her as I flicked her small blade into the wooden potato bucket sitting on the counter in front of her, where it stuck with a satisfying '*thunk*', "I'm down a few coins since my unfortunate setback these past few months and need a quick haul so I can get back on track; and perhaps get some intel along the way if you can make yourself useful," I admitted.

"Of course; do you already have a mark? What are we after?" Nyx asked with a tone of throttled excitement.

"I need to scope out a particular mansion in the ivory district where I was captured to see if there was anything I had missed. You're invited to come along if you think you can keep up?" I slid my words in with a raised brow.

A mixed look of elation and intrigue gleamed in her eyes as Nyx began to boil a stew over the fireplace. The city had already dipped into the winter months these past few weeks and the nights could be brisk this time of the year. A good thief made use of the weather; for the winter season meant there would be fewer guards in the night as they were prone to cower indoors to warm themselves and sneak a few nips of brandy to shake off the cold. The new moon was only a few days away, which was the perfect time for skulking in the night.

The chill winds brought in thick fog from the docks which saturated the city; making it easier to travel unseen. The downside was that there were usually more people indoors, which of course, was where all the loot was to be found; so it was a trade-off in a sense. Nyx and I spent the next few days honing her skills at climbing and teaching her the various types of camouflage that could be utilized in the field. She seemed to find interest in my artistry with tripwires and how they could be used as both traps and warning devices. After trading a few ideas about how to approach the mansion, we made a plan to set out just before dusk so that we could reach the ivory quarter and get in position before full darkness fell over the city.

I had made use of the new tools I had acquired at the black market, and made plans to drop by Vale's abode on my way back through the city to see what additional information I might be able to glean. I wasn't too thrilled about bringing the human-skin parchment with me, but I needed it as a reference to search his apartment for additional clues which I may have overlooked before. We scaled our way to the roof of the lords' chambers where I had been accosted several moons ago, and was slightly surprised to find my grappling hook and rope still intact where it had been anchored on the decorative ledge.

Finding this gear unmolested only confirmed my suspicions that my capture was on someone's personal agenda, rather than just a bout of bad luck on my part.

"So this is where you got cornered like a rat?" Nyx smiled as we quietly scouted the rim of the roof while checking for guards below.

"I had noticed something wasn't right about it," I added in my defense, while refusing to entertain the jest in her comment, "once I had got inside, there was too much loot lying around in the open and too many guards who barged in; they were waiting for me, I'm sure."

"But who tipped them off?" Nyx wondered, her mood mirroring the look in my dark eyes.

"That's what we're here to find out," I whispered just before dropping to the balcony below.

The soles of my boots were cushioned by the new felt lining from the accessories I had acquired in the thieves market. The room itself was dark; which made me realize that this alcove was not the lord's chamber as I had originally suspected. A majority of the furniture which had been present before, was now either rearranged or entirely missing, making it appear like an empty storeroom. I had purchased a map of the mansion from a boy who had claimed to be the son of a chambermaid that worked in the household. This left me questioning myself, if I might have been cleverly duped by a common street urchin.

"A thief returning to the scene of the crime is one of the most foolish rules to break," Nyx whispered as she dropped in behind me as I stood silent while scanning the empty room, "...huh, there's nothing here. Maybe they thought this bedroom was too exposed for burglars so they moved his lordship into a different part of the mansion," my apprentice suggested.

Taking my time to explore the room, I noticed there was no fireplace built within it, which was highly unusual.

Where the bed had once been, there were no markings on the floor; nor were there any tell-tale signs that the room had ever been lived in. This led me to wonder if the entire scene had been set up with elaborate props orchestrated to lure me inside. I had triggered a trap which had been purposefully set to catch a thief. As I stepped aside to listen at the door and peeking through the keyhole, Nyx was a tad surprised when I dared to open the chamber door.

"Where are you going?" she whispered harshly.

"To find some answers..." I brushed back over my shoulder to her as I slipped through the doorway and into the darkened hall.

Nyx slid out of the room behind me as quiet as a cat, following close behind. This section of the manor didn't appear to be lived in either, which struck me as odd considering the size of the estate. There were still guards stationed outside; though fewer than I had seen before, which we didn't find terribly unusual for the winter season. Creeping downstairs, we found there were merely a few lit lanterns positioned in front of the windows to give the illusion that the building was occupied; but there was no one else to be seen. It was as if the entire mansion had been left abandoned.

"I thought you said this was a lord's manor," Nyx noted as she relaxed her wary stance upon seeing that nobody was occupying the place. The lack of furnishings and decor, and the musty odor lingering in the air made it evident that this building hadn't been used as accommodations for quite some time.

"Apparently, this was all a ruse. The real question is, was it a set-up to catch a common thief, or was I personally targeted for this ambush?" I asked myself.

Suddenly, we both heard a dull clanking sound echoing from a distant room. Weaving our way through the corridors to the kitchen, we found the noise was coming from the cellar door. We continued with caution as I tested the latch to find it unlocked and we slipped our way down the narrow stair beyond. An unpleasant bitter musk met us as we approached the landing, but there was little that could prepare me for what we found. The room was splattered with dried blood along with several cadavers lying haphazardly about the room.

The noise we had heard was from a chain wrapped around the body of a handmaiden which had been tapping against the wall. She had been hung upside down and was struggling weakly to get herself free. Nyx gave me a glance of utter horror, not knowing what to say; for she had never seen such brutality in her young life.

I slowly approached the poor servant girl with caution; half suspecting this was yet another trap. Her wounds appeared fatal and were bleeding out from long gashes along her torso. She didn't have long to live.

"Who did this to you?" I asked as I helped to wipe away the bloodied smudges on her face while her eyes rolled in wrenching pain.

"The ...the Dark Weavers ...have awoken," she sputtered in a feeble gasp. I went to untie her bound hands and undo the chains to help her down, only to notice a finger from each of her hands had been removed. Glancing around, I noticed that the other bodies had also been mutilated in the same fashion. The index finger from each of their hands had been cut from them. The wet ropes were difficult to untie and I bade Nyx to help me as she stood there aghast in shock. We finally got the chains removed and the girl fell to the floor in a heap, still muttering to herself about the dark weavers.

"What do we do?" Nyx mumbled, knowing that if we called for the help from the guards stationed outside, that it would only result in us both being arrested and likely charged as the prime culprits of this gruesome crime.

With a sudden stifled gasp, the maiden died; her mortal wounds being too severe. I stood up and searched the room, trying to find a reason for this needless carnage. Someone had vacated the premises and had gone to great lengths to silence any direct witnesses to what had transpired here. It was also quite likely that the guards posted outside had no clue as to the horrible slaughter which had befallen these poor wretches.

"What is that smell?" I inquired, wondering aloud. Nyx herself began to sniff the air. It was something strange and aromatic which overlapped the stench of the dead bodies. The fragrance appeared to originate from a white powder dashed upon the cadavers; hinting of some aroma I could not quite identify.

"Is this some type of spice?" Nyx asked as she pulled a curved dagger from her boot and brushed aside a stretch of the pale powder.

Looking down at the floor, I could see that we had left our footprints within the patches of blood and bleached dust scattered about. It suddenly struck me that there were no other telltale signs of footprints from the persons who committed this atrocity leading back up the stairway. Logic would declare that there must have been another exit from this cellar.

"We need to get out of here and report this to the Guild," I confessed to my apprentice, "and I still have somewhere to be this evening. Get word of this to Koda, and meet me at my place before sunset tomorrow," I ordered.

Nyx nodded in compliance and dashed up the stair, leaving small bloody footprints in her wake upon the wooden steps. I glanced around the room once more to search for another passage out, but a bitter chill fell over me; recognizing it was my gut feeling telling me to leave this place in due haste.

I folded up my blood-stained felt soles as I got to the

steps to keep from leaving crimson footprints in my wake and smeared out Nyx's footprints with a rag as I made my way back up to the kitchen. When I passed through the room I noticed several open jars lining the counter by the door, as if they had been left there and forgotten. Racing up the stairway, I made my way back through the hall to my original entry point; hurrying each step as if some evil and unforgiving anguish was chasing me from the cold shadows. Climbing the ledge of the balcony, I made my way to the roof and reclaimed my hook and rope which had been left abandoned.

Thick fog crept in from the docks this time of night and the hour it took for me to reach Vale's apartment seemed to stretch out like a bad dream. My mind kept revisiting that grisly cellar and the chilling look of dread etched upon the faces of the dead servants. Those victims had seen something meant to be kept hidden, and they paid for that secret with their lives. I had seen cold-blooded murder before, but these deaths were something perverted; almost ritualistic.

It was now well past midnight, and I was fairly confident that Vale would be fast asleep in his chambers as I scampered up the familiar tree outside his study and dropped in through the balcony window. My initial intent was to compare the writings on the parchment that Koda had given me with the drawings I had briefly seen tacked to the wall in Vale's study. I wanted to verify this essential information before confronting Beren about his connection with this grisly manuscript, but I instead stumbled upon yet another morbid scene. Vale's study was a disaster as if he had torn the place apart with his bare hands. Nearly every item in his exotic collection of artifacts lay broken and strewn about the room. The single thing that caught my eye was a jar, similar to the ones left in the mansion kitchen, sitting upright on the central table.

In the place where the skull had once rested, now sat a jar full of human fingers; curled and floating in their own translucent wine. The shock of it stunned me for a moment as I put the pieces of the tragedy together. Had Vale discovered his precious artifact missing and tore his study apart in a fit of rage? He had clearly been either the perpetrator or an accomplice to the murder of the servants in the Manor cellar, but I still could not fathom how the two were connected?

Only a portion of the etchings had been left intact upon the walls, and I compared the drawings upon them and the human-leather scroll the Guild Master had given me. The markings were exactly the same. The strange script upon each image varied in their design, but the emblem was precise. Below the image of the spider, it showed an etching of two hands cradling the skull in a curious way upon a radiating spiral. The image itself gave no clues which I could discern from its odd composition. However, now that I had proof this madman Vale and my baited capture in the manor were linked, the only thing left to do was to confront Beren about this matter.

My temper was rarely excited, but I had been through a great deal of misery and literally came close to losing my head over this bizarre turn of events, and now I was certain Beren held the answers to those bleak questions roaming my mind. His leading me to Vale to acquire that accursed skull, while knowing it must have been more than just an item of leverage. Somehow, Beren had used me to attain that artifact for his own agenda. Having been acquainted with Beren for many years, I knew that he mostly preferred gems and jewelry that could be easily exchanged for coin; but dealing with occult relics was neither his method nor his style.

After a moment of thought, I came to the conclusion that I could cut out the middle-man and get some answers directly from this psychotic collector while I had the chance to confront him. I could sneak into his sleeping chambers and have him hogtied before he awoke, and interrogate him at my leisure. Once I was satisfied with the information obtained, I could make him pay dearly for the innocents he had murdered whose bodies lay mangled and rotting in the bowels of the abandoned manor.

Easing my way down the stairwell, I moved like a ghost in the shadows, peeking in from door to door until I found his bedchamber and snuck in. Before me lay Vale, fully clothed as he was stretched out upon the silken sheets. I fashioned a slipknot noose from my climbing rope to secure his arms before he woke, and cinched them to the bedposts in one swift motion. I stood there glaring down at him as I pulled the small hidden dagger from the pendant around my neck and placed its sharpened blade against the bare skin beneath his chin.

"Wake up Vale, I have a few questions for you," I whispered to his face, only to notice that his pale skin was cold and clammy to the touch. He wasn't going anywhere tied the way he was, so I stepped to the ornate cabinet beside the bed and lit a candle set upon its counter. Moving it over to my captive host, I could now see why he had failed to respond; Vale was quite dead.

The collector's face was unnaturally puffed and his eyes were as blank as silver plates. His tongue was covered in a blackish ink that protruded from his swollen lips. Beside his head lay several lifeless toads which I assumed had been removed from the wet jar upstairs. It was clear that Vale wouldn't be answering any questions this evening.

Golden Spiders

A small silver pendant hanging around Vale's neck glinted at me in the dim candlelight. Embedded within it was some object which appeared to be made from bone. Checking his pockets, the deceased collector had nothing else of value except a ring of keys; which I confiscated. I removed my rope and prepared to exit the bedchamber, only to notice upon his cuffs small tracks of the same white powder that Nyx had found scattered around the bloody cellar of the mansion. Glancing back towards his corpse lying on the bed, I discovered the pale residue was also present on his boots.

Taking the candle, I carefully tracked the pale silt of Vale's footsteps to the rear of the apartment where they disappeared under an embroidered rug. Lifting it to the side revealed a hidden trap door that led to a rough dirt tunnel beneath its heavy lid. Daring to venture further, I took a still moment to listen for signs of occupancy below before stepping down into the dark void. The floor beneath was soft, and the air met me with a thick rancid mixture of wet soil and filth.

The earthen passage broke through a thick stone foundation which emptied into the city sewers. It was clear now that this was how Vale made his passage between the cellar of the manor and his residence; by which course, likely held many other such connections throughout the city districts where one could pass unseen. The bitter odors lingering in the sewer tunnels were offensive, to say the least, and no respectable thief would choose a route through such rat-infested filth and rotting feces. Returning up the narrow ladder to Vale's apartment, I replaced the rug and carefully covered my tracks.

The fog flooding in from the harbor always grows thicker just before the light of dawn, so I made my way out of Vale's apartment and disappeared into the mist. Finding my way back to my safe-house, I tried to get a measure of rest before Nyx arrived that evening. My dreams that morning were restless, with visions of rooms drenched in crimson red and a horrible voice whispering cryptic warnings about the dark weavers. I woke in a cold sweat from the disturbing nightmare by the sound of rustling at my feet.

"Are you feeling alright, Ash? You look pale," Nyx noted after she slid through the window. I had always been a light sleeper as it was a habit of my trade.

"Did you speak to Koda?" I responded as I tried to shake off the disturbing dream. Looking out the window, I could see brooding clouds in the sky giving way to a milky blue as dusk approached over tall snow-capped mountains which wrapped the city in their cold embrace.

"I told him what we saw, and he wants you to remain lying low for now. Koda has other members in the guild that can look into this matter," Nyx answered.

Koda was precautious, and I have seen him handle similar situations over the years. However, cold-blooded slaughter of lowly servants wasn't on the agenda of any thief. You couldn't rob a dead victim more than once; that was common sense. Regardless, the working class was the lifeblood of the city who were just innocent peasants trying to survive like the rest of us.

A lord or lady murdered in a lover's quarrel while entangled in a web of scandal or dramatic betrayal, wasn't entirely unheard of in upper society. However, gruesome torture of innocent attendants was something far off the scale that we have ever had to deal with before. It was only a matter of time before Vale's body would be discovered, and the city watch would put one and one together once they found the jar of fingers sitting in his study. It was vital that I confronted Beren in person to wring out what he knew of this eerie situation before that bell should toll.

"Since we didn't find anything of value at the manor, your assignment tonight is to get out and make us some coin while I wait this out," I ordered to my unhappy apprentice.

"And what are you going to do while I'm away?" She asked with a hint of suspicion in her tone as she glared at me sideways.

"I'll be right here trying to work this out on my own," I lied as I pulled out the scribbled parchment while pretending to study its archaic script.

Nyx was the type of person to be naturally skeptical, which was actually a good trait for a thief. We were both more alike than not, and she could certainly tell that I was a lone wolf. She had no justifiable reason to second guess my intentions, so I sat leaning into my chair and drew my attention back to the scroll as a subtle feint. She left by way of the apartment window, but even without looking her way, I knew that Nyx was waiting across the rooftop for quite some time to see if I would depart after she had left. She of course, was entirely unaware that I had a second escape route from my abode.

In front of a carefully positioned lamp, I hung a feathered strand that swayed gently in the evening breeze; which at a distance from the window, gave the illusion of movement inside my apartment. Once that was in place, I removed a dusty panel from the floor beneath the bed, which hid a convenient hollow where the central chimney once stood. With a few iron spikes set into the stone, I had created a make-shift ladder which would allow vertical passage. Slipping out the back alley via the ground floor, I headed off to confront my old acquaintance at his shop.

Beren's security system was fairly amateur, which was

bypassed by the movement of a few bricks and snipping of a rusted tripwire and allowed me to drop into the cellar through an obscured side vent that I had noticed on previous visits. I wanted to catch my old friend off guard so that I could measure his reaction. Of course, Beren's portly stature secured the fact that he was overindulgent with his food and wine, but even so, he didn't have a habit of talking to himself; which is what struck me as odd when I overheard a one-sided conversation coming from his storeroom. At first, I presumed that he had company, so I approached with added caution so as not to be detected.

Moving closer within the dancing shadows from the glowing fireplace in the corner of the room, I was surprised to find Beren alone; hunched over in his armchair. He was muttering to himself incoherently, accompanied by the occasional wild outburst of untethered dialog.

"Who are you speaking to, Beren?" I asked while I slowly stepped into the warm light of the fire while interrupting his thoughts.

My words seemed to strike him like a spear. Beren jerked around towards me; his eyes wide and yellow, with hot sweat prickled upon his face. It seemed to take a long moment for him to recognize me, to which he gradually lowered the dagger he was gripping tightly in his hands.

"Ah, Ash ...I, I didn't hear you come in," the old shopkeeper breathed heavily as he relaxed his nervous posture.

"You seem a little tense, old friend. Is there something troubling you?" I led on to see what he might confess.

"No, no ...nothing, I'm just not feeling well. Might be the turn of the weather, you know," He brushed off an excuse for his erratic behavior as he clumsily knocked over a wine cup he had reached for. I moved around to the front of the light to see that his eyes appeared to be unnaturally blurred.

"I just dropped by to inquire if you've gotten any word

from this Vale fellow, about who may have put a contract out on me?" I baited him.

"Oh, Vale," Beren fumbled for a second cup as he hastily poured himself another drink. More wine splashed upon the floor than landed in his cup due to his shaking hands, "I sent a messenger to deliver a note about returning his little relic in exchange for some relevant information, but I haven't heard back from him, yet. I, ah ...I'm sure he'll come around soon," he stuttered uneasily.

"We can only hope so, for your sake," I pressed, trying to decipher if he was lying to me. It could very well be that Beren delivered an ultimatum letter to Vale's suite, and that his volatile reaction to the news was what had turned him insanely unhinged. However, it didn't appear that Beren was aware of Vale's death.

"Yes, he will, I'm sure. No worries, Ash; I've got your back," Beren smiled anxiously, "You're my best customer, I wouldn't let anything happen to you; you know that."

"And this old skull you had me obtain as collateral; you have it kept in a secure place?" I inquired directly to read his reaction.

"Um, the skull, yes, it, it's quite safe," Beren muttered in an edgy tone, "once Vale responds I'll exchange it for what he knows about your secret admirer," he tried to joke as he raised his half-empty cup.

"Remind me again what was it that made you think Vale, himself, had any inside information about my stalker in the first place?" I demanded in a flat whispered tone; so that the old man knew I was being serious.

"Well, shopkeepers such as myself keep in certain circles, and Vale is an acquaintance of the trade and well known as a collector of odd and exotic artifacts; and I was certain he had a variety of connections in the Ivory District uptown," Beren responded as he seemed to be desperately searching for his words.

"That's interesting; you told me a different scenario before sending me out to obtain that morbid trinket from his flat," I answered, "in fact you stated that Vale had made more than a few enemies along the way during his stint among the aristocrats."

"Well ...yes of course, that too. You know me, Ash, I wouldn't lie to you," Beren offered with a pleading smile.

"I *do* know you, Beren, that's what has me concerned that you're not telling me everything," I granted with a sigh as I pulled out the human-skin parchment and laid it down on the table in front of him. Upon seeing this, the color immediately washed from the old man's face and his mouth fell open in disbelief. It wasn't surprise, but the cold and sterile look of fear.

"How did you get that...?" he began to stutter, "Ash, you don't understand, old friend, you really shouldn't have taken that," Beren barked as he leaned back with a jolt, only to gaze at the ceiling while his thoughts raced, "I need to get that parchment back to the people it belongs to, immediately!"

"And who might that be?" I inquired with a sideways glance while I paced around his chair.

"A group of people you don't want to know..." he muttered back before gulping down the rest of his wine. I had never seen Beren so unsettled in all the years that I had known him. Whoever this faction was, they had him mortally frightened.

"Since Vale won't be giving me any answers, perhaps I can persuade your new friends to accommodate my needs in this situation," I replied coldly.

"What do you mean, why wouldn't Vale...?" Beren began to moan before I cut him off.

"Vale is dead," I put it bluntly for him.

A mixed look of confusion and dread crept upon the shopkeepers face; which authenticated that Beren was unaware of the Collectors demise.

"Uhh, how ...when did...?" Beren continued to stutter in a quiet panic.

"I'm not aware of the method, but when I found him last night in his apartment he appeared to have been dead for a day or more," I offered as an answer to him, "I need you to tell me exactly what he was involved in, and if these are the same people who are after me," I demanded, although, not electing not to include the gruesome details of the dismembered fingers and tortured servants left to rot in the ivory quarter.

"These people, they're part of some type of spider cult," Beren began to mumble once again, so I bade him to calm down and poured him another drink.

I found friendly persuasion to be as equally effective as mild intimidation in such delicate matters. He was still my fence after all; and I didn't want to sever the business side of our relationship. Beren picked up the parchment with trembling hands to examine it again, then immediately dropped it with a look of horror with my next words.

"My sources tell me that was made from human skin," I mentioned as I paced around his chair.

"So it's true; they're a coven of witches who practice dark sorcery," he muttered in response, "You've got to help me, Ash!"

"Oh, so the tables have turned, and now I must repay the favor after all?" I asked with a shrewd glance back towards the tormented man, "I thought they were after *my* head, and now you want me to help *the both of us*, my old friend?"

"You don't understand, these occultists are mad, Ash, and not to be trifled with," Beren remarked.

"Still, it makes me wonder why they would be after a person like myself; since I've never handled any such archaic artifacts before the one you led me to. So, why don't you help enlighten me, old pal?" I offered with a firm hand to his shoulder, while holding him where he sat with an iron grip.

"Uh, who really knows, maybe you crossed paths with someone they knew, or robbed a lord or lady who's a part of their little sect, or congregation; or whatever it's called..." Beren offered off the top of his head. I could tell that he was reaching for answers again.

What he alleged was highly unlikely, since I worked from the shadows and prided myself in being a ghost when it took to completing a job. I would slip in and out without being seen, my pockets full of coin and jeweled trinkets. The only person who would be aware of my identity and the stolen items I bartered, would be Beren himself. Had he ratted me out to someone for a price?

If so, it would have to be a heavy bag of coin to cross me; for the old shopkeeper knew that would be a fatal mistake. That line of thought didn't make much sense to me either, since any corrupt shopkeeper found violating the trust of the Thieves Guild would be tutored in every form of regret known by the edge of a knife. I had known Beren for more years than I could count and he never struck me as being that particular level of stupid. Unanswered questions still lingered, so I pressed him for relevant facts.

"Who exactly were you leaving this parchment for out on the docks several nights ago?" I breathed with a serious tone towards the nervous drunk.

"I, uh, how did you know...," he began to stammer, but caught himself as he could tell I wasn't in the mood for excuses, "I was trading rare artifacts with a special buyer who had wished to remain anonymous. In exchange for this worthless scroll, they left me this," Beren stated as he fumbled for a silver chain tucked around his fat neck. From his collar he pulled out a silver pendant set with a type of bone at its center. It was a close duplicate to the one I had taken from Vale's corpse.

Holding out my hand in expectation, Beren reluctantly pulled the chain off his neck and handed it to me. Taking Vales necklace out of my pocket, I brought both pendants over into the firelight to examine them, it appeared that the small bone inset in each face of the silver pendant was a human tooth. After revealing this fact to Beren, he refused to take his necklace back.

"Tell me where you attained this mysterious scroll, and why the buyer would give you this morbid trinket for it?" I demanded dully.

"I obtained this scroll last Fall from another five-fingered supplier," which was Beren's colorful term for a thief, "along with an archaic assortment of loot I thought might be worth something. The stuff he had appeared fairly old ...like it had been dug up from a grave; but you know I'm not too picky about my sources – as long as I can turn them into coin," Beren granted as he flashed a dim smile that vanished as quickly as it had appeared.

"And where did he obtain these curiosities?" I pushed him to divulge.

"Well, you know I don't ask and don't tell, keeping to our code, old friend; but this guy was a real rookie and kept bragging about an abandoned mine he found outside of the city walls that connected to a hidden complex full of crypts. This guy was pretty sketchy, so I figured he was feeding me a tall tale to make himself look like he was a big-time burglar so that he could up the exchange price on me. He claimed he would be back with a whole load of priceless relics, but after that day I never saw him again."

"And how did the buyer for this scroll contact you?" I asked the old man while he put down his cup and wiped the nervous sweat from his brow with a scarf.

"One day I found an anonymous note slipped under my shop door, from someone that somehow knew I had come into possession of the ancient artifacts, and they promised to buy them off of me for nearly ten-fold what I had paid; and hell, after considering it, I had to admit it would be difficult to move them out of my inventory, including the fact that I couldn't decipher the scroll or even tell what it was for; so I agreed," Beren conceded, "Several weeks later they left another note instructing me to drop off the parchment at a specific spot near the docks, where they had left me a down payment along with that pendant you're holding," he pointed, "and they directed me to wear it on my person so the buyer could identify me when we finally met in person after our initial transaction, so they could pay the balance for the rest of the goods I had obtained."

Beren's story was too far fetched to be made up, so I took him at his word. It made me wonder if Vale had received the same deal from this mysterious sect as he may have well come across similar bizarre artifacts for his collection at any point in his trade, and this anonymous buyer used these strange pendants to mark the salesman without having to risk exchanging names. Unfortunately, the last person I had seen wearing this ghoulish trinket was dead. Perhaps the members of this cult secretly used these pendants to mark their intended victims, rather than as a token to identify their accomplices.

Since a member of the Thieves Guild had intercepted the exchange at the docks before the anonymous buyer arrived; then it was safe to speculate that they would be more than a trifle upset that Beren had taken the token necklace and their coin, while the scroll itself had gone missing. I convinced him that I would take the rest of the looted goods from the crypt and take his place during the exchange the next time they contacted him, and at this suggestion, the old shop keeper was more than happy to agree. Out of morbid curiosity, Beren took the time to delve into some research into the true value of these artifacts he held, to make sure he wasn't being somehow shortchanged in the deal. What he eventually discovered, was a few lines of script located in the dusty religious tomes from the clergy of the Builders, which had extensive archives on a long-forgotten cult once known as the Golden Spiders.

The old manuscripts were from the frontier days before the City of Stilgrave was founded. Well over a century ago, war ravaged across the land as kings and overlords struggled for power across the northern territories. The foot of the valley was the only passable track across the great mountain ranges where the encroaching armies camped and resupplied during their advance. Stilgrave had started off as a small military camp which had begun mining operations in these ore-rich mountains. It was a lonesome garrison that suffered the harsh living conditions, which eventually cost the lives of many men over the brutal winters experienced upon this silent pass; filling its makeshift graveyard, and thus, earning the cursed name of this solitary township.

This was the history of the city erected by its builders; whose credit was gained through the great hardships that earned them their tribute, which blossomed to a devotional level within the misery-worn society that emerged from its rocky foundations. What were once common architects and masons had evolved into a union of devoted workers, as converts who idolized their superiors to a theological level; for lack of any other deities in these god-forsaken lands, they became revered as the givers of life. As a child, I had heard rumors that there were buried shrines and mosques hidden beneath the mountain upon which the city was built; so given its history, it didn't surprise me to hear that Beren's little graverobber might have stumbled across an abandoned mine where bodies had been buried. I'm sure the mountainside upon which Stilgrave stood was riddled with them.

Any open passages had been sealed off long ago when the veins of ore went dry, and those derelict passages were likely dangerous to navigate. Precarious deadfalls and sudden collapses would bury any fool who dared venture into the bones of the earth. The old tunnels had been sealed for good reason. Their forgotten chapels and shrines which had been carved into its living stone had faded away into legend and lore.

Beren enlightened me that what he had learned in the old tomes was that the Builders were not alone in their search for followers, and that such devotees who were weak of mind were all too easily converted into fanatics. The lowest of the laborers that toiled in the mines found oppression at the hands of their rulers; which led them to forge their own doctrine. A denomination where the living prophets of the aloft Builders who ruled them were reflected by the dead martyrs of the spider cult, which practiced dark rites and unholy sacrament in its place.

Suffered hardship and servitude to another's will always breeds dissent, and in the conditions of forced toil, the shadowy sect of the Golden Spiders grew like a festering wound. In those early days of the city, a deep rift had formed between the classes as the struggling workers died under the whips of those who governed the city under the military rule of the time; while the disparity of labor spread to the point where there were those who slept on dirt floors, while others rested in warm feathered beds. It was a familiar tale of mankind being retold, wherever those that struggle to survive at the expense of a privileged few will eventually seek justice by any means. The icon of their revolt came in the form of an eight-legged creature which dwelled throughout the dark passages of the mines, where so many of those poor souls had lost their lives.

Followers of the spider sect came to believe that their fallen comrades were reincarnated into these arachnids found among the great labyrinth of mining shafts. It was a fable retold over the years which had endured even to this day. Their folklore survives in children's tales to beware of lost souls that lived in the form of the small yellow spiders; as young children were warned that if they misbehaved that their bad deeds would be preserved within their tangled webs to be revealed to their parents.

This revelation led me to think back upon the words of the poor servant girl in the Manor cellar who had been sliced beyond recognition, and her strange foreboding warning about the dark weavers. Crawling around in the forbidden mines as he did, that lone desperate graverobber had stumbled across something he wasn't meant to find, and unearthed a forgotten nightmare in its wake. A lot of innocent people had died as of late, for reasons still unknown. Drenched in thought as I stood there within the flickering firelight of the shopkeeper's basement, I knew I had no other choice but to resolve this mystery and find the culprits of these depraved acts of murder; or I would likely find my corpse among their list of victims.

Michel Savage

Forgotten Souls

By the end of the night, Beren had shuttered his shop and gone into hiding, being able to do so without much strain for all of the dirty money he had collected over the years, and he disappeared from public sight. Before parting, he promised to keep in touch by using the countless orphans and street urchins which roamed the roads and alleyways. I didn't like the idea of letting Beren slip through my fingers during this critical juncture but understood that he feared for his life. The old shopkeeper had a valid point and I realized the logic that there would be no inherent benefit to my dilemma if he turned up dead one day.

My next move was to speak with Koda and inform him of the situation. Slipping through the dark streets and alleyways, I made it back to my safe house to await the return of my apprentice. Before I had slipped away that evening I had left several 'tells' around the apartment, which appeared to have been left undisturbed. A shake of fine dust under a window sill or a thread tucked into a door jamb could let me *tell* if any particular way of ingress had been passed by someone other than myself.

It was an ingrained habit I had practiced for years; allowing me a measure of forewarning to verify if the occupants of a targeted house were present before I encroached. Such tactics also helped to preserve my own safety, such as placing a thin pipe or tool balanced in the jam of a guardroom door that would make a clamor when it fell. In my line of work, one could never bee too cautious. It was these skills of self-preservation that defined a master thief from the common burglar.

I made a quick mess around the apartment to make it appear as though I had been loitering there for the entire evening, and proceeded to get some rest until Nyx finally arrived just before the break of dawn. She appeared a little worse for wear, giving me a story about a job she pulled that evening which had almost went belly up.

"Look at this place; have you been lounging around all evening and making a mess?" Nyx complained as she unclipped her boot daggers and dropped a bag of loot on the apartment floor. She went straight for a container of water and began to wash herself off.

"What else am I supposed to do if the guild master wants me to stay out of sight?" I lied, leaving her unaware of my little rendezvous with my old fence in the lower quarter.

"Well, you could clean up after yourself at least, especially while you have guests," she fussed while stripping away the bits of leather armor she had strapped to her wrists and legs, which helped protect from the rough stone and scrapes one gets from clambering over walls and rooftops.

Nyx grabbed an apple and devoured it while she told me about the robbery she had pulled that night. On any other occasion, a professional thief would never divulge the jobs they pulled, but as my assigned apprentice, she wanted insight from my experience to her dealings that evening. She had followed up on a marked job she had recently scouted-out near the docks, one that she had presumed was an easy target. By her description, I recognized it was the old merchant's warehouse that was usually packed with cargo shipments from abroad.

This time of the year the port was usually quiet, for trade vessels rarely traveled this side of the coast because of the risk of ice. Goods and supplies for the city and shops were kept under lock and key in the warehouse. Barrels and crates, and other items stored there, were usually far too large or cumbersome for a solo thief to make off with; which left the main storehouse as a low-value target.

However, Nyx had her eye on the tubby warehouse manager who always seemed to have a fat bag of silver on his person; so she chose to break in and loot his office of any extra coin lying about.

A quick snatch and grab seemed appropriate for the circumstances, and she had already scouted out a way of entry from a precariously placed rooftop window. Lowering herself inside the chilly warehouse by rope, she had made her way to the office and picked the lock to gain entry. The manager's office was a mess of account books and ledgers that littered every shelf and table. She hadn't quite prepared for the challenge of crossing the sealed safe she had found tucked away in the back of the tiny room.

She could have dealt with a padlocked chest; but this device was constructed of heavy iron with a unique triple tumble lock she had never seen before. As aggravating as it was, she was unable to breach the vault. Unwilling to leave empty-handed, Nyx chose to scour the warehouse for anything of value she could pinch. Little did she know that a pair of desperate wretches from the lower quarter had also arranged a bit of larceny that very same evening at the outer docks.

The pair of would-be thieves had commandeered a tattered dinghy and quietly paddled their way beneath the rafters of the docks, beyond the eyes of the patrolling guards; then forced their way into the warehouse through a section of rotting floorboards. They had gained entry in the moments Nyx was slipping out of the manager's office as she noticed the duo while they argued between themselves as to what items in the large warehouse they should swipe. The scoundrels found several barrels of ore while Nyx eavesdropped as they squabbled among themselves about the crates full of spice and grains and how they would be too difficult to barter for a quick coin, and instead, had chosen to commandeer the metal ore, which was notably more valuable, and they reasoned it would be relatively easy to melt down into ingots.

Not having a lick of sense between them, the pair of crooks rolled two heavy barrels of smelted ore and loaded them into their shabby rowboat, while unbridled greed prompted them to snatch a third container and drop it through the hole in the storeroom floor, and onto their flimsy craft below. Any seafarer could tell you that the weight-per-mass ratio had already been strained by the first two casks, which overburdened the rotting wood of the tiny boat, but the two hefty idiots hadn't even bother to consider adding their own pathetic selves into that equation. While lowering the third barrel into the vessel, its rims popped, and the mistress of catastrophe began to moan a tune of cold regret as each barrel displaced and promptly punched through the floor of the boat and sank into the watery depths. The two men followed in their wake, hollering as they fell into the frigid waters like chased pigs pursued by the king's cooks before a royal feast.

In reaction to their debacle, the guards posted outside heard the commotion and were drawn into the storage hold by the clamor erupting from the pair of unhappy privateers. After falling into the drink, the chilly winter waters soon sapped them of any zeal or desire to resist the guards who were laughing their armored-asses off at the spectacle. Taking advantage of this distraction, Nyx slid out through the open warehouse door while snatching several loose items stuffed within the captain's property box that was stationed beside the guardroom door. As amusing as her tale was, I had to warn Nyx against the undue risks she had gambled upon, and calmly instructed her on the alternate measures she should have taken in such circumstances.

"I'll wager those two fools are chattering their teeth right out of their jaws while they shiver in the city dungeons. The guards will be retelling that story in jest for years to come," Nyx smiled as she plopped down her bag of booty onto the table, "Now, let's see what we got?"

While my apprentice began fingering through the bag full of booklets of ships logs and personal trinkets, her eyes brightened as she popped open a small leather bag. The expression on her face as she regarded the two rogues freezing in their cells, brought my thoughts back to that strange relic I had filched from Vales parlor. In hindsight, I should have secured that particular item from Beren before we parted ways; given its assumed value to the members of the spider cult.

"Is it anything of value that can feed us for the next few days?" I asked offhand while my troubled mind wandered back to that accursed skull.

"Well, looky here," she answered as she pulled out several glossy pearls; the reflection of the small luminous orbs glowing in her eyes.

"Ah, well I hope you have your own fence to turn those into coin, since mine has gone incognito," I mentioned without exposing the entire truth, "Those little sea gems will keep us afloat for the next month, but I think we should head over to the Guild again soon; I have a few words to share with Koda."

Nyx was in a brighter mood after attaining her rare treasure; but professionals in our business don't become attached to such shiny trinkets, since possessing such evidence could earn you a pair of chained cuffs from the city guards or a knife in the back from a rival. We had to drop off our cut from this job to the Guild Master anyways, and report the attempted robbery of the warehouse at the port so that the Guild could educate those two rogues about unsanctioned larceny when they find their way out of jail. Permission for jobs was allotted by the guild master to the equal benefit of all members; which cut down on the resentment by our associates who might feel like the available wealth in the city wasn't equally distributed for the taking. This also relieved a measure of retaliatory conduct between rivals and set standards to make sure our practiced craft was equally beneficial to everyone in the trade, rather than being at each other's throats over every silver coin.

Being a lone wolf, I naturally resisted any kind of control; but I could certainly understand how it kept the young pups of the guild in line and out of the trouble they could effectively get themselves, and our expert veterans, into. Twice a year during the equinox, our branch held a tournament where prospective new members could attempt to prove their skills and gain acceptance into the Guild. Those few we allowed for initiation had to pass a vigorous level of vetting by their piers; which was quite a challenge for a secret Society of Thieves. Needless to say, fresh initiates were sternly warned that anybody caught snitching on the guild or revealing its agendas, would quickly find themselves without a tongue to wag.

Some of us being nocturnal creatures, we slept through the day as the snowfall gently fell across the city. Though I tried, I was unable to sleep; my mind occupied by what Beren had revealed to me about the ancient cult which had awoken from its slumber. Nyx whipped up a quick dinner before we left, proving herself to be a better cook than I had given her credit for; and we set out into the night. The cloudy skies and heavy sleet provided good cover as we wove our way through back alleys and narrow streets until we reached the Thieves Market.

Once inside, Nyx set off to sell her pearls while I sought an audience with the guild master. Koda seemed a trifle upset to see me again so soon; considering the lengths they had gone to saving my neck a few days before. Currently, he was in the middle of orchestrating a heist in the lower crimson quarter; which had gotten its name from the cheap red clay bricks which made up most of the architecture within that parcel of the city. Taking a moment away from his plans, we spoke within the privacy of his secluded antechamber.

"It is in the best interest of the Guild that you disappear from the public eye for the next few moons, Ash. Your presence on the streets puts our fellow members at risk by drawing attention to yourself," Koda advised.

"There's been a new development about that scroll you gave me and my capture," I offered as consolation, "an associate of mine has enlightened me to a certain cult, a faction of the Golden Spiders, as they call themselves, which has resurfaced from Stilgrave's early years." At the mention of this occult order, the guild master's face hardened to one of concern.

"That's a name I haven't heard in a long time," Koda scowled as he turned away in a moment of thought, "it was a dark religion birthed from a resistance of the house of the Builders and their holy parish."

"As Nyx has informed you about the murders of those servants in the Ivory quarter; I now have reason to believe that these two incidents are connected. This cult of witches have pursued a path of bloodshed to cover their tracks by killing off any witnesses," I stated.

"This does not bode well, for when those bodies are discovered the city may very well impose martial law to hunt down the culprits. Any members of the Thieves Guild would present an attractive scapegoat for the slayings, along with any other crimes the City Watch might choose to pin on us," Koda noted as I followed his logic on the precarious position this put us in, "I suggest that you take the initiative and contact this cult directly and we can set up an ambush to bury this mess before it comes to the surface," he ordered with a tight lip.

Koda's plan was simple; after explaining everything I

knew, he agreed that I should take Beren's place and assume his identity for the exchange of goods which had been robbed from the forgotten sanctuaries hidden among the twisting labyrinth of mineshafts under the mountain. Since this mysterious buyer had never met Beren in person, they would be none the wiser; and I could act as the mole until the Guild could arrange an ambush to catch them. Koda and the guild would never consent to outright murder under normal circumstances, but neither did he have any tolerance for a bunch of unhinged fanatics who got their thrills by killing and mutilating innocent civilians.

I wasn't terribly eager to take Beren's place to complete the deal he had set up with their contact, but we had to discover the cult's agenda. They murdered those servants for reasons which had yet to be revealed. That evening, on my way back through the city, I dropped into Beren's closed shop to pick up the array of artifacts he had left in storage, only to find a folded note slipped beneath his door. It was a terse letter demanding the return of the scroll which had been promised to the cult.

The wording within had a threatening overtone to it, but included an offer for consolidations. Beren had been in this purely for payment, which made me wonder offhand how much they could afford. As instructed in the message, in two nights' time, I returned to the designated place on the docks where Beren had first left the archaic scroll. I returned the ancient parchment as the mysterious note demanded, then waited in the shadows for the caller to reveal themselves.

Being unseen and fleet of foot were only secondary traits of a good thief; the top of which, was retaining a good measure of patience. After leaving the parchment at the allotted location, it wasn't until the evening's bell tolled at sunset when a lone individual approached the drop point. A lanky figure of a man wove his way through the docks like a sailor's ghost; as if his passing had gone unnoticed by the dock labor. The man was notably bald with pale white skin pulled taught over his thin frame.

The peculiar man's unhealthy and gaunt appearance was in itself, unsettling. The very sight of him elicited a repulsive response one might perceive upon the appearance of someone with a dreadful disease. I felt something dark and revolting in his image; which was oddly akin to the mild distress I experienced whenever I handled that decorated skull artifact. As much as I personally denied accepting any belief in such superstitious witchery; I felt a distressing knot in my gut whenever I thought about that ancient relic.

The frail figure quickly snatched the parchment from where it had been hidden between the crates, and examined it for but a moment before turning and snaking a hurried retreat back through the maze of barrels and containers lining the docks. I tailed him through the cover of the dark shadows and gloom which soon developed into the risk of losing him in the rising fog. Across from the wharf, he made a sudden turn towards the outer walls of the city to an abandoned division of the port which had been left in a stage of collapse. Here, the city guards and warden did not tread for fear of the disintegrating ruins, which could claim a life in an instant.

Not even the vagrants dared to trespass into this warren of shattered bricks and stone. It was a section of the city discarded long ago and equally forgotten; its broken remnants now left scattered beyond the retaining walls which imprisoned the unwary inhabitants within its cold embrace. This area had become inundated with seawater generations ago when a thin layer of bedrock gave way to the shifting sands of the shore. Spring storms and torrential rains washed away whatever was left, and this splintered section of the city became unlivable.

A great barricade was erected along the shoreline, separating these ruins from the watchful eyes of the metropolis beyond its high stone walls. I had heard rumors it was haunted; which served to protect the secret entrance into the mines that gored their way into the flesh of the mountain. Halfway through the abandoned ruins, I lost track of my mark in the thickening fog which swiftly rolled in. Unwilling to give up, I quickened my pace to catch up with the lone man who had vanished like a ghost in the swelling mists. Silence is a thief's greatest ally; which is why I knew I was making too much noise scrambling across the broken stones in my rush to gain ground on my lost prey.

Stumbling upon a crooked building comprised of large stone blocks, I found fresh wet footprints upon its stoop. With a note of caution, I peeked into the darkness from the open portal and slid my way into the surrounding shadows. Several boxes and crates from the docks were stockpiled here alongside a table filled with lanterns of various sizes. An empty circle in the dust told me one of the lamps had been recently removed from its placement.

The rear of the building itself was tucked into the side of the cliff, and peering behind a heavy curtain I found a passageway which cut deep into the earth. Here the living stone breathed with its cool damp breath. Even though my eyesight was sensitive to navigating the shadows of the night; I found the heavy gloom here thick and unforgiving. Against my better judgment, I lit one of the oil lanterns and muffled its sphere of light with my unraveled scarf.

It turned out to be a wise choice to bring the lamp as the pathway beyond was rife with snares and pitfalls. Progressing down the wide shaft, I snuffed out my lamp the moment I noticed the dancing glow of torches ahead. Exercising every effort at stealth, I crept my way up to the source of light streaming in through a side chamber carved

into the rock.   There I found the remnants of a chapel
where several figures sat in a circle around a central dais.
A voice reached out from the chamber to greet my arrival.

"Come, step out of the shadows my brother.   We don't
often have such visitors to our sanctuary," a breathy voice
spoke with an unsettling tone.   Realizing I had been
discovered, I stood to present myself.   Passing into the
light of the chamber, I saw there were eight individuals,
both men, and women, sitting within the room.   The dais,
itself, was empty, save for the familiar parchment of etched
skin lying at its center.   Oddly enough, only one man
amongst them turned to face me, as the other seven
members sat prone; their gaze not wavering from the stage
before them.

Getting caught as a result of my own clumsiness was
humiliating enough, but at least they didn't appear hostile
at the moment.   Having lost the initiative, I considered the
best tactic was to let my host do the talking so he could
lead the conversation.   The person speaking to me was an
older gentleman, ragged in appearance; though clearly
different from the individual I had followed in from the
docks.   I led him on with a clue.

"Greeting, I didn't mean to intrude; but I had wished to
apologize for the delay in delivering the scroll," I pointed
at the parchment lying open upon the platform, "and take
an avid interest in practicing good relations with my
customers," I presented awkwardly to throw them off and
made sure they could clearly see the silver and bone
pendant hanging around my neck.

"And you are the shopkeeper with whom we've
conversed?" the older man added with a hint of hesitation
in his tone.

"Yes, I'm Beren, with the quaint little shop in the lower
district.   I received your note..." I offered as I showed them
the folded script I found slipped under the shops front door.

"Ah, well then it is good fortune that you made it here safely for these tunnels are littered with bottomless shafts and hollows which present a mortal danger to unescorted visitors who wander alone," he granted with an ominous choice of words, "If you would come with me, I will help to be your guide," the man offered with a raised arm to point me towards another chamber.

When I stalled at accepting his invitation, in distressing rhythm, the other seven members all turned to face me in one motion. As alarming as their gesture was, I caught myself, and quickly jumped back into character, only to nod my approval with a forced grin. I did not like delving deeper into the abyss with my back to these fanatical butchers, but I was currently surrounded and outnumbered, and if I should dare to dash back through the hazards of the dark tunnels, I would likely come to a sudden end. With a quiet sigh, I realized I would have to play out this role a little longer to glean what information I could.

As I stepped forward and the man turned to follow, I noticed that he had an oddly shaped blade hanging upon his belt. It was designed like a crescent axe with an arched hook at its end. I had never seen a device like it, nor could I fathom what possible use it could be used for. Cuts by a blade were deadly enough if the wound got infected, and the city residents weren't the most sanitary of folk as it was. The device appeared too short to be a weapon for self-defense; but I imagined they were fast to wield and could create lethal gashes in skilled hands. With a sudden chill, that grim thought led me back to the dreadful wounds I had seen slashed upon the bodies of the servants in the manor cellar.

With a glance over my shoulder, I saw that two men stood up from the group and followed us closely a few steps behind. Apparently, I had been duped into being escorted somewhere, and wasn't enthralled at the idea of my only escape route being blocked by armed men. I didn't like being at a disadvantage and would have to do something to correct this unfavorable situation. My guide on this unpleasant tour led me through a maze of dreary halls carved from the raw stone of the mountain, and I had to hide my shock as numerous pale faces began to emerge from clusters of hidden corners and crevices as we progressed deeper into the mines.

It was as if an entire section of the city had migrated to this web of underground tunnels. Sickly looking men, women, and children loomed into the dim light; their lifeless eyes were chiseled with despair. These were the poor souls who found no welcome place for themselves among the populous residing above, even within the lowest gutters of the city. They were the unwanted sick and starving vagrants who shuffled their own corpses into this sunless grave.

"What you see before you are the refugees from the tainted city, who have come here to seek asylum," the robed man offered as he motioned to the spiritless faces which turned to watch us pass. One small boy held a tiny spider the color of straw; its bloated abdomen speckled with reflective scales of gold that glimmered in the torchlight.

"I had no idea all these people were down here," I added with genuine dismay.

"I am not surprised to hear you say that," the old man responded, "for these are the forgotten souls; the rejected and undesirable," he granted while gracefully touching a woman and her child gently upon their heads, "here within this sanctuary they find new purpose in their miserable lives ...one of service to a higher cause."

"Ah, well ...as long as the price is right, anything from my collection of relics is yours," I added to turn the conversation, "and who runs this place, do you have a governor or gutter-king, so to say?" I asked in jest. Though the slight was clearly out of taste, my guide presented no recoil, but kept his calm demeanor which I found to be even more disconcerting.

"Yes, yes ...if it is merely coin you worship, then it is coin you will have," the man answered poetically.

Winding our way around a tight corner, we stepped into an enormous cavern filled with a sizable subterranean lake. Before us, several ramps and docks constructed from salvaged boards and driftwood lined its edge while small rafts were moored as they drifted lazily within its waters. Among the shabby pier there were also fishing nets and waterlogged barrels. It was a strange collection of salt-stained debris that made up the sunken wharf.

If I was to guess, I would presume that the pool opened up to the sea by some underwater channel. These wretches scrounged to survive, living off the fish and seaweed, and whatever lost cargo they could reclaim from the harbor. Countless lanterns hung from posts while a hodgepodge of interwoven shelters reflected in the brackish waters below, presenting a fascinating sight to behold. Surviving like this under such hardships was mildly impressive, if not downright disheartening.

Not wishing to be condemned to a similar existence was one reason I became a thief. Among our citizens were the highborn's who dwelled within the city's finest districts, far above the peasants and rabble of the lower quarters. The shiny trinkets, and jewelry, and various treasures they accumulated were but commodities that had no particular owner in the eyes of the Guild. We never stole from those who were desperately poor, even when a given situation was tempting. Stilgrave consisted of the privileged and the paupers, and everyone in between was merely tinged in various shades of gray.

In the eyes of the Guild, it was in our best interest to keep the flow of money circulating. Whether it be from the trading docks and shop keepers to the open markets; the city toiled to stay alive, and there was little complaint as we led fairly comfortable lives outside of the limelight with the small amount of profit we earned. In a way, I could see the same similarities here; though with a much greater level of despair.

The brotherhood of thieves survived by calculated acts of moderation. Steal enough from a shopkeeper, but not so much as to ruin their business, or lift a few trinkets from a blueblood aristocrat, but not their entire family inheritance. It was a symbiotic relationship we held with a measure of conscience. Of course, the City Watch saw us as nothing more than pilfering parasites, which would be a fitting comparison but without us lowly thieves around, there would be little need for city guards. In a sense, you could say the guild offered a measure of job security for those mindless thugs.

My robed guide led us through a central hollow which was notably more decorated by a creative use of wood and bone; all assembled to radiate outward from the central path set before us. This led into a vast side chamber lined with a mesh of tangled and twisting ropes, decorated with twigs and driftwood, and bones of aquatic animals. This great network of knots and debris were anchored at countless points around the ceiling of the cavern; all conjoining to meet at the central vault. In all artistic respects, it resembled a giant web.

While entering the hollow, we passed by several monks standing as armed sentries to the inner sanctum. With a wave of his hand, these guards stepped aside, letting us pass. Within was a dome comprised of fishing nets, with a morbid collection of carved human bones lying upon a circular altar. The intricate designs engraved upon these remains were reminiscent of the archaic symbols I had seen etched within the strange skull that I had sequestered from Vale's flat.

"Those who live in the light above may be the architects of our lives, but here in the darkness, we are the weavers of our own fate," the man uttered as though he was reciting some sacred proverb. He looked down at the sacred bones as I noted there were a few pieces of the skeleton missing, most notably it's head.

As I scanned the room, I could make out additional oddities, such as small eggs and various bottles, including bowls of noxious liquids and powders lying haphazardly upon the floor and numerous shelves. The aroma within the small chamber was heavy and intoxicating, and I felt my senses begin to dull. I stood there in a confused daze as the old man turned directly towards me as he reached out and lightly fondled the exposed silver pendant around my collar as if to inspect it. While looking at the bone embedded into its shining metal; with a sharp tug, he snapped it from my neck and held it aloft.

"This medallion is a token of the faithful and the trusted of our order," the old man mentioned before dropping it into the container of bones as he took a small bottle from the altar, "and to wear it you must first earn our blessing," the monk stipulated as he pulled a sharp pin from the cap of the vial; its spike saturated with the murky liquid within as the two guardians standing behind me suddenly grasped my arms and held me still while the old monk punctured my neck with the tainted needle. Within the blink of an eye, I felt a rush of nausea as a brittle heat fanned out from the wound and rushed to my head. My vision quickly faded as the room around me began to spin, and quite abruptly, everything went black.

The Poison Garden

I awoke in a cell comprised of rotted cargo nets that appeared to have been salvaged from the shipping docks along the shore. The blood in my veins felt heavy; it was a strange sensation as though I was weighted down by some unseen force. The painful throbbing inside my head told me I had been poisoned, and logically a toxin was the only thing that could have reacted so quickly after I had been struck. In a vain attempt to feel the wound upon my neck, I tried to reach up only to discover that my hands were bound by my side as I lay upon a cold stone slab.

The ropes and twine which restrained me were woven in an odd meshwork pattern, as if meant to imitate the intricate design of a spider's silky web. The room itself was unoccupied, although I could hear commotion beyond the perforated walls. I had gotten myself into a real fix from breaking my own rules, by following my mark into unknown territory. I had been captured, and by the look of my situation, I wasn't going anywhere soon.

After several minutes of struggling with my bindings, a tall woman brushed aside the net curtain and began to circle the stone cradle to which I was tied.

"Looking for these?" the woman asked in a strangled voice, which sounded more like the hiss of a snake. Within her hands, she held my armored bracers and their embedded tools. The secret blades I had sheathed within them were now well beyond my reach.

"Why do you have me tied up, what is it that you want?" I asked, realizing that my cover was likely blown. If these were actually the same people who were out to get me, then I had just walked right into their hands. Marching into dangerous situations was not my style, and at the moment,

I felt like a complete fool for getting caught so easily.

"You seem to be a man of hidden talents," she hissed back as she tested the retractable garrote; then dropped the customized gauntlet while continuing to pace about the small room, "these are quite unique items for a mere shopkeeper."

"It's a dangerous business dealing in rare antiquities," I breathed, noting to the current predicament I found myself in, including the sheer irony of my statement. Even so, she seemed to find a bit of humor in my remark.

"Then let us get down to business, shall we my dear?" She bent down to breathe her words into my ear as I lay prone upon the slab.

As she did so, the cowl she wore fell open, exposing an elaborate necklace of human fingers she had tied about her neck dropped before my eyes. Trying as I could not to squirm, I drew my attention back towards this strange woman. Her skin was quite pale, as though it had been bleached of color, and fine black veins could be seen creeping beyond her thin hairline. Additionally, her gaze was unusually dark as if the whites of her eyes had been stained black by some vile infection.

"What is it that you want? More artifacts, a better deal?" I tried to act nervous while keeping in character.

"Your name came to our attention when we were told you may be holding a few items which had been stolen from our sanctuary," she pressed, her cold breath stinking of some unnatural odor I could not place.

"Stolen you say?" I tried to act surprised, "I run a legitimate business and would not knowingly deal in pilfered items," I declared. Upon hearing that, the woman dispensed a quiet cackle as she rose from the table.

"Oh please ...our congregation is made of the vagrants and street urchins that litter the city. Those who were forced to beg, borrow, and steal; we all know the nature of your trade, my friend," she snapped back.

"Well then, I would be more than happy to return your property ...if you would just untie me and I'll go get them for you," I offered with a tug at my ropes. Again, she reacted with that breathy cackle which was unnerving to behold. Turning away, she headed back out the entry from whence she came, while stalling to glance back over her shoulder towards me with a final word of warning.

"You are our guest, and now that you are among us we will find the truth ...and you can trust that we have ways to persuade you to loosen your tongue," she threatened before leaving the tattered cell.

I had seen how they had tortured the servants in the mansion, and though I was not easily rattled, the idea of meeting the same fate did not leave me in a state of calm. Doubling my efforts, I tried to wiggle my way out of the bindings but found that their web-like construct was difficult to resist. I suddenly froze when I heard a hushed voice behind my head, just outside my field of view. My exasperation was soon replaced by a mixed sense of confusion and relief.

"Hold still and stop making so much noise; I'll cut you loose," Nyx whispered behind my head. Taking a serrated blade in her hand, she crept over and began sawing on the netting that bound me, "Look at you, lying down on the job," she mocked with a slight grin.

I didn't know how she had made it down here unseen, but I had to give her points for effort.

"How did you bypass the guards?" I asked, wanting to know the quickest way out of this rat hole.

"I was an orphan stray once too," she answered while she moved to the other side of the slab to cut the ropes binding my other arm, "I had heard tales of this place and presumed the stories were based on a measure of truth; so I simply dressed up as one of these wretches and wandered in."

Her scheme sounded like a great way to infiltrate the cult, but getting me out by the same method might prove to be slightly more problematic. Nyx admitted she had waited for me to return after speaking with Koda, and took it upon herself to follow me out to the docks and kept a close tab as I pursued the thin man along the ruins and into the mines. She, of course, was just following orders from our Guild Master to keep an eye on me, but had also risked her life by doing so.

Nyx stood guard by the doorway with a drawn dagger as I untied my legs and gathered the remnants of my gear. Slipping out through the back of the netted chamber, I followed her lead as we shimmied our way up the side wall and through to an adjacent chamber. These mine shafts appeared to have penetrated into a natural cavern system; creating a confusing hive of irregular routes by which to take. Finding a small channel in the cave set far out of sight from the locals, we stalled for a moment to get our bearings.

"How do you propose we make our way out of here?" I asked Nyx, giving her credit for sneaking her way in here and saving my hide.

"I've heard rumors that there were passages from these mines which connected directly to the sewers under the city," Nyx answered as she peered around a corner, "but finding them in this maze would be futile. You're lucky they kept you alive; what was it they wanted from you?"

Remembering the morbid shrine I had been shown, it was clear to me now that they were likely after the strange skull artifact I had swiped from Vale's study. I was guessing that they were onto him, but the unfortunate Collector ended up dead when he couldn't produce the relic. The fact that Vale had adorned one of their creepy bone pendants and had a jar full of fingers in his study, made me wonder just how long he may have been working with them. It made me wonder if Beren's name had come up in some hushed conversation or by the rattled screams of torture, which eventually led them to his shop?

The cult of the Golden Spiders had been after my hide for some reason I still could not deduce, but they clearly had not known me by my face, or I would have certainly met a grim fate long before Nyx showed up. In all my time scouring the city nicking personal treasures, I had never seen such archaic and primitive artifacts before my visit to Vale's apartment. I enlighten Nyx as to recent events related to the shopkeeper and Koda's suggestion that I infiltrate the sect disguised as Beren. She just gave me a confused look, which didn't surprise me since it was a tall tale to begin with. However, she had witnessed the bodies of the tortured servants and the cruelty of these Dark Weavers first hand.

Nyx mentioned the rumors she had heard as a child about the spider cult and their witchery. They were said to control the vengeful spirits of the poor and the wretched. The impoverished and the suffering were the base of their followers, who saw them as angels of retribution who could cast spells and curses upon the cruel masters whom they served. There were many who claimed to have witnessed their dark magics themselves, and the eerie stories of them had haunted her childhood.

Although, now older and wiser, Nyx still held her own apprehensions of their alleged sorcery and witchcraft. I, for one, was still skeptical; but I had also witnessed how unsettling the presence of that skull artifact had made me feel, and it was not something I would soon forget. There were countless numbers of these poor souls living under the mountain, and the dark clerics held a form of sinister control over their subjects.

We could make our way back to the underwater cavern, but knew it was too dangerous to risk swimming in the icy waters to the outer shore. We chose instead to follow a procession of their guards who wore dark gray-hooded robes. The group of monks led our way as they carried their lanterns through the twisting tunnels while we followed within the cover of shadows close behind. Trying to keep track of our direction became a notable challenge as there was a lack of definitive landmarks along the path.

Within one tall alcove, they ascended up a steep set of stairs carved into the living stone. We didn't want to take the chance of getting caught in such a tight space, so we clambered up the side wall with the aid of a rope to an opening where we spied a shaft of light coming from within the open cavity. Once Nyx and I had squeezed ourselves into the upper chamber, we were amazed as our eyes fell upon a sunlit grotto. A crevice in the cavern ceiling was open to the sky, shining warm sunlight down upon a lush meadow covered in hues of green.

I had entered this labyrinth at sunset and realized that I must have been unconscious for far longer than I had previously suspected. Among the moss-filled hollow, the clergy tended to growths of mushrooms among the tall ferns. A natural spring filled a small pond where we could hear the song of frogs as plumes of fireflies scattered when they were disturbed by the monks cultivating their unusual garden. This cavity was insulated from the harsh winter gales beyond the cliff walls and sustained its stable temperature from warm air rising from the labyrinth of shafts below.

Unraveling my rope and grappling hook, I placed my attention towards the opening in the ceiling high above as our means of escape. Nyx and I practiced our talent of melting into the shadows while we waited for the monks to retreat. The sparse sunlight began to wane while they busily collected an assortment of ingredients from the surrounding flora.

What drew my scrutiny was that this hidden grove of mushrooms and thorned berries, including the array of flowering plants and brightly colored frogs, did not appear native to these highlands. These were exotic plants and fungi not naturally seen in the territories outside the city walls. The plants they were collecting were taken to a set of heavy oak tables, where they were being dried and ground into fine powders and mixed into bizarre concoctions. Among the ingredients were what appeared to be tufts of seaweed and bowls of algae, alongside many other strange additives we could not readily identify.

It appeared that this strange alchemy was the source of the poisons they employed; created from the toxic roots and deadly essence of this serene but lethal garden. As we waited in the shadows, the ghoulish woman who had interrogated me earlier came wandering into the clearing. She appeared to be overseeing the cultivation of the herbs and was approached by one of the sentries. Eavesdropping on their conversation, we made an alarming discovery.

"My priestess, we have received word that the Lord Regent will be arriving tomorrow, and his attendance at the affair in the Ivory district and meeting at the manor have been confirmed," the guard related to the dark mistress.

"And our agents are in place, and everyone is aware of their roles; I assume?" she hissed in her strange voice.

"Yes Milady, all participants are familiar with the plan and are ready for their performance," he assured her.

"Very good, for they are also conscious of the price of failure, are they not?" she bade while picking up a bowl of noxious herbs from the alchemy table and stirring its contents with her hands. I could see now that she and the other workers in the grotto had blackened fingers, as if the vile poisons had stained their bodies with their taint.

"They are..." the monk began to respond, but was curtly dismissed by the dark priestess who seemed satisfied by his reply.

The thieves' guild had been aware that an important diplomat was arriving within the city in the coming days, but a shroud of secrecy had been forged to the individuals' identity. The only Regent we knew of was the lord protector of Blacktide, which was a large maritime metropolis to the north. Its beaches were made of dark sand from whence the port got its name. It was, however, an opposing faction in this region, which was once a naval garrison back in the days of war between the territories. If anything happened to the emissary during his visit, it would be a catalyst that could flare hostilities once again.

The city of Stilgrave was in a defensible position, but retained a weak military force. Any hint of war would neither be good for its citizens nor for the Guild. If a diplomat from Blacktide came to any harm within the city walls it would threaten the frail treaty between the two regions which they had upheld for so many years. This cult priestess was up to no good, and from the sounds of it, they were using the same mansion in the Ivory district where I had been ambushed to conduct this scheme.

We had to bring this information to the attention of the guild master. Once the priestess left, I realized we might not have much time until they realized that their captured guest had gone missing. Contemplating if we should risk making a rush for the rift high above us; I realized doing so would be too much of a gamble. There were too many workers laboring in the grotto and the climb appeared relatively precarious, to say the least.

In a brash move, I chose another option; one of which my apprentice did not care for.

"We have to follow her," I demanded.

"Have you lost your mind?" Nyx whispered back in a curt tone, "She is probably heading back down to your cell, and the last place we want to be is two steps behind her when she sounds the alarm!"

"We can't make that climb without drawing attention to ourselves, there are too many eyes here," I argued, "and we have to find out what she is up to."

I quickly placed the pieces together in my head, realizing that the abandoned mansion in the Ivory district was being used as a stage to bait their targets. The roles of their agents were to put on an act to trap their prey. The gruesome deaths of the hired servants in the basement made sense now, and these fanatic cultists would be decoys taking the place of the murdered attendants for this covert operation. These cult leaders were proving to be clever and sophisticated enough to coordinate such an elaborate enterprise in order to ensnare their unwary victims.

I had to uncover whatever diabolical scheme they were orchestrating upon the visiting Regent, and expose their hidden agenda. If I was lucky, I would find out what animosities they held against me along the way, and the Guild could take measures to subdue this threat. The cult priestess made her way back to the lower levels with two guards following in her wake. Nyx and I stalked her movements as the tall woman chose an alternate route and entered a network of passages, which led back through a system of older tunnels.

Here and there, aged brickwork could be seen cropping up through the architecture as the bare bedrock was eventually enveloped by worn bricks and cobblestones the further we progressed. After several moments we began to hear rushing water echoing up through the tunnel. The foul waft which accompanied the trickle of water told me we were approaching the sewers, which reminded me of Vale's studio and his hidden passage to the drains which branched out beneath the city.

By this hidden ingress, the cultists could make their way in an out of the city walls without being seen. The sewers were grated with heavy bars in most parts of Stilgrave; but as I had witnessed in the Collectors flat and his makeshift tunnel, Vale had connected a direct route under the streets and was able to convey himself between the abandoned mansion and his study, beyond notice of the city guards. After entering a side chamber, the priestess stalled to inspect several crates stacked within the narrow alcove; so Nyx and I crept closer so we could see what she was doing. Within the antechamber, she was pulling out several small vials and carefully placed them within a leather satchel at her side.

"It smells like the sewer system, we can make our way out of here and get back to the Guild," Nyx suggested with a curled nose as she covered her face from the rancid stench with her scarf.

"My guess is that those are crates of poisons they've been harvesting in the grove above," I whispered back, "we need to grab a sample as proof before we head back to meet with Koda."

Nyx just shook her head at me as if I was some sort of belligerent child who couldn't be satisfied. The hand of fate stepped in when we suddenly noticed another monk approaching us from behind. With practiced stealth, Nyx and I nimbly slipped behind cover so as not to be seen as the man stepped forward to meet with the woman. Eavesdropping upon their conversation, the messenger related to the priestess about a certain prisoner which had gone missing.

It didn't take much to realize that I was likely the person they were referring to. Upset at this news, the priestess turned to follow the messenger back through the sewers while leaving a sole sentry behind at the stash of crates. From experience, I knew this was the opportunity I was looking for and I wasn't going to let it pass by. Nyx turned a glare at me in wonder as I slipped the latch from my bracer; letting the weighted flail slip silently to its full length within my hand.

I waited for the first moment the guards back was turned, and without pause, I danced across the passage while avoiding the puddles of water that could give away my approach. The trim flail was devastatingly fast as it spun with a quiet whistle before striking the sentry in the back of the head at full velocity. Stunned by the initial blow, the monk staggered forward, and with a simple twist of my arm, the heavy leather loop of the flail curled around my wrist to free my right hand and yank the retractable garrote from my left sleeve. Looping it around his neck, I pulled it taught and spun my body behind him to cinch the cord.

Nyx rushed out from hiding to help, but by the time she reached me the guard was already down. I didn't kill the man, but choked him hard enough to the point he would be incapacitated long enough for us to make our escape. Rummaging through the crates, we found several sets of both servant's clothing and regal outfits, which were likely costumes for their theatrical roles when they posed as staff within noble households. With care, I cracked open a small iron chest to find it heavily padded inside with velvet. Within were a selection of vials filled with a variety of liquids and powders.

"What are you taking those for?" Nyx asked in confusion as I stuffed several wrapped bottles into the hidden pockets lining my doublet.

"Koda may know an alchemist who can determine what these are for and might be able to create an antidote," I answered back, "and it might also help if we had some evidence should we get nicked along the way."

A good burglar doesn't linger at the scene of the crime, and a wise thief is tempered with an acute sense of timing when they've overstayed their welcome. Within moments we had disappeared into the darkness of the sewers as we

Michel Savage

followed the flow of water into the womb of the city. Though Nyx kept constantly complaining about the stench, I explained to her that we were following the stream downhill which would eventually take us to the lower districts of the city. Luckily for us, it was still daybreak outside and the dim passages were lit by shafts of light streaming in through several cracks and grates. Once we had breached the city walls, the sewers spanned out into a vast labyrinth of channels.

"I don't know about you, but I'm taking the first exit out of here!" Nyx commented as she folded her scarf up over her mouth to stifle the septic fragrance which began to choke our breath.

I really couldn't blame her and wasn't enjoying the discomforts of the city sewers myself, but after a moment of gathering our bearings, I noticed something unusual which caught my eye. It was the glint of gold from the shadows which caught my attention. Drawing closer to inspect its source, I discovered a small brand of the spider cult embossed in polished gold upon the sewer wall. The image was tiny enough to be overlooked as the symbol was only the size of a genuine spider.

Below it was the rough scrawling of some dialect I could not decipher, but which appeared similar to the strange markings I had seen drawn upon the parchment skin Koda had given me. Taking a moment to check around the tunnel branches, I spotted several more of these emblems carved into the corridor junctures above head level. This made sense, as these small icons could easily go unnoticed by any passer-by paying attention to where they were stepping and not actively looking for these marks. Following the marker upon the nearest tunnel, we noticed a breach in the wall where the brickwork had caved in. Peering inside, I recognized the earthen tunnel which laid beneath Vale's apartment.

Climbing up the crude ladder, I listened for a moment at the hatch for signs of any occupants and slowly lifted the door. It was heavy upon my first attempt, for it was still covered by the large carpet masking it, so Nyx helped me force our way inside; now glad that I had left it unlocked during my last visit to his study. What we found within was even more of a disaster than I had seen before during my last call to his flat. The Collector's apartment had been thoroughly ransacked. A quick visit upstairs revealed that Vale's body was now missing.

Any residual evidence of what had happened to him had been removed, and several of the artifacts in his collection, which had been present before, were also missing; all that remained were a few discarded and broken fragments left scattered upon the floor. It wasn't clear if this was the work of the city guards, or members of the cult; though either way it wasn't good news. After carefully covering the secret hatch with the rug, Nyx and I were on alert and waited in silence until dusk arrived so that we could make our way to the guildhall a few streets over in the Ivory district. Our arrival that evening at the hall was met with a sense of urgency by the stationed sentry who directed us to meet with the guild master immediately.

We were quickly ushered inside and left in a private chamber without other guild members allowed to converse with us directly while we waited. Left confused as to what was going on, it was nearly an hour later when Koda finally stormed in, showing a mixed look of concern and unrest sculpted upon his chiseled face; both of which moods were typically uncommon from his usual poised character.

"Ash ...Nyx," Koda curtly nodded as he greeted us and sat down at the table before us, "the murder of the collector in the Ivory district has stirred up a great deal of commotion with the upper hierarchy which governs the city," he noted as he grabbed a scroll from a bin and rolled out a map of the city before us.

"Last night I was at the docks and used that strange parchment as bait, and ended up following one of the cult members to their lair; and can affirm that it appears they are conspiring to either abduct or murder the visiting regent from Blacktide," I conceded, "That little excursion also revealed that there is a significant group of refugees currently dwelling within the abandoned mines beyond the city walls."

Koda seemed stirred at this revelation while Nyx nodded as she affirmed that fact. The guild deals in secrets and rumors as its life-blood for information, but having what were once merely bizarre stories and wild myths confirmed by two trusted associates were no less shocking.

"We have to keep this information under wraps for the moment since I don't want such gossip spreading throughout the Guild and into the streets," Koda warned under a hushed breath, "My sources have recently told me that the northern Regent was due to arrive tomorrow to stay at the lord's manor after his delegation with the city governor. Given what you've seen, Ash, what direction do you suggest we take from here?"

"That could be a significant problem," I granted, "the manor in the upper district where I was captured is apparently being utilized as a kill box, which the cultists use to stage its activities in the Ivory quarter. We suspect that members of this spider cult will be posing as servants and members of the lord's entourage to entrap their victims. Which is what happened in my particular case," I added.

"Did you determine why you were one of their targets, Ash?" The guild master asked with a hint of interest.

"Well no ...not as yet," I responded with a heavy mind, for it was still a part of this troubling mystery which eluded me, "however, we did acquire these," I mentioned while carefully pulling out the vials of various poisons and stacked them on the table before him.

Picking them up, Koda examined several of the small corked bottles which had been sealed with wax. Their contents were only labeled by exotic symbols painted upon each lid. Fortunately, the guild had access to doctors and alchemists who worked within the black market whenever circumstances required their skills. In spite of their respectable reputations in the public eye, one might be surprised to whom such scholars would offer their services in trade for a stack of silver coin.

Koda would forward these toxic samples to his specialist to have them analyzed for their properties and effects, and see what we could do to counter them. Poisons weren't the way of the Thieves' Guild, and it was generally considered a cowardly way to take a person's life; even for such disreputable rogues as us. Although, use of such bane was commonly practiced among members of high society, who would apply such venomous concoctions to off their rivals during ugly scandals between jealous lovers and family affairs. From a certain perspective, such dishonorable conduct among the highborn could make us degenerate bandits and burglars look like saints.

The real question now was how were we going to intervene in this situation? If the Regent's life was put at risk, the backlash from the authorities in the city watch would have dreadful repercussions upon the lower wards. Guardsmen would likely double their patrols in the streets and security would be tightened across the city; making the pursuit of our livelihood ever more scarce and the risks far greater. Such stifling of coin and travel throughout the districts would only germinate a great deal of anxiety and dissent among the members of our Order. Any guild master knew that such desperation only births greater problems, as snitches would emerge from the woodwork to rat out a fellow crook to the city guards for a mere piece of silver. To keep his position and measure of order among the members of the Guild, Koda would need to exercise due diligence to keep peace within the city, and thereby protecting our own interests as well.

Interfering with the dealings of the upper echelon of lords and nobles who ruled Stilgrave from its interior was inherently risky, and not an ideal solution, but we had no choice in this matter. Military conflict with a neighboring province would only bring bloodshed and hardship for everyone in the city. The best solution was to take care of this problem ourselves and see that no harm came to the visiting regent. The elaborate scheme Koda came up with as a resolution to this situation was a complete surprise to us all.

The Pale Dancer

After Koda convened with his closest advisors they came up with a plan to pull some strings and a few bribed favors with a handful of dirty city guardsmen who were on the Guilds' payroll. Rather than pass a note of this grave situation to the city chancellor and risk exposing select members of the Guild; Koda proposed to abduct the Lord Regent himself. It was a wild plan which seemed even more bizarre than what dangers the spider cult had posed. The Thieves Guild would intervene in this affair and protect the visiting diplomat by removing him from harm's way; but the timing of the plan was crucial so that we could expose the members of the cult when they made their move and let the city ward accost these fanatics. It was a bold but risky plan; and one that could go south at any point if the pegs we set didn't fall into place.

Since I had already wagered two different personas with the cult leaders of the Golden Spiders, who now new my face, Koda determined that I would make the perfect bait to draw them out at the right moment. Needless to say, I was not fond of this idea from the start. Koda suggested having our scouts track the visiting Envoy's route and make arrangements to accost him at the most opportune moment so as not to alert his personal guards or that of the City Ward. This all had to be timed to nab him before the cult members could exercise their cruel plan.

The city governor had prepared a lavish welcome for the regent from Blacktide at his private abode above the royal court. Security would be tight, so I opted to revisit Beren's storeroom to pick through his costumes once again. Koda had implanted spies into the banquet and on the rooftops to keep an eye out for unwelcome guests. Nyx found herself recruited as one of the serving girls, much to her loathing.

Koda had finally convinced her that they needed someone at the party skilled with a blade in case unforeseen circumstances called for her prowess and proficiency. The guild master had played on her ego and convinced her to concede. We knew the lord's manor down the avenue from the royal court would be filled with cult members acting as servants and staff, but we had no idea how many of them may have penetrated the guest list of the governor's party. Koda had snuck me onto the list as an anonymous uncle taking the place of an Earl to the royal family who ruled Stilgrave and the southern territories from abroad, citing that the earl was unable to personally attend for health reasons.

Koda left the character I was to portray up to me to contrive and he appeared comfortable that I wouldn't disappoint his expectations. Unwilling to go unarmed this round; I chose an outfit of darker colors layered beneath with generous sleeves to hide my tactical bracers under the tailored ensemble. Except for my small neck knife, I had to forego the rest of my gear to fit into the regal attire for the affair. With a practiced level of class above the rest of us in the guild; Koda had arranged a well-bred steed for me to ride up through the Ivory quarter to the chancellor's banquet.

I was pleasantly surprised to get my stallion at the stables, which had been decked out with a velvet caparison whose elegant design matched the gilded bridle and polished saddle. The embarrassing truth was that I hadn't been on a horse for more years than I could count, and it showed. So at the cost of comfort to my aching rear, I bobbed awkwardly in my saddle as I rode up the cobblestone streets through the Ivory quarter until I reached the council hall, whereupon I was redirected by the line of guards posted there towards the main entrance. I was genuinely happy to dismount my steed, and tried to casually stifle the soreness I had suffered from the ride when attempting to walk normally without drawing attention to myself.

The guise I adorned was necessary at this stage, as the district around the court was lined with city guards patrolling the area. Among them were other guests arriving by mount and carriage in the chill of the night. One guard with a sash was checking invitations and personnel entering the grounds, who stopped me to take my name before I passed through the gates.

"Good evening Sir, if you could present your invitation to tonight's gala," The burly guard asked with his armored gloved open in expectation.

"Why certainly," To act my part, I put on an accent for the sentry while I handed him the forged document. Reading the invite slip, he double-checked his register and gave a confused look.

"Your name is *Rogue*?" he asked with a flicker of doubt as he looked me in the eye. Without a flinch, I gave a snooty response with my head raised and stared down my nose at the audacity of being questioned by a lowly gate guard.

"Sir, it is pronounced 'Ro-jou' the Earl of Larcené, and I am his lordships uncle Filché of the Ro-jou' estate," I answered with a puffed chest.

"Ah, yes I see a Sir Filch listed here as the Earls representative for the event, but I still..." the guard began to question further before I promptly cut him off in with an annoyed tone.

"No-no-no, it is pronounced 'Filché," I demanded, "and the Regent is expecting my presence at this affair, and I do not approve of being further detained by an untitled sentry. Where is your superior officer?" I barked as my voice grew ever louder to gather attention as I glanced around in overreacting agitation.

The guardsman squirmed and seemed unwilling to draw unwanted scrutiny to the duties of his post by the chancellor, and abruptly folded my invite and stuffed it into his satchel with the others he had collected from previous guests, and tried to de-escalate the situation.

"My apologies Sir Filchy," the man blubbered, "please, enjoy the evening's festivities," he waved me through as the other guards shot him nervous glances.

With an audible huff, I stomped past him and towards the mansion at the rear of the court where several torch braziers lined the walkway. I had gambled that my brazen attitude would not only draw away the guard's suspicions but that they were also fearful of losing their jobs. I knew that only the lowest of their ranks would be posted outside in the bitter cold while the seasoned watchmen would be stationed within the comfort of the household. I did not envy these men who had to put up with the pompous nobles and aristocrats on a daily basis; who were not only arrogant and conceited but clearly received some sort of twisted enjoyment from rubbing their heels into the dignity of their servants, and anyone else whom they deemed of lower stature.

Making my way up the steps to the chateau stationed on the road above the court building, I slipped into the arriving crowd in an effort to blend in. After grabbing a taste of the delicacies and making the rounds to scope the layout of the manor, I spotted Nyx in the crowd. I must say that I was not only pleasantly surprised but mildly impressed by how she cleaned up. The outfits they gave to the house staff were slightly more provocative than the usual attire of the common chambermaids.

Her dark hair was cut short which framed her face as the rest was tied up in a ponytail decorated with golden lace. For the first time, I noticed that she bore an intricate tattoo of some dark-winged creature which clad her left thigh. A closer look revealed this decoration to be the artistic rendition of a black sparrow; hence her nickname among the members of the guild.

She was carrying wine-filled glasses upon a tray, and not looking to entirely excited about her job serving the gentile and bluebloods among the throng of party guests. I approached her and snatched a glass from her tray without pause; but in response, she grazed me with an offensive glare for a split second until she almost burst out laughing at seeing me in my ridiculous outfit.

"Calm down servant girl," I whispered under my breath for her to keep in character, "have you seen the Regent as yet?"

"Well, don't you look dapper, my lord," she snorted back while catching her suppressed giggle, "the Regent arrived about an hour ago and met privately with the chancellor in his study; so I assume they should be out before the main course is served and the scheduled entertainment begins."

"And how would I recognize him, this emissary from Blacktide?" I whispered covertly to Nyx as I dabbed an embroidered handkerchief over my lips to hide our conversation from prying eyes.

"He's a tall man with a trimmed gray beard and mustache; wearing a silk jacket decked with enough medallions and badges to choke a horse ...you can't miss him," she added so that I could identify my mark.

There were also a few other members of our guild on the property who had infiltrated the event as temporary stable hands who could identify horses and the various carriages used by the guest, and even as cooks to scout the kitchen staff for members from the spider cult. Our objective was to identify any sect members and be ready to step in and protect the Regent if need be. Unlike common pickpockets in our field, my personal preference was to avoid working in large crowds; but we needed to gather intelligence on the Golden Spiders, and determine a strategy to undermine their objectives this eve to accost Blacktide's diplomat. We could quietly dispatch any spies they had among the staff, but our Guild Master preferred that we capture a few for questioning as an alternative.

From what we understood, the Lord Regent was merely a temporary official who was acting on behalf of the inheriting ruler of the Northern Territory until they came of age. If the Regent had come to any harm, then the underage ruler of Blacktide might react with anything less than a mature mind and retaliate with force that would lead to bloodshed between our two territories. As Stilgrave was a small port of trade at the edge of our eastern province, the city was ill-equipped to deal with an all-out incursion. We wanted to quell this dangerous situation without provoking the city ward, which would most certainly disrupt our way of life.

A few of the guild members floated the idea of not only kidnapping but also ransoming off the Regent back to the city; however, Koda quickly stifled that idea. The results of such a scheme would have proven as both an unforgivable embarrassment to the bureaucrats that ran the town; but would also have made a bad impression to the neighboring territories that our city had a reputation for being rampant with crime. Such rumors would dissuade any traveling noblemen who were overburdened by their wealth from visiting Stilgrave; which would only tighten our belts and leave but slim pickings among the local merchants and the upper class residing in the cobbled streets of the Ivory quarter.

By the grandeur of decor and guests in attendance, this evening's venue was promising to be interesting to say the least. Our governor was a bloated goat of a man, who wore his popularity and wealth like a badge of superiority. He, like many other aristocrats embedded in the upper crest of local politics, had been born into wealth and didn't get that way because they were intelligent or exercised a sense of morals; but because they took the credit from the hard labor of others, and milked their wages on top of it.

It was a whole different level of thievery I wanted nothing to do with. In comparison, my petty misdeeds were far less sinful than those who ruled without ethics or accountability. My views on this also fell equally upon the religious zealots who called themselves the Builders; and of course, the fanatics of the spider cult were equally repugnant toward my own personal tastes. A person should live by their own deeds rather than blame their slights and offenses on some obscure deity or concocted theology as an excuse for their misconduct.

I let Nyx go about her business and proceeded to mingle into the crowd without drawing attention to myself whenever possible. Standing at the back of the room where I could get a good view of the scene, I finally spotted our obese governor as he wandered into the room via the second story balcony floor while he stood at the rail overseeing the festivities below. Beside him stood the Regent in his decorated sable coat. He had the look of a rigid man who had seen much hardship in his long years, ones with bitter roots that had shaped his style of rule.

Several handmaids quietly made their appearance along the railing upon the 2nd-floor tier and began placing red-tinted glass upon each of the hanging lanterns and chandeliers which lit the banquet hall. Within moments, the room was bathed in a rich crimson light to the elated gasps of the guests below. From down the central stairway came a woman bearing an exotic white costume carrying a long rod. Her skin was as equally pale as her outfit, and across her face she wore a veil that hid her eyes; adding to the mystery of this ghostly beauty standing before them.

Everyone inhaled with delight as she flicked her wrists and both ends of the staff lit with a vivid flame that radiated in the rusty ambient light. Everyone cleared the center of the room as she began to spin the double-tipped torch in a slow and graceful dance; as if she was daring the audience to draw near to be burned by its purring flames as they swirled through the air. Bells on her wrists and ankles added to the beat as drummers and string instruments joined in from the handful of musicians stationed above the crowd; adding to the step an sway of her body. It was an exotic sight to behold, for few acrobats or entertainers of her quality had ever graced this dismal city.

After teasing the crowd with her fire dance, the beat of the drums met their climax and the torches abruptly turned a brilliant blue and snuffed themselves out in a cloud of smoke. The crowd was stunned for a moment, followed by roaring applause as the rising vapor revealed that the dancer's outfit was now covered in a shimmer of golden flakes. Her costume glittering like a finely cut crystal as the maids removed the tinted glass from the lanterns, and the party resumed as the musicians changed their tune to a softer rhythm. An almost rugged smile could be seen crossing the Regent's face as he leaned in towards his host upon the balcony above.

"Who is that exquisite creature?" The regent asked the chancellor standing beside him, as he referred to the unusual dancer.

"Ah, an exotic beauty is she not?" The governor answered with a lecherous smile, "She goes by the ominous name of 'Lilith', which is her stage name no doubt in the realm of such actors and performers; although her real name is a mystery to me. Come, let me introduce you..." he bade for the lord regent to follow him down the flight of stairs to meet the curious woman.

Governor Oren waddled his girth down the wide stairway and onto the main floor where cocktails were being served to the guests who were flocking around the entertainer. As they met face to face, her eyes were still veiled by the jeweled headpiece that she wore. Her dark lipstick only enhanced her striking appearance as the Regent stepped forward to greet her. He noticed that her skin had been bleached with a type of chalk and that her fingers were stained black; likely by the charcoal of her flaming staff he assumed.

"Lady Lilith, may I introduce to you the Lord Regent of Blacktide," the governor motioned to his royal guest, "the Regent will be with us for another day or more to address matters of diplomacy between our two territories along the coast," he smiled as he left them to get acquainted.

Lady Lilith bowed gracefully as he bent to kiss her hand, but she withdrew it before his lips could touch her exposed skin.

"You have traveled far, my Lordship, I hope my performance was worthy of the trip," she smiled as her lips were exposed from the shroud that masked her upper face. The Regent's eyebrow rose for but a moment as he heard her strangely breathy voice break the silence between them.

"It was Milady," he nodded courteously, "may I get you a drink ...if you would prefer a distraction of some polite conversation?"

The exotic dancer nodded in agreement with a wicked smile crossing her face as the Regent motioned a servant to bring over a few glasses of distilled wine. Having kept watch on the two, Nyx saw her cue and weaved her way to the pair and handed them two crystal flute glasses as she overheard the entertainer offering the regent to join her at her accommodations in her manor after the party. Nyx took the opportunity to give the dancer a quick scan to size her up without being noticed and disappeared once again into the crowd. Without making herself obvious, Nyx snaked her way back through the group to deliver the last remaining glasses on her tray to a circle of guests standing beside me.

She then took a brisk moment to inform me of what had transpired under her breath as she passed by.

"I'm quite certain that's the head priestess we saw in the mines," Nyx professed as she shot a quick glance towards the masked dancer.

Looking through the costume and makeup of the entertainer, I could see that my apprentice was right. The cult priestess had made contact with their mark and was luring him back to their private manor in the Ivory quarter. Any attempts at directly dissuading the Regent from accompanying the exotic artist would be a hard sell at this point. This only complicated our plans, whereby we would have to accost the Regent as he left the governors' chateau. With a nod, my apprentice snaked her way back through the crowd to inform the other agents of the Guild of this new facet.

I scanned the room once again, knowing it would be foolish to think that the spider priestess would have come alone, which drew my attention to the musicians which had accompanied her for this evening's performance. They remained on the upper level playing their instruments as the guests mingled below; so I chose to wander up to the second balcony to keep an eye on them as I placed myself in a position where I could also observe the movements of the Regent moving among the crowd below. I watched as the priestess tilted her head up towards the players on the second floor and gave a nod so slight that it would have gone entirely unnoticed had I not been wary. Out of the corner of my eye, I watched as one of the musicians stopped playing her flute quite abruptly and turned to depart through a side door; so I took it upon myself to quietly follow her into the chamber beyond.

The girl went into a dressing room and quickly changed into an outfit similar to the attire of the serving maids and took a platter of food that had been left for the musicians, and rearranged the delicacies to make them appear untouched. I watched from the shadow of the door as she removed a small familiar vile from a leather pouch and sprinkled its contents across the morsels; being careful not to touch the mysterious liquid with her bare hands. I melted into the closet as she picked up the tray of tainted food and turned around to rejoin the festivities as I slipped out behind her a moment later. Realizing that she had poisoned the cuisine on the serving tray, I made the rash decision to thwart her plans.

The girl stepped out of the backroom with her hair now tied up and walked with an entirely different demeanor than she had during her act as a musician just moments before. It threw me off for a moment when she gleefully offered the tray to the instrumentalists until I witnessed them all politely decline with a shake of their heads and she turned to offer the appetizers to the surrounding guests before starting to make her way down the stairs and into the crowd on the ground floor. I quickly snatched a half-empty wine glass off a nearby table and stumbled down the stairs, intentionally tripping myself as I cascaded down the side rail. My body came in square contact with the unsuspecting girl as I grabbed her tray arm to keep myself from falling. This sent the food upon it flying to the floor as the tray and its various appetizers went toppling down the carpeted stairs.

There was a stall in the music as the band stopped playing, while the surrounding guests turned to gasp at the sudden commotion as the silver tray clattered to the floor. Putting on the act of being quite inebriated, I stood up to brush myself off and helped the girl to her feet with blubbering apologies. The poisoned contents of the tray had been ruined, and I caught her giving a distraught glance towards the cult priestess as her face turned sour.

Quickly recovering her dignity as the musicians began to play once again, the serving girl scurried back up the stairs while refusing my offer of assistance.

No one was the wiser for what had just happened, and the patrons went back to their intoxicated conversations and revelry; that is, all except the pale dancer in her sparkling outfit who turned to the Regent and whispered something into his ear before she calmly divorced herself from the other guests and headed out the front entrance in haste. I quickly caught sight of Nyx who had witnessed the episode unfold, and with a secret hand signal, I issued her to follow after the priestess who had just departed. Having placed my apprentice on her tail, I turned back to see that the Regent was now shaking hands with the plump chancellor and bidding him goodnight as he planned to retire from the party for the evening.

I had no doubt that in her exotic guise, the cult priestess had invited him for a private rendezvous at her manor after the party, where he would most assuredly come to no good end. The attempted poisoning of the guests' appetizers would come secondary to pursuing the Regent for his own protection; so I shadowed him as he swiftly headed out the gate to call for his personal carriage. Our original plan was to draw the Regent aside to a private room during the party, where we could secure him away from his personal entourage and sneak him off the grounds in the dark of the night. However, our plans to that effect had gone wildly astray.

There were far too many guards present to outright accost him, so I had to make a quick decision in this contingency and headed straight for the stables. It wasn't protocol for a guest to gather their own mounts, so I put on an act of being a drunken lout that was sick by taking a swig of wine and coughing it up at the feet of the closest guard who jumped back to avoid the mess as I spit up the fake vomit.

They would be glad to have an intoxicated guest off their hands, especially one who retched his dinner upon their polished armor. The ruse worked better than I could have hoped, and without further resistance they let me grab my horse from the young stable hand as I galloped off into the night in pursuit of the Regent's carriage.

I was a little distressed that I had seen neither Nyx nor the costumed priestess at the entrance before riding off into the cold night, but they had been a few steps ahead of the Lord Regent before he departed. I trusted that my apprentice was adept enough to pursue her prey; especially so after having saved my skin back in the mines. I pressed forward without hesitation, for I knew where the regent was heading. I crisscrossed through several side streets in the Ivory quarter, where a lone horse could travel beyond the limitations of a carriage, in order to reach the manor before his arrival.

In all honesty, I was not looking forward to returning there knowing what horrors lurked in the cellar. I would be lying to myself if I believed my usual calculating demeanor wasn't affected by the chilling scene I had witnessed that day. I could have just as easily ended up dead by the hands of these cultists, with my corpse strung up and sliced to pieces alongside the other servants that Nyx and I had discovered. It deeply bothered me to wonder if this cult truly wanted me dead, for if so, then why had they gone through the trouble of handing me over to the city watch and left me to rot in the dungeon for months when they could have disposed of me right then and there?

The riddle of this gnawed at me as I dismounted my horse several yards from the back of the manor and patted the stallion on the rear to let it run off into the night. Although I was still in my costume for the party, I had not come unprepared. Within my hat, I had hidden a gauze scarf to use as a mask, and quickly removed my tunic and turned it inside out to reveal the dark material lined beneath. Though I was grossly lacking in my usual gear; my two armed bracers and concealed dagger hanging around my neck would have to suffice.

The sash I had worn was woven of thick thread, and with a quick loop tied into both its ends, the cloth served as a short climbing rope to help me shimmy up a pillar in the rear of the building as I gained access to the rooftop. I had scouted out this estate before and was confident I knew every room and hall. I was not surprised to find the property currently occupied as I saw movement through the glazed windows. Making my way to the front of the mansion, I watched as the Regent's carriage arrived in the courtyard below.

There were a few guards from the City Ward present to greet him in the yard, which further confused me as to their participation in this scheme. However, upon the arrival of the carriage, a butler wandered out from the manor to greet him as I overheard the Regent tell his driver to pick him up at dawn, while a pair of the Lord's personal guards stepped from the carriage and relieved the city guards of their posts, and took their place. With a nod, the driver took off into the misty evening as the clatter of hooves across the cobblestones disappeared into the dark, while the city guardsmen returned to their barracks. As the Regent calmly stepped inside the manor, I became pressed for time to find my way inside to thwart the attempt against his life by the members of the cult. I could only hope that Nyx was also somewhere upon the grounds if she had been successful in pursuing the spider priestess back to her lair.

Koda and I had assumed that the Regent would be disposed of by the cult while behind closed doors here at the mansion, where he wouldn't have the protections of the City Ward, and only had a pair of personal guards stationed outside. His sentries had seen him come in, so it left me wondering how these fanatics could think they would get away with murdering a visiting diplomat? I had suspected that there was likely another secret route in the cellar which led through the sewers back to the mines; but with a little investigation, the City Ward would undoubtedly find it even if the entire staff of the chateau fled through the hidden route back to their subterranean den. Their actions would eventually bring the entire city guard down upon their heads should the authorities raid the labyrinth of mineshafts and eradicate the cult if they did something so brazenly foolish.

It just didn't make sense. Certainly, their hatred of the royalty and wealthy aristocrats, who ruled the upper echelon of the city, wouldn't lead them to a suicidal war of the classes. The city guards were far too well-armed for the scamps and dredges we saw lurking in the abandoned mines; and if prompted, any violent skirmish would surely result in a massacre. There must be an end game here that we had overlooked.

Being the winter season, I didn't have the luxury of multiple points of entry and freedom of movement since the windows were mostly boarded up this time of the year to ward off the cold. Being wary of entering through the upper balcony as I had on previous visits, I used my utility knife to slip open a latch on an exterior shutter to let myself into a darkened privy. Though not the most lavish of entries, I had managed to get inside unnoticed. I began to wonder what had become of Nyx as I snuck down to the lower level while evading the occasional staff which passed through the candlelit halls.

Acting as insulation in the winter months, the heavy curtains covering the bare stone walls were a blessing to a thief; and their presence allowed me to meld with the shadows cast by the sparse lighting spaced throughout the manor. I was actually impressed by how quickly they had refilled the villa with new furniture and paintings; giving the space an entirely different ambiance than it had before. This was a theater to them, and everything within was a prop to create an atmosphere to match the scenery of their stage. The manor was currently covered with an interesting array of gaudy decorum; which I considered would have reflected the personality of an exotic artist such as the role the spider priestess was now playing to lure in her unwary prey.

I heard voices coming from the rear of the grand hall, which encircled the central hearth that held the source of heat within the building. Slinking ever closer, what I spied there made my heart sink. The spider priestess was standing there, still in full costume, while the Regent rested in a high-back chair across from a stool upon which Nyx sat slumped forward, with her body bound by ropes. I watched as the priestess calmly walked over to a table with her back turned to them both, which hid what she was doing while she poured two glasses of wine from a decanter, then quietly sprinkled a few drops from a small poison vial into both drinks.

I noticed there weren't any armed guards inside the manor, however, several handmaids stood silently in the background of the room where they kept at attendance while the priestess returned to her guests and handed one of the blighted cups to the Regent, while she held the other before her in front of Nyx as she struggled at her restraints. Moving as close as I dared, I could overhear their conversation above the crackling fire of the hearth.

"So, my dear, why would a mere serving girl follow me from the governor's party?" Lilith hissed in her strange voice while she swished the tainted contents of the glass as she noted Nyx's outfit from the banquet.

Nyx just flashed her host an ugly glare, though she was more aggravated than anything else for having gotten herself caught. The young rogue had seen the carnage of the dead servants in the cellar and knew her situation was dire. What I hadn't expected was that the Regent would be calmly accompanying the interrogation of the captured girl; when in all respects, they should have just handed her over to the city guards before they were dismissed. I felt a tense flash of indecision when the Lord Regent smirked at the dancer's remark to their captive, and took a swig from his poisoned glass.

I felt as if I had failed the Guild at that moment by not rushing out to stop him from drinking the lethal wine, but doing so would have likely gotten both Nyx and I killed in the process by acting so rashly. I had to bide my time and wait for the right moment before making any move to free my apprentice; so I quelled my rising anxiety and watched to see what would happen next. As the moments passed, I was a little perplexed when the Regent took another drink and emptied the glass he held; showing no ill effects. The priestess, Lilith, still held her glass before her subdued prisoner, as if to taunt her with it.

"Ah, an excellent vintage," the regent remarked as he took a stiff breath while removing his gauntlets to warm his hands by the fire. In doing so, I could see that the tips of his fingers were also stained black, as were the priestess and her monk alchemists we had seen in their toxic garden. Nyx had followed the dancer to the manor in a vain effort to protect the Regent, as I had, although a look of puzzlement crossed her face, as did my own from the distant shadows, to this curious revelation.

"Indeed so," Lilith smiled with her vicious grin, "...oh, you look confused my little dear," the priestess noted with a condescending tone as she grasped Nyx by the chin while the young thief's eyes grew ever wider, "Ah, there now, you are beginning to understand, aren't you?" She chastised the young rogue, "As you can tell, the Lord Regent and I have had previous acquaintance for quite some time. In fact, we share the same goals for Stilgrave and those depraved nobles who tarnish this city with their obnoxious presence," she hissed once again as she turned a polite smile towards her exalted guest.

This was a turn of events I was not expecting, nor by my apprentice by the subtle bewilderment that flashed within her scared eyes. The rulers from Blacktide and the elders from the cult of the Golden spiders had been allies all along. My gaze fell back upon the Lord Regent where I noticed a familiar pendant hanging from his neck, which bore a single embedded tooth within its cold silver casting. Clearly I had misinterpreted the conversation both my accomplice and I had overheard from the spider priestess; which only served to add more mystery to their nefarious scheme.

Confessions

"Just to enlighten you, I was actually born into a noble family who enjoyed the privileges of position and influence among the circles of upper society," the cult priestess admitted to Nyx as she paced before her with the poisoned cup in her hands, "perhaps it was the hand of fate which one day led me to befriend a poor servant girl against my fathers wishes; a friendship which eventually led me to the outer banks of the docks where this young girl and her mother lived. I must admit, exploring the realms outside of the lavish manors of the Ivory district opened up an entirely different world to me; but though they were poor, the people there were kind and accommodating and didn't care about my family title or to which class I belonged. They were merely common folk struggling to survive day by day and to be as happy as their miserable lives would allow. What they couldn't reap from the sea to fill their bellies they earned by hard labor to the highborn," Lilith related to her captive rogue as the Lord Regent listened with a dry grin drawn across his cheeks.

"If so, then why do you now conspire against the nobles and risk bringing war to our shores?" Nyx dared to spout at her masked interrogator.

"Ah, but there's a crux, and you haven't heard the entire story, little one," the priestess answered, "...children of the imperials live very protected lives, which are twisted and controlled as we are taught to see others with less as if they are merely assets, rather than equals. And as such, my small act of rebellion to escape the confines of my family's estate offered a measure of excitement as a great adventure to see these new sights and surroundings. One day, while playing with my friend along the cliffside shore near her hovel, my impoverished friend and I discovered the abandoned mines left deserted ages ago, and as children are curious little creatures, we snuck our way inside to see what mysteries we could find," Lilith paused to reflect as if she was reliving the moment, "we dared not step too far into the darkness, but that was when we saw several glints of yellow light, like a swarm of fireflies sparkling from the inner walls. I alone, dared to delve deeper and approached one of these curious specks which glimmered upon the rough walls, and reached out to caress its alluring gleam reflecting in the dim twilight of the cave; believing it to be the sparkle of gold. However, it was at that very moment when my life forever changed."

Lilith looked at her hand through her veiled mask as if experiencing the event itself long ago when she was but a small curious child. Those days of naive innocence were now lost as a distant memory but not entirely forgotten. Hearing Lilith's tale, the Lord Regent flashed a smug look towards Nyx; as though he knew she was about to experience something especially unpleasant which she would most certainly not enjoy. This gave me further cause to worry as I tried to read his body language to foretell what might transpire next; for any action I took henceforth would require that I give up my sanctum in the shadows to save Nyx from an unsavory fate.

"If your family was so privileged, then why are you putting them and everyone in Stilgrave at risk?" Nyx squawked as she glanced about the room uncomfortably, looking for some means of escape from this dire situation.

"When I was that small child, my girl, I tried to clutch that little speck of light I thought to be the glitter of gold, only to be stung," Lilith announced as she looked at her blackened fingers, now tainted and stained from countless years of handling noxious poisons, "You see, those little specks of light swarming the cavern walls were merely reflections from the golden patterns which adorn the bodies of a rare species of spider. Their venom is highly toxic, especially so to a small child. After I was bitten, I rushed out of the dark mine, and as I began to fall ill the people who lived on the shore sent a messenger to retrieve my father in the upper district; but by the time he had arrived, I had turned pale and fallen unconscious. Afterward, I had lain comatose for several weeks as my family called upon every doctor and alchemist in the city to try to save me from death while I grew increasingly fragile as my life was slipping away. It wasn't until I awoke several months later when I discovered I had lost my voice as a side effect of the poison, which took many years to regain my ability to speak again, as it is today," she noted towards her oddly hissing voice, "it wasn't until I regained a measure of my health from being bedridden that I had learned, that in my parents grief, they had presumed I was going to die. I was horrified to discover that my father had taken it upon himself to retaliate against the impoverished citizens who lived along that desolate shoreline; as he personally blamed them for the curse which afflicted his only child," the priestess added.

"Lilith, tell her what happened to those poor souls at the merciless hands of the city governor during those dark times," the Lord Regent advised as he lounged in his seat while fiddling with the small silver pendant hanging around his neck.

At hearing his suggestion, the priestess swished her fingers in the poisoned wine cup and dabbed a few drops onto Nyx's lips before the girl could react.

"My father was a prideful and vindictive man, and he used his wealth and position to sway the former Chancellor to order soldiers from the city ward to exact his retribution upon these people, whom he believed had harmed his child. What is now left of that accursed place is but a cluster of broken and forgotten ruins scattered along the shore and the mangled remnants of shattered families who had lost everything they possessed. Those few injured who managed to survive the onslaught by the vengeful attack, escaped into the mines; what was left of their orphaned children are the lineage of crippled and destitute vagrants you see in the city gutters begging for scraps," the priestess confessed.

As I listened to her story from the shadows, the formation of the underground society of the poor and destitute began to make sense. They had been driven underground many years ago by the anger and vanity of a vengeful nobleman who had seen these underprivileged as a threat to his family and way of life. As the priestess continued, I understood how this once highborn heiress was robbed of her future by the caustic actions of her own family. It turned out that the attack on the shoreline-ward had fanned the flames into a cruel blaze, one which swept upon the poor across the lower city districts; creating a crisis among its people.

When these refugees flooded into the abandoned mines, they discovered the old shelters left by the first settlers of this mountain town. It was there that the poor and wretched found refuge from the resentful tyrants in their silken gowns who ran the city by brutal dominance. Those impoverished victims had endured great hardship after their homes were destroyed and forced to abandon their decaying dwellings along the shore, so as not to draw the wrath of the City watch to their sanctuary deep within the labyrinth of forgotten passages.

It was within those buried mine shafts that they found the temples dedicated to the Builders that were praised by the elite, but in their rage, these ancient sanctuaries were soon desecrated and replaced by shrines to the cult of the Golden Spiders. I could imagine the disdain these fortuneless people had for high society and the arrogant leadership which had stolen their dignity and kept them pressed beneath their thumbs. They had toiled away the best years of their lives for mere crumbs, while the lazy aristocrats feasted at their banquets in their mansions and manors. I understood because I was one of them, but I honed my skills as a thief to reclaim what had been unjustly withheld from our pitiful lives.

"I had seen you among the attendants at the chancellor's festivities this evening," the Regent professed towards Nyx, "now why would a mere servant girl be following Lady Lilith to her manor?" He demanded with an inquisitive tone. Nyx had shadowed the dancer on her journey back to the mansion, only to find herself surrounded by these cult followers who had been expecting an intruder.

"Either she is a spy for the city governor or here to attempt to relieve me of my money, or my life," the priestess speculated.

The mild poison Lilith had placed upon her captive's lips had started to take effect, while Nyx felt her head begin to swim. Noticing the drugged look in her eyes as Nyx began to waver, the priestess started the interrogation of her captive.

"Members of our sect have built up a resistance to many types of poisons over these long years," the priestess granted as she displayed the tips of her blackened fingers to the bound girl, "yet in low doses there are several varieties which have, let's say, more *interesting* side effects on those who are not initiated in our ways."

Nyx appeared dazed for a moment when her head began to sway as she tried to shake off the effects of the drug. Observing from my corner of the room, I had wondered if Lilith was going to kill the young thief with her tainted concoctions, and knew I had to do something before she was administered a fatal dose. Beside the Priestess and the Regent, there were four other handmaids present and the glint of the curved blades hanging at their sides did not go unnoticed. There would be little chance of rushing out to cut Nyx loose from her bonds and successfully making an escape, especially in her current condition.

"We need to find out who she is and who she works for," the Regent declared to his accomplice, "small increases in dosage of the poison will make her ever more compliant, but as you know, too much may kill her," he cautioned.

The spider priestess was quite aware of that since she worked with various toxins for many years and was well educated in their effects. Her assumed persona as an exotic dancer was one way she was able to fraternize and mingle with the nobles and upper society without fully revealing her true identity. Given that without her mask, the priestess would appear like a demonic wraith to an average commoner who beheld her darkened eyes and ghoulish skin. Such unsightly features were easily covered by the adornment of lavish costumes and makeup usually worn by such entertainers of the theater.

"Perhaps we need to explain what is about to happen to you, little one," Lilith announced as her tone turned sour, "the more poison I apply, the more drained and flexible your will becomes; so don't fight it, for too much of this elixir can cause permanent damage," she warned the bound thief.

I could no longer bear to watch Nyx being tortured, nor could I risk letting her die at the hands of this vile priestess. My opponents in the room were armed with their vicious blades and poisons left me clearly outmatched, and I realized the odds were stacked against me. Even so, I could not watch Nyx suffer, nor let her meet the cruel fate of those servants whose mangled bodies littered the blood-stained floor of the cellar below our feet. Hastily checking my gear again, I realized I was ill-equipped for this conflict, and conceded that my only hope at gaining the initiative was to create a distraction.

Like the hand of fate, a sudden loud banging from the main door echoed throughout the hall. Both Lilith and the Regent appeared surprised by this rude interruption to their plans. The sound of a scuffle and a clashing of blades pierced through the heavy wooden doors a moment before they burst open, and the cold air of the night rushed in. Like a dark wind, several masked brigands flooded through the entry and fanned out into the grand hall. In reaction, the cult maidens brandished their hellish weapons and stepped forward to defend their priestess.

Lilith dropped her glass of poisoned wine and backed away as the Lord Regent followed in her wake. Turning towards this new adversary, I slunk deeper into the shadows to analyze the situation before making a move. It took but a moment for me to recognize the emblem on the leather armor of the marauders. A masked man with a familiar stature stepped forward and ordered his crew to capture the cult priestess; apparently, the Thieves Guild had interceded to save one of their own.

A pair of archers stepped forward with their crossbows and took down two of the armed handmaidens where they stood; their wickedly curved blades dropped from their hands, clattering to the floor before, they too, fell beside them with bolts protruding from their chests. Behind them, the priestess slipped beneath the thick tapestry secured upon the wall, and disappeared. The Regent lunged forward to follow his accomplice until my tossed knife found its mark in his thigh, crippling him. With a violent clash of swords and daggers, the remaining occult maidens fell while a pair of thieves rushed forward to accost the wounded Regent where he had dropped to his knees.

Lowering his mask, Koda's gaze turned my way as I

stepped from the shadows beside the stairwell. A brother thief dashed forward to peer behind the heavy curtain for a moment, before reporting back to the guild master.

"She escaped through a secret door," he declared as he was unable to find the hidden switch that opened the portal behind the wall.

"You wounded the Lord Regent..." Koda seemed to question my actions, though he was wise enough to know I would have a good reason to do so.

"Everything is not as it seems here..." I began to explain before he cut in his response.

"It usually never is," he smirked back with a hard glare while awaiting my answer.

"The Regent here is colluding with the cult priestess, Lilith, who was posing as the dancer at the governors banquet," I motioned towards the wounded lord who was scowling at one of our men that was busy binding his leg with a tourniquet, who ripped out my small knife from his thigh before handing it back to me, "they confessed to have been plotting to overthrow the Chancellor and seize the city," I declared.

"Which would be a violation of the long standing treaty between our regions," Koda finished as he turned towards the two guild members holding the Regent and motioned for them to take him away.

"A little help here..." Nyx cried in her drugged stupor as another member jumped forward to cut away her bindings, "before you guys start hugging one another and celebrating; maybe one of you could go catch that ugly bitch before she escapes back into the mines."

Nyx was right of course, and we would lose our advantage if the priestess was allowed the time to assemble a defense within the great labyrinth of passages deep within the mountain. The Regent from Blacktide was secured and taken back to the guildhall where he would be held for questioning regarding his treason, while Koda and I took a few men to search the cellar of the manor for the hidden entrance to the sewers. A half dozen of us grabbed lanterns as I forewarned them about the bodies in the basement before we entered the scullery. We found the kitchen cupboards and counters were now stocked with fresh meats and produce as we made our way down the narrow cellar stairs.

Creeping below, I was mildly surprised to see that the bodies of the tortured servants were now gone. All but bare traces of their presence had been swept away; however, they could not mask the faint stench of their dried blood and decaying corpses which lingered in the stale air. Searching the room thoroughly with our lamps, one of the men found a hidden panel behind a barrel that swung open when its lid was turned. The wooden rack pulled away from the wall to reveal a narrow gap within the foundation, a quick glance inside revealed it led into a well-kept corridor beyond.

It made sense now that this manor had been equipped with secret doors and hidden passages to allow the cult to perform their covert missions. They operated much in the way Beren had hidden corridors beneath the streets to accommodate his smuggling of stolen goods between the city districts. It made me wonder how long this obscure cult had been interfering and manipulating the politics of Stilgrave over the generations. I wouldn't be surprised if the sudden deaths and mysterious disappearances of several peasants and officials in recent years had been dealt by their stained hands.

The corridor opened up into the sewers where I paused and held up the lantern to the walls. Before us, glinting in the spec of light, I spied a small gilded spider embossed upon the wall as I pointed this out to the other members of the Guild.

"Search carefully for this symbol," I instructed the men as I pointed at the design.

We fanned out along the sewer system and heard the cry of an owl echo up the hall; which was our way of signaling by night to other thieves without drawing attention to ourselves. Rushing forward, we assembled where we had been called towards an opening that had been carved into the solid rock beyond the architecture of sewer drains. It held the familiar scent of dank earth I recalled from my last visit to the mines, where Nyx and I had escaped the clutches of the cult. Making our way in, we slowed our pace to the practiced stealth of our trade.

Hand signals replaced speech as we crept deeper into the labyrinth of tunnels and shafts that spread out before us. Tracking our prey, we noted droplets of fresh blood scattered among the dusty floor until we found a wet arrow shaft lying in the dirt, and realized that one of the bolts from our crossbows must have found its mark in the priestess as she fled. As we drew deeper, I saw a familiar pattern in the layout of the tunnels and recognized where we were. Instead of returning to the depths of the mines, the priestess had headed towards the garden sanctuary in the grotto.

We quietly approached a pair of armed monks standing guard at the entrance to the chamber, who were easily distracted by a tossed stone down the hall beyond them. As one sentry left his post to inspect the disturbance, with practiced stealth, a pair of thieves lashed out with a weighted scarf around the remaining guard's head; covering his face to muffle him. Pulling it tight, they silently yanked him out of the bloom of torchlight and into the shadows, where he was introduced to a stout club to the skull. The returning sentry looked around in confusion for his missing companion before a tossed club flew in from the darkness and clapped him sharply between the eyes with an audible snap.

We pulled their limp bodies into a side chamber, and bound them so that they could not move when they awoke. As a precaution, one of us stayed behind to warn the others in case more company crossed our way so that we wouldn't become trapped within this dead-end corridor with no means of escape. Our comrade donned one of the monk's robes and pulled the hood low so as to remain in disguise if anyone approached. As he took his post, the rest of us made our way up into the chamber as the cool night air swept in from the natural opening in the cavern high above.

With silent hand gestures, Koda directed another member to scout the perimeter of the double-tiered chamber to forestall any unwelcome surprises, while Koda and I made our way to the garden on the upper level. Scanning the area from the shadows, the cult priestess was nowhere to be seen. Only a lone portly monk sat at one of the alchemy tables, quietly looking at something which he held within his hands. I turned and signaled to Koda that I would capture this cult member for questioning while he stayed at the entrance stair in case one of our men raised the alarm.

Sneaking through the shadows until I was beyond the monk's line of sight, I crept up silently behind him with the garrote from my arm guard dropping to the ready. As I crept up behind him, I detected something familiar as the man was muttering to himself in words too quiet to hear. With a sharp jerk, I snatched back his cowl to bind his neck but paused in a moment of dismay when the man turned his frightened eyes my way. What was Beren doing here dressed as one of these cultists?

"Ah... Ash, my old friend," the shopkeeper stuttered in shock, but drawing a blank in words for not knowing what else to say. I looked down to see that he was holding yet another bone embossed pendant in his hands while also noticing that the tips of his fingers were now stained as dark as slate.

"What is this Beren; what have you done?" I demanded with a tone of condemnation. The resulting look of guilt embedded in his eyes told volumes, which only cemented my assertion of his betrayal.

"I'm sorry Ash, I should have told you; but I know you would have disapproved," he began to mumble, "either way my old friend, its too late now... *cough**" he began to choke.

"What do you mean?" I responded in sincere confusion; though glancing down I could see a tell-tale sign of the means of his ailment.   Upon a plate before him sat remnants of blue petals and poisonous berries. The look in his watering eyes told me he had taken them.

"There is no cure for this," he choked through a hoarse breath as he glanced down at the toxic plants, "...I was hoping the poison would act faster, at least before the city watch raids the mines," he added with a somber smile, "I'm a coward, you see, Ash. I'm sorry I got you into all this, but honesty is not exactly one of the highest qualities for men like you and I," he added with a painful grin.

"What are you talking about?" I charged back, "You told me you were afraid of these cultists, yet..." I began to accuse before he interrupted.

"Yet here I am," Beren interjected as he grabbed my arm for support when his balance suddenly faltered.

I could tell he didn't have long. I had known Beren for many years, ever since I was a kid myself picking pockets and robbing merchants in the streets. Our relationship had flourished over time as I matured and my skills as a thief had sharpened. I had always held a measure of trust in him; until now.

"What are you doing in this place?" I inquired more gently to the nature of his deceit.

"My old adversary, Vale, had acquired a rare relic beyond

his knowledge of its true historical value; and I knew there was only one man in this wretched city who possessed the skills to steal it from him," Beren's painful red eyes turned up towards me, for it was I of whom he spoke of, "At the cost of a few coins and scraps of bread I set you up with a few tidbits of information from the lips of a local street urchin; about an easy job at that particular mansion within the Ivory district. It would be a mark which I knew you couldn't resist," he revealed how he had baited me with what had appeared to be an easy heist. "I had to set you up, Ash; but for good reason. Several months prior, I had the unfortunate luck of crossing paths with that priestess witch and her wretched cult, and she threatened me with an unpleasant death if I failed to obtain what she desired," and at those words, Beren attempted to chuckle at the irony of her threat, for he had failed to escape that fate as he now sat dying in her poisonous garden, "so I paid off a few guards to let you stew in the dungeons to soften up your temperament, and a pretty sum to the Thieves Guild to rescue you from the gallows," the old man muttered.

"You risked my life for a rotting skull?" I shot back with a cold glare.

"I'm sorry, it was all a sham to get you to cooperate in acquiring that relic, which is some sort of heirloom to this Spider Cult. If I had tried to get anyone else to steal that artifact, they would have likely sold it themselves to another fence, but I knew I could trust you to retrieve it," Beren choked out his words. "I returned the relic to these fanatics as they had demanded, but that bitter wench, Lilith, reneged on her agreement and demanded that I was to remain here as her captive until she had taken over the city; since she was afraid I would sell my information and ruin her plans."

"You could have just told me, Beren, and we could have worked something out..." I reached for a rational answer in the last few moments of his pathetic life.

"No, no... *cough**" he gasped, as he began to grasp at his throat, "These people are sick of mind and twisted by hate because they have been deprived of any sense of decency in their lives.   They are unable to comprehend any impression of balance; but only revenge and death to all of those who had ever crossed them.   They can only see the rich and affluent upper class as evil and wasteful; while unable to recognize that all their envy and anger has poisoned their souls; making them just as monstrous as those for whom they hold so much hate."

"We have to stop Lilith," I demanded, though the callousness of my tone softened as Beren's posture began to falter and his face turned pale, "where can I find her?"

"There is a hidden chamber beyond the shrine of bones. You can corner her there," Beren answered weakly.

I knew we were in a dire hurry, but I didn't want to just leave my old acquaintance there to die alone.   Though he had used me through an act of betrayal, Beren was the closest thing I had to a friend in all of my years in this miserable city.

"You were too young to remember, my boy, but I was there on that fateful day when the city watch massacred the peasants and burned down their homes along the waterfront all those years ago," Beren muttered as his grip on my arm began to weaken, "that was where your parents died, and I found you sitting alone in the burnt husk of your home covered in soot and ash ...which is why the name stuck," he confessed with a sickly grin, "you weren't crying like the other children who were robbed of their parents and left as orphans that accursed day, but instead, you held a cold look in your eyes as a child possessed with the stature and strength of a survivor.   Ash, I only hope you can stop this madness...*" he choked again as he slumped from the wooden chair and onto the soft ground in uncontrolled convulsions.

"Do you want me to help you?" I offered grimly as I slipped my finishing knife from my waist as an act of mercy to help him end the pain. For the first time as long as I could remember, I felt a glint of remorse within me; proving that my heart had not turned entirely black over these long, lonely years.

"No, my old friend, I ...I deserve this," he muttered through his pale lips as he gently pushed my blade away, "you must stop these people, for they will murder everyone and bring a blight to the city through their dark magics."

"But they aren't real witches," I responded with logic, "just alchemists who use poisons."

"No, you don't understand... there is something far more evil here at hand which you haven't yet seen," Beren grasped my arm tightly with unusual strength, as if to urge his point that I was making a deadly mistake to underestimate the true nature of this vile cult. His eyes widened at the gravity of his affirmation as if he had once seen this malevolent wraith of which he spoke of. As long as I had known him, Beren had never believed in the occult or dark spirits, but as hardened as I was from my long difficult years living in the streets, the look he held in his eyes still scared me.

With a final sigh, his hand slipped free from my wrist in which I held the sharpened dagger, as his head tipped to one side with that fearful stare petrified in his open eyes. I took the silver pendant he had held in his hand and slowly turned back to meet Koda upon the stair. Seeing me approach alone, the guild master assumed I had taken out the lone monk in the garden without knowing his identity or what had transpired between us.

"Didn't give you any trouble did he; what did you learn?" Koda asked.

"Gather the others, I know where to find the priestess," I

responded with a hardened glare which hid the growing chill I felt prickling up my spine.

I turned and left behind a friend, a weary man with broken morals who, once upon a time in his miserable life, had actually possessed something far more noble than the weak character he held in his final days. I was inclined to forgive him, for it was this hard and unkind world we lived in which whittles away at our dignity, inch by inch, and robs us of our courage to dream of a life better than what we know.

Beren's still body lay crumbled beneath the soft moonlight pouring into the cave from the rift above. In a moment of thought, I found it a cruel irony that he lay surrounded by the beautiful scenery of a lush but poisonous garden; which, in a way, reflected the illusion that flawed men such as ourselves, who live our cursed lives as we struggle against all odds to overcome our past, always knowing deep within our wounded souls that men like us would eventually face a sad fate we could never truly escape, no matter how hard we tried.

Dark Shepard

Koda and I darted back to the lower chamber as we gathered our forces while our group penetrated deeper into the cavern. Following my lead, we rounded a corner and crossed upon the grotto which fed into the sea. Several peasants were milling about as they made their way through the causeway that hugged the rim of the lagoon. Pulling out my blade, I drew a crude map of the passages ahead in the soft dirt at our feet as we huddled together out of sight.

"There is a shrine at the end of the lake, here," I pointed as I tapped the tip of my dagger upon the dirt map, "the priestess can be found there."

"Time is short and we have reason to believe the Ward may raid these tunnels within the hour. We must eliminate this threat," Koda confirmed to his men.

"And if we catch her?" One of the thieves asked.

"We can't afford to take the chance of her escaping again," Koda clarified, "if any of you get the chance, take her out!"

I realized he was right, of course, but also worried that her execution would make the cult priestess a martyr to these fanatics. Cultists were an unpredictable lot and I didn't want to find myself mobbed by a bunch of suicidal lunatics if we killed their leader. As thieves, we weren't exactly warriors but relied on stealth to slip in and out of danger. A crowd of angry peasants cascading down upon us in these tight quarters could go sour in an instant; let alone we had no beef with these vagrant outcasts.

One of the men found a pile of abandoned rags, and we heaved them over our shoulders and arranged them as hoods to hide our faces. Grabbing a few nets and buckets, we headed out into the causeway in our effort to meld into the crowd; hoping to go unnoticed while the rest of our men circled the chamber along the walls. Their route was far more precarious and rife with obstacles to slow their progress, but we didn't have enough fabric for disguises and staying together in a large group would likely draw unwanted attention from the monk guards posted at the top of the alcove.

Koda accompanied me along with two other men as we made our way down to the edge of the lake while donning our disguises. Hefting pails and gear we found sitting alongside the path, we lowered our heads as several peasants passed us unsettling glares. I glanced ahead as we approached the entrance to the shrine of bones, noting the two heavyset guards posted there with their wickedly curved blades glinting in the torchlight.

"Well, any idea what we're going to do about those two?" I whispered over my shoulder to the guild master as he walked behind me.

"We'll improvise," was all Koda remarked as he too stole a glance towards the pair of monks at the top of the step. Taking them out in full view would immediately expose us, so we had to think fast. Growing up on the harsh streets as a child, being a successful pickpocket relied on exercising a fine balance between the art of distraction and sleight of hand. Refining one's skill meant the difference between a full belly or going hungry, and being light of foot either meant a clean escape or a lashing from the city Ward. The trick was to slip away with the goods you lifted before the mark knew they had been robbed.

Of course, being a good cutpurse also meant exercising your own set of defenses against becoming a victim yourself. Dexterity and distraction was an effective tool; although quite useless against someone who saw it coming. If a would-be thief was so unfortunate to have been identified by their victim and was able to escape; they would have to change their persona and appearance to go unrecognized in public. At a young age, the street urchins had learned to change their character like other people changed their clothes.

As we approached the first guard, I held the large vase I grabbed on my opposing shoulder to hide my face, and quickly eased into a staggering limp to make myself look decrepit and crippled. Squinting one eye as if injured, I displaced my jaw in an awkward way as to change the appearance of my features as I casually swabbed a few fingers of dust from our ragged hoods and smeared them across my face. My objective was to have the sentry pay more attention to my face than to the finer clothing I was wearing hidden beneath the sparsely laden rags.

"You there..." I gurgled in a creaky voice as I stumbled up the steep stone stairway to the shrine, "help an old man would you, this load of poison berries from the garden is too heavy for me to handle with my bad leg," I muttered in a strained tone.

One guard shifted his eyes down towards us as I timed my next move just as I faked a stumble, and let the jar on my shoulder fall straight towards his chest. As I had hoped, the man caught the flying vase with both arms and staggered back in surprise. While his hands were full during that vital moment, he was unable to grab the curved blade hanging upon his belt. Following my lead, Koda leapt up and covered the second guard who had turned to aid his companion; and we pressed them back into the landing of the shrine beyond the sight of the peasants milling below.

A quick tap to the back of their heads with the flail knocked them out cold. Murdering unconscious men wasn't our style, so we hogtied them with their own belts. The group of thieves gazed in awe at the shrine spread out before them and its disturbing collection of bones woven into the lattice of webs stretching far above.

"Over there!" I motioned to the others after searching for the hidden chamber Beren had mentioned, lying behind the gridwork of rope and twine cinched around the countless bits of cartilage.

Creeping around the central altar, a quick glance revealed that the entire collection of carved human bones was now missing from their central display. One of the men took the lead and was the first to pass into the narrow corridor which led into the room beyond. We heard a sharp 'click' and the man gave a stifled gasp as he turned back towards us with a look of confusion burning in his eyes. Several short spikes were now protruding from both his head and neck; their metal shafts sticky with some vile black substance oozing from the wounds.

Without a sound, his eyes rolled up into his head and he collapsed where he had stood. The rest of us took a respectful step back, lest we trigger the same trap which had suddenly ended the life of our brother thief in such an unpleasant manner.

"It's booby-trapped!" One of the other men spouted the obvious under his breath.

A moving shadow followed by a scuffle beyond the doorway told us we had been heard by the occupant within, but there appeared to be no alternate entry into the chamber beyond. Rushing around the lattice of knotted ropes, I grabbed a few lids from the crates scattered about the sanctum, but our attention was drawn away from the sound of a signal horn which began to echo throughout the caverns. A clatter of footsteps was heard approaching as one of the men leaned over the lip of the high chamber to observe the activity below.

"We have company," was all he said before darting back into the shrine.

"Up there," Koda pointed as he motioned to the network

of ropes surrounding the chamber. Their anchors were set within the supporting timbers and rock face high above. Koda watched as I grabbed the lids from the crates and impaled a pair of throwing blades into the soft wood for use as crude handles. "Don't let her escape," he asserted as Koda patted me on the back while I hefted the wooden pallets by their embedded knives.

The rest of the thieves began ascending the tangled net that hung above the room as though they were seasoned sailors climbing the yard shrouds upon a ship. Holding the pair of lids to either shoulder, I took a deep breath of courage before leaping through the narrow corridor into the room beyond. All too late, I noticed that the plank set upon the floor had been fitted with a lever. Any small weight upon it triggered the mechanism which spat out the poisoned spikes, which pierced through several sections of the thick wooden lids.

Stepping into the chamber beyond, I promptly tossed my makeshift shields before the rancid residue dripping from the spikes could touch my hands. The room was gripped by a heavy musk from cauldrons of burning incense. Beyond the fragile webs of smoke hanging in the air, I saw that the entirety of the candlelit chamber was decorated with a strange array of idols and frightful statues carved by the hand of some disturbed mind. To my discouragement, a quick search of the small room told me it appeared to be unoccupied, so I began to look for another exit hidden within the chamber.

While stepping around the central pillar within the room, I caught a movement out of the corner of my eye. With a quick duck to the floor, I dodged beneath the arch of a sharpened blade reaching for my neck. The cult priestess had stepped out of a niche in the wall where she had assumed the guise of one of the many tall statues lining the room where she had stood prone, waiting for the right moment to strike. She donned a stony mask matted with gold leaf and her torso was now caked with dust, which helped to camouflage her presence among the collection of statuary.

"Hmm, I recognize you now," the priestess uttered with a grunt, "the pretentious charlatan; you will pay for your arrogance, thief!" she hissed with noted aggravation as she backed away.

I became distinctly wary of the wide curved blade she wielded which had been smeared with some caustic green film; knowing that one cut might spell my demise.

I loosened the flail hanging from my wrist, making ready to strike; but her attention was suddenly drawn towards the commotion of shouting men just outside the chamber door. Backing away, she flung aside a winged statue set against the wall and fled into the narrow tunnel hidden behind it. Diving after her in pursuit, I stalled for but a moment to grab a lantern to check the floor for more devices lest she draw me into another trap. Daring to follow, I raced forward with the small lamp to light my way into the enveloping darkness.

The passage beyond opened into a wide corridor which had been lined with a railing made of rope set into the wall by several spaced anchors. A few steps more and I quickly discovered the reason for the oddly placed rail. On one side of the tunnel, a wide chasm opened upon the floor revealing a precarious fall to anyone who might overstep the narrow path. As I paused to peer into the fissure my foot hit a loose stone that went tumbling into the void below. I slowed my pace, not wishing to take a slip into the rift where my broken body would be forever lost within the belly of the mountain.

I turned a corner to find the priestess standing at a precipice where the remnants of a wooden bridge had once been anchored. What was left of the catwalk was now nothing more than rotted planks and tattered rope left hanging over the edge. Lilith sensed my presence as the light of my lantern fell upon her. The priestess turned as she ripped off her mask so that I could see those terrible black eyes of hers, glistening like a pair of murky shadows. She let the mask fall from her hands to the stone floor and swept a cruel grin back towards me.

"It's over..." I stated after an awkward pause, while noting that she was now cornered. She merely answered my taunt with a sadistic cackle.

"You grew up on the streets of this wretched city, crawling your way up from the curse of poverty through the filth and garbage to gain some pathetic illusion of self-dignity," the priestess declared as she turned to face me, "and look at you... what have you attained after all those years of risk and struggle? You're nothing more than a petty burglar, stealing the wealth of others, and no better than those vile aristocrats who rob the lowly peasants they exploit."

Fundamentally, her raw perspective had a tinge of merit to it, which was clearly meant as a feeble stab towards my sense of honor. However, any such distinction I might have once held in my youth towards such lofty ideology had been long since discarded. I knew her posture had been warped by a series of unfortunate events in her life which had molded her fate, but the killing of innocent people and considering them as mere casualties towards her personal vendetta against the upper class, was not an acceptable consequence. Our Brotherhood of Thieves were not the architects of the turbulent political climate which governed this cruel city; we were merely opportunists trying to survive by navigating the ruins of its scarred and broken landscape.

There was nothing left to say; no speech I could give that would sway the outcome of this final encounter. The priestess had to die.

I let loose a quick spin of the short flail attached to my bracer, which caused Lilith to parry with her poisoned blade in defense. At the last second before coming into contact with her weapon, I dropped my footing to one knee and rotated around to my side; catching her off guard as the tethered weight caught her at the ankles. With a snap of my shoulder, I tugged at the snare, pulling her feet out from beneath her; whereupon she toppled off balance and over the edge of the rift.

Like a miner's pick, her toxic blade slashed down and stuck deep into the crumbling brim of the rocky shelf; to which Lilith held onto by one arm as she swayed above the dark abyss awaiting below. I rose to my feet to stand above her as the priestess gave me a disdainful glare with her horrible eyes; knowing her last moments had arrived.

"Those without faith, lead a life without regret for their evil deeds," she professed with a mild snicker, rambling off some line which sounded like an obscure verse from their warped theology, "know that the Dark Shepard is coming for you all; the one who will invade your dreams and your waking life, and there will be no escape from the nightmare that is to come," the priestess hissed.

"Hmm..." I pondered as I bit my lip in deep thought of her curious threat while I jabbed my foot forward to kick the handle of the dagger by which she clung, "I've been tormented by unpleasant dreams all my life, priestess, and I've learned that the only way to end a nightmare, is to kill the monsters that taunt us."

Her blackened fingers slipped from the handle of the blade when it suddenly wrenched from the stone, and it followed her as it tumbled into the darkness below. The unsettling cackle of the priestess echoed through the cavern as she disappeared into the embracing shadows, a sound that would forever haunt me; leaving me uncertain if it was but a figment of my imagination. Her poetic fate which was written those long years ago, would end with the final page being scripted in the very mines where her story began as a curious little girl.

In a way, I suppose that the priestess was right. In our society, run by those who are rich and depraved, a man's importance is measured by the clink of his coin rather than by his deeds. Thieving those small bits of treasure and trinkets from the wealthy now and then may have very well led to the misfortune of the impoverished from whom they were leeched. But then again, those of the prosperous upper class were known to possess an insatiable hunger beyond any degree of moral conscious.

I stood there for a long moment staring into the empty darkness swimming below, awaiting the hint of a distant thud of her body, a confirmation which never came. The last words from the priestess mentioning a 'Dark Shepard' left a restless and uncomfortable weight in my mind. The Lord Regent from Blacktide had been a party to this entangled plot against our people; but the longer we kept him captive would only worsen our position.

We could not hold him or risk setting him free to enact his treasonous plan. However, that was an issue to attend to only if we were able to escape these catacombs with our lives intact. I picked up my fallen lantern and surveyed the chamber. Apparently, the priestess had presumed this avenue would provide a means of escape; however, the rotted bridge had been left to fall into ruin and disrepair, and it appeared as if its securing tethers had been severed.

The shattered catwalk was in a state of decay and was clearly unsafe to traverse; which left me perplexed as to why she would choose an escape route that was clearly a dead end. It could be that the priestess was so absorbed with the pursuit of vengeance against the hierarchy which ruled the city, that she had failed to consider a backup plan.

It was a hard notion to regard; since the basic rules of a master thief would be composing a contingency plan in the event any initial strategy went awry. This labyrinth of caves and winding shafts had been her home for countless years. Even though the priestess had proven to be of shrewd mind and possessed the guile to think ahead, somehow she had failed at this one task.

Knowing I had to leave and get back to the fight to defend my guild brothers; I had to surrender to the fact that I would likely never get the chance to return to these forbidden passages. Rushing back out into the hidden room of statues, I found the mechanism which operated the trap and crippled the device by inserting a rod obtained from a nearby statue, which I jammed into its gears. Being convinced the trap was secured, I hastened through the narrow corridor to find that Koda and the others had trimmed the anchors to the webbing, which in turn, acted like a weighted net that fell upon the monk sentries below; effectively snaring them in its heavy bindings.

Koda hopped down from the far wall where they had scaled the rocky surface, while several of the men were playfully jabbing their swords into the mess of writhing occultists caught in the bone-laden net.

"It's done," I stated with conviction as the guild master approached my position.

"Good. We should make our way out the way we came. I don't want to be here when the city ward shows up armed to the teeth and starts taking names," Koda answered.

We struggled through the chaos of unarmed peasants who were rushing through the passage in alarm. After reaching the tunnels, I advised our crew upon the alternate route we could take once we reached the sewers; one which would take us through to the collectors study in the Ivory district. After making our way into Vale's apartment, for our own protection, Koda instructed the rest of the men to immediately relocate the guildhall to another quarter of the city. It was a process we were familiar with, and I knew before the break of dawn over the snow-capped mountains that the thieves market beside the Raging Stallion would be dismantled and abandoned, with nothing left as a trace to our presence.

If we were lucky, it would be a few days before the chancellor started looking for the Lord Regent and realized that their royal guest had gone missing; as he was currently being held captive at a secret location. While spending a majority of my time at my apartment recuperating from the encounter, I was pleasantly surprised to see Nyx skirting in through the open window several days later.

"It's nice to see that you've recovered," I bade her welcome as I motioned towards a bottle of fine brandy I had pilfered from Beren's shop; while noting that she wasn't adorned in her regular gear. She was wearing ragged traveler's clothes as if she were a pilgrim. Before answering, she snatched up the bottle of brandy and popped the cork with her teeth. After spitting it out across the room, she took a long swig which was followed closely by a resentful sigh.

"I was as sick as a dog for a few days, but the poison finally ran its course," she answered curtly, though I could tell something else was on her mind.

"What's with the disguise, are you pulling a job today?" I asked curiously.

"It's not a costume," Nyx answered as she set down the half-empty bottle, "get your gear; Koda is sending us to Blacktide," she explained with a straight face. Though by the hardened posture she took I could tell she wasn't happy about the assignment.

Blacktide

I wasn't too thrilled about the mission our Guild Master had set us up for either. Nyx explained that Koda had planned to keep the Lord Regent hostage for the moment and was sending us as emissaries to deliver a forged document from our governor stating the Regent would be late on his return. On the surface, there appeared to be a lot of holes in that story, especially so regarding the Regent's private guards who were killed outside during the attack at the manor. Since I had been staying out of sight for these past few days, Nyx caught me up to speed in regards to what had been happening after we escaped the lower mines.

"Koda moved the guild hall to the Crimson District which is where I stayed with a healer who was able to bleed out the poisons," Nyx admitted, and she looked a bit worse for wear from the ordeal, which made me wonder why Koda would be so eager to push her into a new assignment before she had fully recovered, "The abandoned mines were eventually raided by the city ward when they came searching for the missing Regent and found the bodies of the cultists in the manor. Koda had paid off a few girls at the brothel to testify that the Lord Regent had been staying with them that eve, and that he was recovering from his sexual exploits at a private abode of the Madam who ran the Raging Stallion in the upper quarter; claiming he had paid well not to be bothered and preferred our Governors discretion so that his wife in Blacktide would not get word of his exploits during his extended visit here in Stilgrave."

It was an elaborate cover story, I admit; but that still didn't explain where the two of us fit in.

"I don't know what he's thinking, but you don't look like

you are fit to travel, Nyx; especially in this weather," I offered as a small measure of compassion towards her weakened condition.

"I agree, but Koda said my ailment would only help as a convincing disguise during our trek," Nyx mentioned as she repeated Koda's words, "I'm not quite happy about it either; but after some persuasive torture, the Regent revealed a few disturbing details that convinced our guild master we had to investigate the situation in Blacktide."

"And what might that be?" I asked as I swished the half-empty bottle of brandy Nyx handed back to me while contemplating recent events.

"Apparently, the Lord Regent was working hand in hand with the cult to undermine the political rule of the city and usher in a climate of chaos, by unsettling the peasants from the lower districts into rebellion," Nyx admitted, "they had planned on killing off several lords and ladies of the upper society, and then blame those deaths on their rivals. When the civil discord began to get out of control, the Regent was set to have a few key officers in the city ward he had bribed to intervene during the revolt and castrate the administrators running the city," she finished. Although, it was a little disturbing to watch her mime a phantom blade cutting off the testicles of an imaginary assailant while she made her point.

It sounded like an elaborate plot; one that was worthy of the aristocratic back-stabbers that permeated the gilded halls of upper society. Death and drama were a part of their daily gossip; but if the headcount got too high, then they would certainly turn on one another like hungry wolves. I had to admit, it sounded like a decent plan that had a high probability of succeeding.

"Paying off a few guardsmen wouldn't be enough to pull off such a coup," I muttered aloud in thought at her words, "it's far too easy to be double-crossed or betrayed in that pit of vipers," I professed, "the only way the Regent could hope to have any success in that scheme would be to send a large detachment of soldiers."

"And that's where we come in," Nyx conceded while interrupting my line of thought, "as you know, the Lord Regent is merely the acting authority to the young daughter of the royal Minister of Blacktide. It was reported that the Duchess will come of age next summer, and thus, we presume the regent is attempting to seize power for himself. He would be lynched if he had tried to pull such a plot against his own people, so the Lord is attempting to shoulder his way into the ruling council of Stilgrave, before he should lose his exalted position when the young duchess assumed her official title and coronation.

A man grasping for power was always the sign of desperation, and such a ploy carried many risks. Such men usually associated themselves with kindred delinquents who were just as worse, if not as equally depraved, despite their embroidered silk robes and weight of coin held in their fat coffers. Wealthy wretches were the worst kind because their feeble minds would crown themselves with a troubling measure of self-entitlement, and those with such a delinquency of character would readily betray or sacrifice anyone who got in their way. The affluent filth who resided in the upper districts bore a lack of ethics and integrity that would put any petty thief to shame.

It would be a long journey to the fortified walls of Blacktide which rested along the northern shores. The road across the border wound its way through several steep mountains, and the risk of avalanches was a hazard throughout the winter months. The Lord Regent had arrived in Stilgrave by means of a private convoy, and the corpses of his slain bodyguards had been disposed of at night by the way of heavy stones tied around their boots as they were unceremoniously slipped off the edge of the docks to a watery grave. The guild was risking a great deal by getting involved in this scheme; but Koda had convinced our brotherhood of thieves that war between our territories would ruin many lives and fortunes, and along with it, our livelihood.

I had to admit, our current guild master had a way of dominating a conversation and swaying the attitudes of even our most dubious members. Personally, I was left with no other option but to agree that military conflict would cast the brotherhood to the four winds and bring about an era of gloom and despair; and the extra clink of coin would be a scarce commodity among the nobles. Conflict has a way of tightening purse strings, and treasures quickly find themselves buried or hidden from prying eyes. It would be a dry season for any thief to find surplus revenue during such trying times.

While I was packing my gear, Nyx revealed our travel plans and points of contact once we reached the city of Blacktide. Koda had a boat waiting at the docks that would ferry us to their main port. I was not fond of this idea as the icy waters were known to be treacherous to cross this late in the season, and the thought of drowning at sea was not worth the personal risk. However, the long road by way of the mountain pass this time of the year could be far more precarious without proper armed protection from bandits, or the scattered border outposts where our presence would fall under suspicion and scrutiny.

Nyx finally convinced me that the shorter journey by sea along the coast was the preferred method of travel at this juncture. Packing every hidden blade and picking tools I could scrounge, I adorned the tattered cloak my apprentice had brought for my use to help conceal my gear lying beneath its drape. It had taken many years to gather the accessories of my trade, and each blade, pick, and tool, had its own compact placement upon my person. I didn't want to be caught unprepared, but it was the idea of stepping onto the unfamiliar landscape of a new city that I found the most daunting.

Thieves prefer the familiar, and the confidence that comes with knowing every twist and turn of the city streets alongside every nook and cranny of the narrow alleys in the field. I had only heard stories about Blacktide and learned that it was a maze of high walls and stunning architecture. Koda wanted us to infiltrate the house of nobles and determine the extent of the treachery the Regent had engaged upon in his grand plan before we released him. Gathering a few names of his accomplices would be adequate leverage to hand over to the Duchess and the royal guards should the Regent choose not to cooperate and bring his mad plan to an end.

My one worry was that we would run into yet another murderous cult once upon their shores. Apparently, Koda wanted the best man on the job who could exercise discretion and retrieve any documented plans the Regent kept in his private chambers on the royal grounds, and effectively deliver them back into the Guild Master's hands. With such evidence, Koda was certain he could persuade the Governor to turn a blind eye to the interference of the guild in such political matters. We were all trusting Koda was making the right decision to help preserve the peace in the region.

Once our gear and attire were set, Nyx and I made off for the docks where we met our departing ship at midnight. We boarded under the light of a pale moon and into the hands of a skeleton crew and its captain, who was well paid not to ask questions of his special passengers. Personally, I was not too thrilled to be aboard a watercraft, for the rocking of the ship disturbed my balance and churned my gut in unpleasant ways. After departing the port, we had settled into our cabins for the journey around the coast, when Nyx tossed me a heavy bag of coin.

"There's 500 silver in there for use as bribes and expenses," Nyx stated as she revealed she held a similar pouch of her own.

"Hmm, that's quite a ransom..." I admitted, considering the 1000 silver pieces we held between the two of us was more riches than either of us might see in a lifetime, "a lesser man might be tempted to disappear into the night and let the fates sort out these unpleasant affairs on their own."

"...Or a lesser woman, 'if' they were willing to face the consequences," she answered back with a dry smirk, for she knew I was only testing her loyalty to the guild. If either one of us skipped out on a mission with the goods, we could only expect to find our throats cut in the night as retribution, no matter how far we ran. There might not be honor among thieves, but crossing the Guild was a thought worthy of pause.

We had been provided a basic street map for the layout of Blacktide, showing the location of the royal residence and a sparse number of alternate passages to-and-from the port. There once existed a remote branch of the Thieves Guild within the castle city of Blacktide, but by order of their parliament, each and every one of their members had been hunted down. Such strict laws and merciless consequences for getting caught by the city guard were powerful deterrents for resurrecting another guild within their walls. Blacktide was a harsh environment for anyone in my particular line of work.

The journey took a little over two days by way of the coast. Many areas of our passage were thick with ice but we were blessed with calm seas; unlike the summer months when maritime trade was common, but ships that came to harbor also risked the stormy gales that lashed the coastal regions through late Fall. Our time together in the cabin gave me a chance to further my apprentice's education, as I taught her about coded words and shadow symbols, which were utilized among our brethren.

"These etchings are markers are comparable to road signs for our kind, usually carved into the foundation stones of sites and locations of interest. Such tags are designed to be inconspicuous, but act to revealed the purpose or contents of the building they adorn," I mentioned while drawing out various symbols upon a spare parchment for her to memorize.

"I'm a little confused, Ash," she shrugged, "Why would a thief advertise his marks for others to cash in on?" she inquired, which was a valid question in itself.

It made sense to inscribe warnings of guards or dangers within a given estate to fellow guild members, but to exhibit a wealthy mark for other burglars would be counterproductive to one's own earnings. More than once I had scouted a wealthy abode to loot, only to enter to discover it had already been burgled the day before and parted with nothing of value to show for my efforts. This was one of the main goals of a Guild, which was to establish permissions for certain activities so they wouldn't become so repetitive at prime locations that they became points of interest for the local ward to ramp up patrols, or entice the authorities to set a trap for the culprits. This also helped alleviate the strain of competition for those thieves who got too greedy and made things risky for the rest of the brotherhood.

Shadow marks were used to help warn other members of unseen dangers or to avoid certain areas that were too hazardous to explore. However, there were the few who were crafty of mind to put false hazard symbols on lucrative marks in order to retain those rich targets for themselves. Greed and self-indulgence in our field was as natural as breathing the air, so I salute the ingenuity of those who came up with that ruse; but it still caused issues among the remaining guild members who soon learned to ignore the shadow marks altogether.

"So then, what is the point of me having to learn these symbols if they are obsolete?" Nyx inquired with a scrunched brow of confusion.

"That problematic issue came along after the guildhall in Blacktide had dissolved. Thus, I would imagine any such markings we found would still be valid within the Regent's city," I offered, which she conceded was an adequate answer to her question.

Later that evening, Nyx pressed me for details as to what exactly happened during my confrontation with the cult priestess. I intentionally chose not to mention my surprise encounter with my old fence, Beren; however, I repeated Lilith's final words about a 'Dark Shepard' which was a riddle that had left me mildly perplexed.

"Well now, a dark Shepard, huh? That sounds pretty foreboding..." my apprentice mocked, even though she was fully aware their fanatical members were unbalanced of mind, to say the least, "it sounds like she was trying to manipulate you and get under your skin," Nyx expressed as she passed it off as an empty bluff.

I didn't tell her of the dire warning which had been conveyed by my dying friend; for I witnessed a quota of genuine fear locked within Beren's eyes before his life faded away. I usually don't fall victim to frivolous superstitions but the premonition woven by my old friend and the priestess was more than just coincidence. Like an ill omen, the thought of it became an uncomfortable weight resting in the back of my mind, which continued to grow heavier in the days to come.

We went topside when the stronghold came into sight. The high walls of the castle reflected the hue of the stark cliffs surrounding the main harbor. Heavy mists drifted lazily across the port below this foreboding structure, enveloping the staggering sentinel which stood like a ward against the sea. Rising from the depths was a sandy beach as dark as coal; born from the ebony cliffs that towered above the crashing tide. I was impressed by the architecture of this keep which had made Blacktide into an impenetrable fortress.

The outer walls were far too steep to scale by any length of rope, and the port was protected by jutting towers. At the outer edge of the bluff stood a lighthouse; it's glaring beam cutting through the cold salty air. The castle of Blacktide was a formidable sight, which in comparison, made the port of Stilgrave appear as an indefensible lamb ready for slaughter. Several tall warships were moored at its banks, each twice the size of the merchant vessel we currently occupied.

I was eager to get my feet on solid ground once again and the stone-cut docks were a welcome change to both my gut and my unsteady legs. The guardsmen here were both well equipped and heavily armored. The helmets they wore were forged in a way that they bore the faint resemblance to that of a crab shell, as was the sectioned flairs of their plate armor. They were bearing spears adorned with vicious hooks, which I imagined would work well against both horsemen and marauders alike. Such a weapon could easily snare its prey and keep them at a secured distance at the end of its long spike.

Observing their gait and character, I could tell these watchmen had superior training over the city guards that patrolled Stilgrave, who had grown soft and arrogant from serving the affluent in the upper districts. Nyx and I would have to be extra precautious to not run afoul of the city sentries while we were here. By referring to the map provided to us by Koda, we wound our way through the mysterious city until we reached a quaint little hostel called the Ramshorn Inn. The shadow marks etched into the foundation stones were still barely perceptible; designating the location as a safe-house for those of our distinguished profession.

The place was little more than a tavern with a flophouse above, where travelers could find bedding and accommodations for the night. It had a quiet and mirthless atmosphere where the locals eyed us with suspicion as we entered the door. Per our instructions we received from the guild, we asked for the proprietor about our reservations for the attic room. With a glare of skepticism, the barkeep stepped to the far end of his counter and clumsily untied a small cord fastened to an iron peg set against the wall; disturbing the bundle of cobwebs which had grown upon it over the years.

When the bartender tugged a rope, we heard a distant bell chime from the floor above. Several moments later, a greasy little man tromped his way down the stairs to greet us, although our reception was a little less than cordial.

"Who be you two?" the balding man stammered as he met us at the landing, and by his thin squint we could tell his eyesight wasn't too keen either.

"Uh, we're guests seeking shelter," Nyx responded to the direct question, which was profoundly out of line for a guild host to be asking names in such a public setting, "...within the attic room if you please, good sir."

"*Humph*... good sir?" The little man gave a gruff chuckle, although his beady eyes softened as they passed from me to fall upon my apprentice and the sharp features of her alluring face. She was answered with gaps of blackened and missing teeth in his lecherous smile with a grunt of sensual desire.

"Yes, fine. Follow me," the manager motioned as he turned around and tromped back up the narrow stairs; scratching his rump in front of our faces as we ascended.

"I think he's taken a shining to you," I whispered under

my breath to Nyx, who promptly elbowed me in the ribs for my lacking sense of humor.

We reached the top floor as the squat little man paused to carefully look around for any prying eyes before he removed an old iron key hanging around his neck, and began to unlock a rusted padlock on a tall cupboard at the end of the hall. Unlatching it, the creaking hinges complained as he swung the panel open to reveal a secret door hidden behind it. Stepping up into the faux cupboard, we ducked our heads as Nyx and I scurried inside; turning around for but a moment when we heard the decrepit little man making a scene of clearing his throat while holding out his wrinkled hand in expectation.

Nyx brushed passed me and dropped a pair of silver coins into his greedy little hands.

"Thank you, kind sir," she offered with a forced smile, as the man swiftly covered the loot from sight and stashed it away in his soiled pockets.

"...Kind sir, *heh, heh*," the little man repeated as he giggled to himself with a devious grin while he turned away, satisfied with his small profit.

Nyx turned back while snapping a sideways glare in my direction, as if to warn me not to make any humorous remarks, so I bit my tongue.

The steep narrow stairs were rife with cobwebs and grit, revealing that this section had not been accessed for many years. Entering into the chamber beyond, we found a generous room with windows that opened up with an overlook facing towards the noble house; which certainly made it a perfect location for spying on the ministry. There were a number of unkempt beds along with several crates and a wardrobe where piles of gear had been left abandoned. Apparently, this hidden chamber had not been discovered by the authorities of Blacktide in their purge of the Guild from their harbor city all those years ago.

We removed our distressed robes and Nyx slipped into an appropriate gown befitting for her visit to the quarter of the nobles; in effort to deliver the forged letter from the Regent to explain his postponed return. While she was there, Nyx would collect names and assess the layout and security detail of the castle to identify any weakness for points of entry. Our purpose here was merely a stall tactic and to gather as much information as possible; then quickly report back to the guildhall in Stilgrave. I was hoping things would go smoothly, but my experience told me that such missions usually don't go as easily as they are planned.

I refitted my gear, and we donned our concealing robes as I accompanied Nyx out of the Inn and through several side streets as a precaution to flush out anyone who might be tracking our movements. When we were confident nobody was following us, she removed her cape and exited the alley in her rich apparel along with the forged note for delivery to the Duchess. Her green and gold embellished gown stood out in stark contrast against the dark stonework of the city as Nyx made her way into the viper's nest. I quickly backtracked my way to the Inn and kept an eye on her progress from our secret perch high above; keeping watch as she made her entry into the grand citadel.

I trusted Nyx, and knew she would be safe but this was still a foreign city with unknown dangers. We were both aware that her lone arrival, in place of the Regent's return to explain his delay, would be received with a certain level of scrutiny; and we knew that if anything went drastically wrong during this mission that we would be left to our own devices. The merchant ship we used for transport would arrive back at port in a week's time to collect us, but the captain had been given strict orders not to wait for us should we fail to produce ourselves at the appointed hour.

After surveying the layout of the city from our secret roost, I removed myself from the window to search through what had been left behind by the previous occupants. Pleased with my luck of finding a map of the city that was penned with additional details and notes of interest, I studied its contents; memorizing every road and alley, including every guard post marked upon the parchment. There were also several flagged points drawn around the citadel which weren't explained as to what they signified. Unfortunately, the interior of the castle itself was sparsely inked in at all as to be of any reliable use whatsoever.

There were no dates or names upon the documents, nor scattered scrolls or notes within the room itself, which might reveal a hint at the history of the Guild which once presided here.   I did, however, find several lengths of blackened rope in a box that would be useful to scale the dark stone walls of the tower. At the bottom of the crate, I saw a glint of an object, which I pulled from the cluttered container. This item revealed itself to be a bronze dagger with a strangely curved blade, thickly engraved with worn cryptic runes, and upon the tip of its pommel, I found the familiar crest of a small golden spider.

The Duchess

Once she gained entrance into the citadel, Nyx passed herself off under a false name and guise as the Governor's messenger from Stilgrave. These northern lands were run by a structure of reigning monarchs that had divided the territories to each ruling family. Their system of leadership here varied wildly from the wealthy politicians of the southernmost regions such as Stilgrave. We had candidates who competed for popularity to gain favorable positions, while the royalty of the North merely demanded the loyalty of their subjects.

The sitting Governor of Stilgrave and his cronies were corrupt to the core and usually bought their way into office by one form or another. Opposition and dissent were how the nobility of the north viewed competition; which was most always quelled by the chains of shackles or from the tight end of a noose. Thieves and brigands do not relish the idea of titles, nor bowing or offering obedience to those who haven't earned it. In our years, we had seen rulers come and go, rise and fall, and free men like us were always left behind to pick through the rubble.

"May I introduce Lady Kashara, messenger for the Lord Governor Oren of Stilgrave, with a personal letter for your eminence," the guard spoke aloud for all to hear in the massive reception hall.

Nyx glided in with grace in her emerald shaded dress. The circular room was adorned with bronze statuary lining the rim of the chamber, among the myriad of lit chandeliers which reflected upon the polished floor. Near the far wall, a woman in red wearing an eccentric headdress stood opposite of a soldier adorned from head to toe in ceremonial armor. Between them sat a young girl with a painted face in a white silk gown, who was perched on the strangest throne Nyx had ever seen. The seat was as wide as a bench with a fanned backing that resembled a giant ribcage embellished with gold, which appeared to be composed of gilded whale bones.

The woman in the crimson gown turned a harsh glare towards Nyx with a rude scowl etched on her lips, as if her arrival had been an inconvenient interruption. The older man with grayed hair also turned to gaze upon their new guest. In response, he spun to greet her as his boots clacked upon the smooth marble floor.

"Lady Kashara, a pleasure to make your acquaintance," the man offered cordially as he took her hand and gave a slight bow. Nyx was a little rough on her curtsy but managed to pull one off with a touch of haste.

"I have a message for your lordships ...and ladyships," Nyx quickly corrected as she gave a shy glance towards the young duchess whose curious glance flashed her way.

Nyx offered the envelope to the armored gentleman, who seemed to regard the wax seal upon it with a passing interest, then opened it and made its contents known to his colleagues.

"It appears our lord Regent, Sir Ryan, appears to be delayed in his return for a fortnight, your highness," he offered to the child in white. With that revelation, Nyx could swear she saw a flicker of concern cross the young girls face.

The man then handed the letter over to the woman in red who snatched it from his hands and proceeded to inspect its contents thoroughly.

"Lady Kashara, thank you for delivering this letter to the court," the soldier offered, "but forgive my lack of manners; I am General Stalker and this is lady Shiva Graystone, the high council to her royal Duchess," he offered with a gesture towards Shiva and finally to the young girl who sat motionless on the strange throne between the pair of nobles.

"Charmed ...I'm sure," Lady Graystone answered dryly without tearing her eyes away from the letter.

"A pleasure it is, Milady," Nyx answered while staying in character, "Is there anything else the court may require before I depart?"

"Perhaps there is..." the general responded, "we don't get many visitors from Stilgrave these days. We would be honored if you would join us for dinner this evening before your return home. He offered as an invitation.

Nyx thought about the request for but a moment and realized it would be the prime opportunity to case the castle and gather information. With a graceful bow she accepted; though noting that the young duchess seemed a bit perplexed by the proposition of her advisor. Giving the general her consent, Nyx would be expected to arrive later that eve. Stalker pointed out that there was a bell tower above the castle that would mark the hour, and she was prompted not to be late.

Nyx bade the duchess and her advisors farewell and departed the chamber. The guards were advised of her expected arrival later that evening as their royal guest, but Nyx took the opportunity to take a casual stroll as a scenic tour of the grounds before she departed the citadel. As she left the room, the young rogue failed to notice the suspicious glance Shiva shot her way as the sour baroness crumpled up the delivered letter with one hand at her side, beyond the sight of the Duchess.

Nyx arrived back at the inn just before dusk. I had spent the hours of her absence performing some mild cleaning of the room and beds while checking them for lice and removing the accumulation of cobwebs. Keeping to routine, I did manage to lay out everything of possible use which had been left abandoned in the sealed room so that we could take an account of our available inventory. Apparently the curators of this Inn had continued to honor their contract with the former guild and declined to pry into its shuttered secrets after these many years of absence.

"Ah, I see that you found us a few things in this garbage heap," Nyx snorted as she proceeded to undress into nothing but her undergarments, "I can't stand to wear these gowns, a girl can't move properly in them without tripping over herself."

"Hmm, then I guess you'll never acquire the refined tastes of nobility," I smirked in response as I sat at the table, busy memorizing the map of the city, "so, how did things go in there?"

"I delivered the letter, and they seemed to have bought it for the time being," Nyx hesitated, "however, it was apparent they were anxious to speak with me further, so I have to attend a dinner at the royal table this evening."

"So ...it's a trap?" I stated with drawn conviction.

"I imagine so," Nyx agreed, "but if I had outright declined or should fail to show up this evening it would only serve to heighten their suspicions; so I pretty much got cornered into accepting."

"Which is exactly how traps work," I pressed for her to proceed with care, "...and what else did you find?"

Nyx stood over my shoulder and began to draw in the missing lines within the citadel, which the ragged map had omitted. She had taken a short tour of the estate while taking mental notes with every step; eyeing windows and architectural regions that could be correlated with the exterior points of the castle, which were referenced upon our map. She sought anything that could be used as a point of entry for a skilled thief, including places one could hide after gaining entrance. In a thieves mind, the shadows were our armor and it was common practice, if not habit, to seek areas which usually go unnoticed by others as an angle of advantage in our line of work.

I was impressed by her mapping skills and for recording the interior layout so precisely. The banquet room was located at the rear of the throne room, but public access was only available around its long curved hall from the level below. My apprentice marked out several points that led directly to these areas, but a quick glance out the window towards the castle proved these sections to be high upon the sheer rock wall, which would be a perilous climb in itself. Another option was to gain access from the upper battlements which would prove to be safer footing; however, that was an even longer climb along the nearly featureless surface of the fortification at the rear of the structure facing the harbor.

Nyx had also discovered that uninvited guests weren't allowed on the castle grounds after nightfall, so having me follow her in disguise was not an option at this point. After studying the diagram and weighing the risk of scaling the high walls, I began to consider another option. I then recalled the lighthouse located upon the high cliff which had a direct overview of the castle itself. Its strategic location was unattainable by sea due to the violent waves and the sheer cliffs, but was readily accessible once inside the walls of this seaside fortress.

The dinner invitation would start long after dusk, as darkness fell early during the winter months in this region of the coast. That would give me little time to make my way to the far side of the castle and up the steep embankments to the lighthouse stationed above the citadel. Once there, I would have to find a means of entry to the castle and assimilate what Nyx had learned from her limited reconnaissance, and proceed to pilfer any useful evidence I could find left by their acting Regent. Whether such information was to be found in his personal quarters or their war room was up to me to discover while Nyx was keeping her hosts distracted during her attendance at the private banquet that evening.

The plan was to follow up by dropping by the dinner hall to make sure Nyx was safe before slipping away. If there was any sign of trouble, at least I would be close by. A quick in-and-out was my strategy this eve while Nyx would try to pry what information she could through subtle conversation with the nobles. Once we acquired any solid information to go by, we would rendezvous back at the safe house and await the arrival of our transport ship for passage back to Stilgrave.

I packed as much of the climbing equipment as I could carry on my person and donned a large traveling cloak to help disguise myself while traversing the city streets. Nyx slipped into a fresh evening gown for the formal dinner while taking the opportunity to hide a small dagger or two in her corset as backup protection. The bell tower directly across from the citadel rang as dusk fell across Blacktide; waking ravens that scattered from the rooftops as its toll echoed through the city streets. Realizing time was short, I bade Nyx a silent nod to be careful, and she returned the gesture in kind before I slipped out the door.

Both of us had been through similar risks before and realized that you can't always trust your comrades to get you out of every scrape you might get yourself into. Personally, I preferred to work alone; and having an accomplice only complicated matters, which could become a problematic distraction if you're left worrying about someone else. I've seen many jobs go sour when one loose end snags up a perfect operation, or fellow thieves get caught because they went back to help a comrade. Both instances were grave mistakes, and it went against my basic philosophy because other people's sloppiness can get you killed.

I made my way swiftly through the city streets while

recalling the inked map in my head. I would pass by closing markets while torchbearers began to light the oil-fed braziers stationed at the crossroads. Peasants bearing lanterns started to appear along the darkened alleys as the glow of sunset began to wane, so I quickened my pace towards the solitary road to the lighthouse which clung to the edge of the barren cliff. Halfway up the road I came across a guarded gate, one which had not been previously indicated upon our outdated map.

What might have been an impasse for others, I took in stride. I casually let my pace slow as I ascended the narrow road just as I noticed a horse-drawn cart turn up the route towards the gate. Taking a seat and pretending to tie the bindings upon my boots, the wooden cart rattled by as the clopping of the horse's hooves helped to disguise my swift slip into the underbelly of the cart while using my grappling hook as a means to secure a hold on the planks between the wheels. I had been far enough away to have gone unnoticed by the guards; realizing their sight must be poor in the dying light and due to the obstructing design of their helmets which effectively hampered their field of vision. Without hesitation, the pair of guards greeted the driver with a few courtesies and opened the gates to let him through with the load of wood he hauled for the lighthouse stationed beyond.

The heavy iron gates creaked closed behind us as I peered from my roost beneath the cart where I clung. In truth, I nearly fell off half a dozen times while the rickety cart bumped and rocked as it rolled over stones and into potholes; but managed to hold on long enough until my knuckles turned white and my limbs nearly gave out until we had at last reached the plateau. Dropping myself and rolling off the gravel road out of sight, I waited until the cart met the lighthouse and dumped its load of tinder by the tower. I got anxious as the evening bell tolled again as I sat camouflaged among the rough boulders littering the terrain while watching the old woodsman stack the dropped logs under an easement.

After spending an aching amount of time ranting to his ill-tempered horse, the driver finished setting the wood and finally began his way back down the road as the glow of sunset faded and darkness fell like a heavy curtain. After I was certain he was out of sight, I crept up to the edge of the cliff just as the last rays of sunset glimmered on the horizon across the foreboding sea. A glance towards the tower proved it to be manned by a single night watchman, whose duty it was to keep the lighthouse fire burning till dawn. Behind the lantern, a large polished shield swayed back and forth by some mechanism driven by the high winds striking the bluff.

Strolling farther down to the edge of the cliffs, I crossed a perfect overview of the citadel. The trick now was to reach it, but I had not counted on such strong winds buffeting the rock face. The edge of the castle was now below my relative altitude, though still at a great distance; and it would take a perfect throw of a hook to latch a rope. The uncomfortable truth of the matter was that in perspective, what Nyx was now doing dressed in her embroidered gown among her hosts within their gilded halls might be considered far more precarious than scaling these craggy walls.

I had packed an odd device I had found left by the old guild members back at the inn, and unstrapped the equipment. The pieces appeared as if they had been redesigned from a broken-down crossbow and fashioned back together without all the bits. The completed apparatus fitted together to work with a grappling hook, and with a few attempts to couple the various pieces in the dark, I finally managed to assemble it together. Having never shot it before, I set in my hook on its rails which I had fitted with a light rope and aimed high for the castle turrets.

Pulling the trigger, the equipment worked like a charm as the hook was sent flying much farther than I could have thrown. The rope whipped and whined where I had laid its length in a neat figure eight pattern upon the ground to keep the cord from snagging as it unwound. With a touch of regret, I realized I had been overzealous in my aim as the hook overshot the crenel and fell on the far side of the rampart. The aim was good, just too long, which left me less rope than I would have preferred to anchor on my end.

Carefully drawing in the slack, the hook clipped on the wall and held fast; and I tied it off on a nearby stone cropping until it was secured to my satisfaction. From the crude drawings upon a scroll I had seen which had been left as instructions for use of the device, I removed the coiled bar from the bow and wrapped it around the taught rope while testing my weight upon it. Holding onto the handles on either side, I assumed one glided across it like an upside-down tightrope walker. As it turned out, I was very wrong in my initial presumption.

With hesitation, I stepped off the rocky cliff and hung tightly upon the wrapped iron handles as the ring channel slid across the taught rope. Halfway across the gap, my pace rapidly accelerated to an uncomfortable speed as I flew helplessly towards the stone ramparts, with nothing but a narrow space between the battlements racing up to cinch me. I had not foreseen this eventuality, and glanced below me at the long fall into the angry sea and jagged rocks that would dash me into pieces if I should release my grip. My mind raced in the sparse moment I had left as the hard stone walls rushed forward to greet me.

It wasn't until the last second that I remembered an acrobatics act from my childhood, when I had watched traveling entertainers in a market square one delirious summer lost among the years of adolescence. The rope walker had bounced on the rope, which in turn, acted like a spring; taking the performer who had faked a fall at the gasps of the crowd and suddenly bounced back upon their feet to the awe and astonishment of the spectators. Kicking my legs up, I gathered the momentum and yanked myself down hard, causing the thin rope to pull down upon the edge of the rampart for added tension. On the jolt back up, I slipped past the rope with one hand and landed crouched on my knees upon the very tip of the wall.

I stayed there for a few seconds as I gathered my balance, almost not believing how I had just cheated death. A quick glance over my shoulder at the deadly drop off the edge was enough to motivate me to hop down and place my feet upon the solid roof. Scanning the area, the ramparts above the castle appeared to be entirely unmanned as though they were designed for decor rather than for actual use. While inspecting the rest of the battlements I was mildly surprised to find several stake posts positioned around the rim, along with a pile of dummies fitted with fabricated wooden or damaged weapons and bits of scrap armor and shields. It took me a moment to realize that these were merely decoys used for tactical trickery.

I imagined these mannequins were taken down during the cold season since there was little traffic to the harbor, as there was sparse chance of an invasion by sea during the hostile winter months. The brigade erected these decoys upon the ramparts during the rest of the year, to make it appear as though they had more eyes and arms manning the battlements than were actually on duty. At this great distance from the height of the castle ramparts to the harbor below, no one could tell the difference nor would they be the wiser.

Tracing the upper bailey to the central tower, I found the worn double-doors to be locked by a simple latch. The space between the panels was just wide enough for my blade to slip between them and lift the plank of wood from its securing clamp. I sealed the door behind me and proceeded with practiced discretion as I made my way into the walls of the keep.

The air became chill as night fell upon the city. A whisper of wind whistled through the worn gaps in the rooftop door as I crept down into the bowels of the castle. I often paused to detect the slightest of sounds which might reveal the location of a posted guard as I descended the steep stairwell. The upper levels of the citadel were not as well maintained as the ground floor, likely due to the fact that the upper ramparts were merely home to decoys rather than actual soldiers; and thus it was logical to assume there was little, if any, foot traffic here until the return of the spring thaws.

The monarchs of Blacktide didn't have to fear military assaults from the plateau, as any incursions by land would be funneled up the narrow valley to be met by the formidable gates which shielded the city by land. Any naval offense would be risking wrecking their vessels upon rocks and reef as the bottleneck into the harbor was designed in such a way to limit access to only a few ships at a time. Any warship barging its way in would likely find its bow and hull crushed by the stone shore supports sunk beneath the waterline. Blacktide had endured many attacks by land and sea over the centuries and survived them all nearly unscathed.

Before this eve, I had only seen rough outlines and artists impressions located on topical maps, which had displayed this fortress city at the end of a narrow band of mountain ranges that converged at the coast. In truth, the sight of the city from the vantage point of the lighthouse was truly inspiring. They had walled up the kingdom between two high cliffs; the lanterns glowing in the winding streets below gave the illusion that the medieval metropolis resembled a river of dancing lights encased by a forest of stone.

Whale oil was a valued commodity throughout the region, and Blacktide retained the monopoly on its source and trade. Their stranglehold on the market made the royalty exceedingly rich, even though neighboring harbors were better known as a trading port for a wider range of goods. However, the metropolis of Stilgrave was located in an unfortunate area of the gulf that was plagued by ice during the winter season. This forced other vessels to make anchor at the port of Blacktide during a fraction of the year, even though their duty taxes were far higher.

I crept down several levels of the tower until I crossed upon an open section in the stonework which revealed a framework of supporting rafters beyond. The tart smells of cooked crab wafting up from below made me presume the scullery was located directly beneath me. The opening presented an easy way to gain access to the upper chambers without being seen. Being the main fishing port that Blacktide was known for, I grinned to myself at the passing thought that Nyx would likely be feasting on a five-course meal of seafood at the banquet this night; which was a type of cuisine she firmly despised.

I wiggled my way into the narrow opening the moment I heard a pair of guards chatting to one another while the light of their lanterns and heavy footsteps ascended the stairway from below. I hugged the wall within a narrow sliver of shadows, and became as still as stone while I listened in on their conversation as they passed by.

"...ah, Stalker closed the banquet hall this evening. They had the maids all running around earlier getting the private dining room prepared; what was that all about?" One of them asked.

"I guess they got some special guests they're hosting

tonight. Eh, who cares, that's for the men on security detail on the upper floors to deal with. You and I have to..." the other man answered as his words faded away out of range.

I bit my lip upon hearing the revelation of the change of venue for the royal dinner as I eavesdropped on their discussion. Unfortunately, Nyx had only sketched in the location of the main banquet hall upon our map, but I had no clue as to where the private dining room might be. My time was short to infiltrate the Regent's private chambers and snatch whatever I could find; let alone having to scout the rest of the castle from the narrow rafters. Nyx had noted where the Duchess was residing in the rear chambers located above the throne room, so it made sense that the Lord Regent would have his suite stationed somewhere nearby.

Meanwhile, Nyx had shuffled into the main entry and gave the name of her false identity to the guard stationed at the tall ornate doors, to relay that she was an expected guest that evening. The gray-haired man gave a snoot as he looked at her down his nose, for she had been more than a few minutes late.

"Good evening to you, Lady Kashara, you will be attending tonight's feast in the private dining chamber. Please follow the servant promptly ...the royal Duchess does *not* like to be kept waiting," he pressed a little rudely.

Nyx gritted her teeth and forced a smile as she passed in the doorway where she was met by an elderly butler who was as thin as a rail.

"...Pompous jerk!" Nyx uttered under her breath; though her remark was aimed at the doorman who was now out of earshot.

"Excuse me, Miss?" The butler asked as he paused and perked his head, having not understood her comment.

"Oh, nothing," Nyx shot back another fake smile as she hiked up the sides of her dress to keep from tripping on herself as she ascended the stairs, "I was just admiring the architecture ...it's fabulous work!"

"Oh, ah, yes," he agreed with a baleful stare, "...is this your first visit to our coastal city?" The butler asked as Nyx caught his sideways glance while they walked, "your fashion is ...shall I say, somewhat interesting," he uttered with a surly tone which carried a color of insult.

Nyx had come prepared for this encounter, having used a layered traveling cape which she had specially designed to be reversible. The spare amount of clothes she brought had been sewn double-sided for a quick change of costume. She had turned the same dress inside out and unpinned the hem, which now flaunted itself as a blue velvet gown stitched with gold thread. Her matching azure cloak was lined with hidden pockets for concealing blades and a convenient place for stashing goods.

She had tied up her hair with braids on either side to resemble a tiara, which had been the current fashion in the few tapestries she had seen over the years. Royalty liked to adorn themselves with jewelry, as it was the custom to wear one's wealth as a symbol of status. Nyx also possessed a few fake gemstone rings and a flashy brooch which she brought along on this excursion for the purpose of fitting her role. Koda had been wary of her presentation for this mission, and didn't want to give them the impression that a mere lowly servant had been sent as the city messenger; so she had to look the part in every facet.

"Why thank you for noticing, Sir, I do try to look my best," Nyx responded in a sugared tone that was endowed with an accent of sarcasm; although the butler realized it wasn't his place to argue with invited guests. With a cough to clear his throat and choosing to keep his mouth shut, the butler guided his guest to the upper floor and into the entry hall where she could leave her cloak and freshen up in the side room. Taking a moment to primp her dress and make sure her hidden blades were concealed and secured, Nyx took a deep breath and put on a fake smile before strolling into the reception room.

There she found the General and Lady Shiva who was adorned in a deep shade of maroon, along with two other gentlemen of notable age. They were surrounded by servants who busied themselves serving drinks while other members of the castle staff stood silently at attention along the wall. Nyx took her time coursing the room and exchanging pleasantries while leaving General Stalker to wait his turn, even though he had noticed her the moment she entered. Making his way towards her, Nyx turned to meet his eager gaze.

"Lady Kashara, I do hope our frigid weather is not too discomforting. I understand it is much different from the climate farther down the coast. How is Governor Oren's health these days? I heard he had fallen ill after a gala he held in the Regent's honor."

"The Chancellor?" Nyx paused while searching for her words, "He seemed quite fit the last time we spoke ...just his usual self," she pressed to change the subject, "I'm sure the Lord Regent will have many tales to tell when he returns."

"Yes, yes ...I'm sure he will," Stalker responded with a dry smile just as everyone's attention was drawn away by the ring of a bell held by a servant.

"Dinner is to be served, please take your seats," the butler announced as he placed his tiny bell on a tray and stepped out of the way of the door to allow the guests to enter. The table had been set with an extravagant feast, consisting of an ensemble of fruits and exotic dishes piled high. Nyx was offered a seat next to the General, while Shiva and the other guests took their assigned places. The only seat left empty was the slightly raised chair at the center, to which the Duchess herself, was absent.

"Would someone *please* find her ladyship, and escort her to the dinner table," Shiva bit at the servants with a terse smile. It was clear this royal council was at a disadvantage to handling the young duchess without her usual babysitter; Sir Ryan, as the lord regent himself usually took the reigns in these matters.

A handmaiden quickly scurried off out of the room, while a few spots of idle conversation filled the time as they awaited for her grace to arrive.

"I do apologize, this is highly unlike her royal highness," Stalker granted as he turned towards Nyx, "our young princess can be shy among new faces ...even pretty ones at that," the general offered as a compliment.

Nyx couldn't decipher if Stalker was a gentleman or a letch, for his pretentious demeanor was a blur between the two. Scanning the length of the dinner table, it was piled high with enough stables to feed the impoverished wretches of the entire Crimson quarter in Stilgrave for a month. Gritting her teeth, she began to detect the aromas of steamed squid and shellfish. Her nose began to curl as she noticed cooked seaweed mixed among the greens, and cracked crab legs powdered with paprika.

"Do you have caviar available in Stilgrave?" Her host offered as Stalker presented Nyx with a silver bowl of glistening amber fish eggs. Nyx didn't have the stomach for salty foods, let alone fish and their odd and unpleasant taste. With a shrug, she realized she would have to nitpick the entire meal and would likely end up leaving hungry despite the presented feast.

"Why yes of course," Nyx responded as she hid a scowl of disgust with her handkerchief, "the Ivory quarter in Stilgrave is known for such exotic delicacies," she boasted while the servants began to pour glasses of wine for the evenings guests while they made their way around the table. "Oh, would you excuse me, my Lord; I have a frail bladder and ask if you could possibly point me towards the privy?"

"Oh, ah, but of course," the general replied, and with a snap of his fingers he had a servant girl take her chair and show her to the amenities. Reaching the outer room, Nyx addressed the servant girl directly.

"If you don't mind, if you could just point the way, dear," she asked the servant who wasn't used to being treated with obvious kindness, "I actually need to get some items from my cloak first ...personal female issues, if you can understand?"

The girl became clearly embarrassed and pointed her in a direction out of the hall, "Certainly Milady; when you're ready, just find the second door to the right of the entry," she bade and quickly shed herself of prying any further into such a private matter of a women's hygiene.

Nyx gave her a kindly smile until the servant girl disappeared out of sight, and she quickly turned back to the coatroom to make sure her cloak had been left untouched. Pushing the various shawls and embroidered capes hanging within aside, Nyx was surprised to find the Duchess curled up as she sat on the floor holding a kitten, hiding behind the curtain of coats. The little girl gave Nyx a doleful gaze and put her finger to her lips in a motion to be silent as a court servant suddenly rushed past the entry, calling out in search of her ladyship. Nyx complied and knelt down out of sight of the castle staff.

"Why are you hiding here?" Nyx finally whispered once the servants were out of range.

"Are you the messenger lady from Still ...Stilgrave?" The girl stuttered as she struggled with the name.

"Why, yes I am, your highness," Nyx replied, a bit enamored that the princess played this game of cat and mouse with her attendants.

"It's Cricket," the little girl answered with a pout through the thick powder of makeup upon her face, which was a common fashion for such aristocrats; though it looked oddly out of place on a child, "you don't have to call me by my title, it's silly anyways."

"Okay ...Cricket," Nyx replied with a gentle smile, being mildly surprised the Duchess wasn't the arrogant little brat one might expect her to be, given the company of her royal guardians, "and who is this?" Nyx offered in a gentle tone as she reached to pet the small kitten.

"This is Juniper, she is my only friend," the duchess replied with a cuddle to her furry pet. Most felines roamed the cold city streets as feral cats who fed off mice and vermin, but this one had the luxury of being finely bred, well-groomed, and graced with royal care as one might expect.

"I'm sure both the General and Baroness are also your friends," Nyx answered trying to console the little girl.

"No they're not!" Cricket spouted back in defiance as she hugged her kitten with a glint of a tear welling in her eyes, "...They want to throw me into the sea."

As shocking as it was to hear the little girl say those words, Nyx could see by the look in the child's eyes that she was telling the truth.

Delivering a Lie

Scaling my way through the upper rafters of the castle, I abruptly found myself at a dead-end located somewhere in the middle of the citadel. There was little more progress I could make without descending to ground level and creeping my way through the halls of the keep. Dropping to the floor in a narrow corridor, I became confused with the schematics of the building. It wasn't common to find myself so disoriented, but I was having trouble navigating the curious slender passage I now found myself in.

Exploring the length of the corridor, it clearly branched out into several segmented sections; yet I could find no discernable doors. It took me several moments of contemplation to realize that I had stumbled upon a network of secret passages hidden between the various rooms of the keep. This accidental placement made my task ahead much less burdensome. Within these secret halls, I was protected from being discovered or stumbling into wandering guards.

A small amount of ambient light leaked into the passage, but as my eyes adjusted to the dark I began to notice several more shafts of illumination streaming in from odd placements upon the walls. At nearly waist level upon one wall I found a thin cloth covering a peephole. I lowered myself to the height of the crevice and gazed inward, finding its line of sight fanned into a servant's quarters where several maids were busy folding sheets and other items of laundry. A few more steps down the narrow hall and I found another slit that peered into a weapons' locker where swords and various arms were being stored.

Past the armory, I hunted the walls for tell-tale signs of more spy holes and discovered one with a direct view into

an empty study. Searching further, I found a latch attached
to a steel wire which was woven through a series of
pulleys. After an experimental tug of the cable, I was
rewarded with a portion of the wall next to it popping open
to allow egress into the room beyond. Stepping through, I
could see that the door was designed to appear like a
decorative panel from the other side, which operated by a
hidden hinge within its base.

I folded over the felt lining from my boots to cover the
soles and began the familiar waltz of snooping through the
darkened room. A thick ornate table sat against the far wall
that sat beneath a tall stained glass window. Recognizing
their formation, I realized I was now in the main chamber
which overlooked the harbor below. There were stacks of
scrolls and various writing instruments stationed about the
study, along with a wide bookcase full of heavy tomes.

The fireplace nestled next to the tall double-door entrance
was cold, its embers long since extinguished. Testing the
entry door, I noticed it was locked, but without a proper
key I would have to use my tools to try to pick it open.
Returning to the desk, I shuffled through the documents
lying there; making sure to carefully replace them back in
their exact position where they had lain. One folded letter
which caught my attention was addressed to the Lord
Regent himself.

Taking the parchment over to the moonlight beaming in
from the window, I verified it was marked for Sir Ryan; but
the contents of the letter left me baffled. Looking around, I
concluded this had been the Regent's private study to
where he held his business of state and private meetings.
Risking it would be missed; I placed the private letter into
my vest pocket as its contents were of particular concern.
After sifting through the drawers and array of cabinets
contained in the large study, I took particular care
searching the long bookshelf.

"What I like about the upper class is that they are always so predictable," I whispered to myself as my fingers drifted softly across the rows of bindings until my sense of touch found a false stack bound together.

The set of tomes was a facade which hid a small iron chest behind them. I had always wondered why the aristocrats made it a habit of squirreling away valuables in their bookshelves. I imagined in their world that owning a personal library was seen as a status symbol rather than for true academic study, and the nobility were far too busy ordering servants around and attending their own self-interests to be caught wasting their time nose-deep in a dusty volume. In their minds, a bookshelf was somehow the ideal place that would avoid any kind of scrutiny by servants or guest; which was why I was usually never disappointed looking in similar places whenever I burgled a wealthy abode.

I dislodged the false spines which revealed the concealed chest hidden within. Attempting to remove the small coffer proved futile and I realized it had been cleverly secured to the heavy shelf, which was an effective way to protect the small safe from being carried away by looters. Koda hadn't mentioned anything about the Regent possessing a key on his person, so it would likely be hidden somewhere in his private chambers or stashed away in this very room. I didn't have the luxury of time to search every nook and cranny for something as small as a key, so I pulled out the fine hooked wires I kept stashed within my cuff for such circumstances.

Picking a lock is done by touch, especially so since there was usually very little light available to navigate such a delicate operation when one is trespassing somewhere they shouldn't be. The lock itself contained an interesting set of tumblers I was not familiar with, but I was adept enough to have brought a bendable wire. A little cinch with the teeth made it easy enough to change the subtle curves in the mechanism to bypass the locking clamp. Once I felt the vibration of the clasp begin to spin, I held steady until I heard the satisfying click and release of the pin.

I lifted the lid merely a hair at first, while gently exploring its rim with the thin wire. When I detected a resistance in a spot where there shouldn't be any, I pulled out my clamping wire and secured the hidden obstruction within to the hinge of the chest. Stepping aside, I lifted the lid the rest of the way at a safe distance by the blade of my dagger. I was rewarded by a sharp click and pop from within the iron box and cautiously peered inside once it was clear.

"So what was worth hiding in this trapped chest?" I breathed to myself as I inspected the mechanism designed to trigger the fine needled blade which would have shot out and impaled the hands of anyone grasping the lid. The sharp bitter smell coming from its razor edge told me that it had been coated with a brand of poison that the Regent and his fanatic associates were so fond of. I was hoping to find schematics, a list of associates, invasion plans, or evidence equally revealing towards the Lord Regent's strategy to overthrow the hierarchy of Stilgrave and gain control of the territory. However, all I found inside was a small roll of paper along with an elaborately engraved alloy block.

I couldn't fathom the use of the rectangular chunk of etched metal, though it was fairly heavy and appeared to be composed of polished bronze. The small scrap of paper had several strange designs upon it which were reminiscent of the glyphs I had seen before associated with the spider cult. Searching the rest of the study proved futile, for I found nothing more that was of any relevant value. Resolving myself to seek out the Lord Regent's private chamber for additional clues, I practiced my skills on the lock to the study entry and crept out of the doorway and into the hall beyond.

The trick to not getting caught is to physically become a part of the architecture, for the eye usually only senses movement. The poor design of the armored helmets the guards wore undoubtedly obstructed their peripheral vision to some degree; thus, the ability to become as still as stone was a skill to master, along with effectively merging one's own silhouette into the shadows. The use of a blackened cloak helped to camouflage my position, and it was equally vital to avoid wearing anything which reflected the light. The art of silence was also key to becoming one with the shadows, and with a little patience, a good thief could roam almost anywhere entirely unhindered.

I obtained my skills over the years at the cost of being nearly caught on countless occasions. I did not wish to repeat the episode where I had so blindly stumbled into the ambush in the manor of the Spider Priestess, those many moons ago. That event forced me into a time of self-contemplation; not on subjects so foolish as to turn my life around and enter an honest trade, but rather of encouragement to better hone my skills as a master thief. Unfortunately, over the years I had witnessed many innocent and honest folk who had been dragged off to the Bastille to suffer torture or left to rot in the dungeons on fabricated or trivial charges, and I cared not to be counted as a casualty among our system of injustice.

Slipping down the hallway, I avoided the generous lamplight and several stationed guards arranged along the high rail which overlooked the throne room below; all the while having to quietly dance out of sight from passing servants. The inner chambers were graced with the same ebony rock which colored the outer cliffs. The richly carved wooden doors to each room were decorated with polished brass moldings and iron rivets. Along the lone corridor which led to the royal chambers, I found a solitary guard stationed below an elaborate crest covering a pair of draped banners surrounding a heavy door.

By his tired posture, I assumed the guard was on the last hour of his shift, and there appeared to be little foot traffic down this corridor. I recognized the embroidered crest of their acting Regent upon the banner, but I refused to be thwarted by a lone guard. My position at the hall entrance was precarious since a member of the castle staff wandering these halls could turn the corner at any moment. Their cotton laced shoes would provide little warning of their approach compared to the clank of the armored boots worn by the castle sentries.

Like a bad premonition, I caught a fleeting shade as it shot across the foyer out of the corner of my eye as I slunk back into the shadows just as a handmaid scampered by within arms length of where I sprawled flat against the wall. She hustled her tiny feet up towards the guard near the end of the empty hallway.

"Have you seen the Duchess?" the maid inquired in a curt but stressful tone towards the lone sentry.

"Uh, no ...is she in danger?" he responded while stepping forward in concern as he put his hand to his sword.

"No, no, nothing like that," the maid responded to calm the guard down, "her eminence is likely just being mischievous again and has skipped out on the formal dinner. She does this every time we have new guests," the woman ranted, "...help me search her chambers in case she is hiding again."

"I, uh, I can't leave my post..." the guardsman tried to shuffle as an excuse to the troubled woman.

"I heard the Lord Regent won't be arriving for another week, and you're only guarding an empty room. Everyone is attending dinner at the moment, *except* for her ladyship, so you have nothing to worry about. Come help me for just a moment to find her, would you dear?" The handmaid pleaded as she motioned the sentry to follow her to the royal chambers.

The guard huffed for but a few seconds before he felt wounded by guilt at the pleading look in her eyes as the maid begged him for help. The guard affirmed to himself that it was his essential duty to protect the young Duchess, even if she wasn't in real peril, and was likely just hiding in her chamber. So with a puff of his chest, the sentry removed his hand from his sword and turned to follow the servant as she scurried down the hall. As the guard shifted his sword, I could see a ring with a single key attached to it dangling from his belt.

Unlike a rookie thief who might have hesitated at such an opportunity, I scampered forward with defined stealth to close the distance between myself and the guard as he marched after the maid. With dagger in hand, I stretched forward in a single swift motion, achieved from years of practice, and slit the silk cord on the ring of his belt and caught the key before it hit the floor. The two of them never even knew I was there as I melted back into the shadows while they continued into the royal bedroom beyond; entirely oblivious to my presence. I looked at the shiny key in my hand and smiled, for it was times like these that I felt a sense of well-earned pride from the specialized skills I had mastered in my trade.

I had to admit, there was a certain thrill at being able to come within a hands' breadth of getting caught and being able to fade away like a ghost. I backtracked to the Regent's room and quietly unlocked the door. A quick peek inside told me there weren't any obvious traps or anyone lingering inside, as the maid had mentioned moments before. Slipping within, I secured the lock once again and turned to find myself in the Lord Regents' private chambers. What I had found there was not entirely unexpected, but surprising nonetheless.

*   *   *

Back in the coatroom, the cunning rogue was trying to
console the young duchess who was playing hooky from
the formal dinner. As Nyx stole a moment to search the
assorted cloaks in the confined chamber, the little girl
began to question what this strange visitor to her castle was
up to.

"What are you doing?" she asked innocently as Nyx gave
each of the garments hanging there a quick inspection for
loose keys, notes, or anything else of interest.

"Oh nothing," Nyx fibbed, "I just misplaced something in
here when I arrived," she added with a fake smile, "If I
may ask, what makes you think the royal officials of the
court would want to do you any harm?" Nyx responded in
her attempt to change the subject as she turned back to the
little girl petting her kitten.

"Sometimes when I hide, I hear what they say about me
when they think I'm not listening ...and it's not very nice,"
she pouted.

"Well, I'm sure it's not as bad as you think, your
highness ...I mean, Cricket," Nyx responded while trying to
console the girl while addressing her by her nickname.

"They say mean things about my father, and they don't
treat the servants very nice either," Cricket elaborated,
"they don't want me around, not really."

Nyx began to feel for the little girl, seeing the rebel in her
character which she could identify with. This young child
had been cast into a role she did not wish for; even though
she was blessed with wealth and privilege, she faced the
consequences forced upon her by those who aimed to take
advantage of the girl before she was formally affirmed into
a position of power. Although she was beloved by the
citizens of Blacktide, this little girl was in a precarious
position as she was surrounded by officers of the court who
cared far more about themselves than the people of this

maritime city. The apprentice thief began to wonder if she could somehow protect this girl while also being able to complete her mission.

"It's not very ladylike to eavesdrop on people, Cricket," Nyx led on as if she was scolding her, but quickly turned her lips into a smile, "but I'll tell you a secret ...I actually used to do it all the time when I was your age. So you say you're good at hiding?"

The little girl's worried look turned into a grin of acceptance when Nyx smiled at her, and the child dared to share a little secret of her own. Pointing up towards an inconspicuous hook set upon the wall at the back of the room, the duchess revealed the means of her mischief to her new friend.

"Well, I usually hide within the walls. My father showed me a safe passage from my room in case I was ever in trouble. Nobody knows its there except me ...I think," Cricket declared as she gave a slight pause in afterthought.

Nyx turned her gaze upward towards the coat hook switch, and with a little scrutiny, could see the fine slit which revealed the hidden door buried within the back wall of the coatroom. It was very well hidden.

"Tell you what, why don't you join us for supper, and afterward you can show me these passages after dessert?" Nyx offered as a bargaining chip to the little princess.

With a sigh, the little girl nodded and stood up as Nyx offered her hand to help her stand. They both left the coatroom and entered into the dining chamber where the jumbled cacophony of whispers, absorbed in their hushed conversations, suddenly dropped to an awkward silence as everyone turned their heads to watch the pair enter.

"Ah, you found her," the General affirmed, "Come, your Grace, please have a seat so we can begin," he offered with a motion for the Duchess to take her chair. A pair of servants escorted the young girl who reluctantly let go of

Nyx's hand and took her place at the table.

"Lady Kashara, you seem to have a way with children," Shiva noted coldly as her eyes shifted over towards the General and back with a hint of suspicion.

"The duchess is more grown-up than you might think," Nyx shot back, but remembered to tone down her usual saucy personality and kept in character, "but from one lady to another, we come to learn our place."

The curt comment was a masked insult to the woman in red, who seemed a little ruffled by the remark from the puffed look on her face. The duchess coughed out a giggle at the slight Nyx had lain upon the baroness, but caught her tongue when Shiva shot a harsh glance her way. Nyx had excused herself to search the garments in the coatroom for spare keys, and had hoped to steal a few moments to explore some of the private rooms; but running into the young duchess was entirely accidental. However, the chance encounter did have the unexpected benefit of the girl revealing the hidden passages veiled behind the walls, and Nyx planned to explore them before leaving the castle this eve.

In the meantime, some exchanged pleasantries in conversation might allow her to press a measure of useful information from the Regent's accomplices here in the keep. Now that everyone was seated the servants began to dish out various platters to their guests, Nyx tried to forgo a majority of the entrees offered as politely as she could. Taking a nibble here and there, she managed to cloud the taste of seafood with a large goblet of wine.

"My lady, what exactly is your position?" Stalker inquired as their guest was enjoying her meal.

"I beg your pardon?" Nyx wondered with a bit of confusion about the question.

"What do you do for the Governor of Stilgrave?" he responded.

"Oh, well now," Nyx tried to recall the background story she had made up for her mission while she and Ash were traveling here on the ship, "...I'm the chancellor's personal assistant whom he trusts with such delicate matters of diplomacy."

"It is strange though, because we've never heard of you before, Miss Kashara," one of the older men at the table announced through his cracked and withered voice, which had grown acidic with age.

"Or is it *Mistress* Kashara?" Shiva spouted as a snide remark to repay their guest for the taunt she had suffered earlier.

"Our relationship is purely professional, I assure you," Nyx responded, "and what may I inquire is your duty here, Lady Graystone?"

"I am her ladyships' royal advisor and tutor," Shiva slammed back in a pompous tone as she flung a glance towards the duchess; who was busy playing with her food while pretending two small shrimp were battling one another on the arena of her plate.

"And I assume you run the garrison, General Stalker. That is a very interesting name; I've never heard of your family lineage as far south as our city," Nyx inquired to the oddity of his surname.

"Ah, yes, most guests to our city from the southern borders get a might confused as to its origins," the General answered, "I admit, the name 'Stalker' sounds a bit *presumptuous*," he chuckled, "but my namesake is merely a title which is earned through service to our legion; much like a badge of honor."

"So you're known as a predator within the circles of your military career?" Nyx surmised with a raised brow.

"Why yes; in centuries past our ancestors used such names as symbols of prestige and tribute, and we simply continue that tradition to honor our heritage," the General

Michel Savage

granted to his guest.

"How interesting..." Nyx responded trying to pretend she was impressed, "and do you have any ambitions for flexing your power into the southern territories?"

The older men at the table looked a little shocked at the bold question; however, general Stalker took it in stride.

"Blacktide is an ancient port, and our people pride themselves in their resilience to both the land and the sea," the General stated with an air of dignity, "over a century ago our lands were invaded and occupied by other realms who sought conquest; but we held fast," he finished with a clench of his fist as if to signify their feat of stability and strength.

"Others might consider those invaders, as you put it, were nothing more than pioneers seeking new lands to prosper in their pursuit for a better life," Nyx countered. A harsh glance shared among the hosts at the table told Nyx that her comment was unwelcome.

"My father wouldn't want people to fight each other," the Duchess declared aloud, "its un-ne-ces-sary," Cricket finished as she struggled with the big word.

"Well, your father isn't around anymore, so what he said doesn't matter," Shiva spouted back in a childish tone at the young girl.

"You're mean!" the Duchess growled back towards the woman in her crimson dress as the child's face curled in anger while slamming down the tableware upon her plate.

"Ah, well that's enough for the evening's meal, and it appears her ladyship has grown bored with our company. It may be time for her to retire to her chambers while the adults talk and entertain our distinguished guest," the General responded to defuse the situation.

With that, a pair of servants got the little girls' seat, and escorted her out of the dining hall while she stomped and shot ugly glares towards Lady Graystone as she left the table and departed the room. This sudden change of events left Nyx wondering what she should do, considering she had made plans with the girl after the banquet. The General, however, had already made other arrangements for the evening's entertainment and the departure of the young princess was the catalyst for the events they had planned for their invited guest. Nyx tried not to shuffle uncomfortably as the mood in the room darkened with dramatic speed.

The older men relaxed their composure and rolled their eyes as if to insult her highness who was now out of sight, and Nyx could have sworn she heard one of them ask in muffled whispers how long they would have to endure the little brat. This made the young thief realize that the fears the young girl had portrayed earlier were very real indeed. Shiva herself was making jests in her effort to mock the heiress, and doing so behind her back, which Nyx found distasteful. The general relaxed his civilized attitude, while he found mirth in the antics of his comrades at the dinner table as the rest of the servants were ordered to leave the room.

"I'm sorry ...but how is any of this funny? Don't you hold respect for the young Duchess as your sovereign ruler?" Nyx breathed in disbelief as the doors to the dining hall shut behind the last departing servant.

"Well now, that presumption really depends on if she actually reaches her royal coronation," Shiva replied in a threatening tone while the nobles were left in privacy to speak their minds beyond the ears of the castle servants.

"You seemed confused, Lady Kashara, and rightly so," the general responded, "You see, everything here is not as it seems."

"That is becoming quite obvious," Nyx replied while cleaning her hands with a napkin as she took another sip of wine from her cup to chase down a bite of fish. She had not foreseen the vindictive nature of these lords who put on an entirely different demeanor in the presence of the guards and the castle staff. There was clearly a measure of ill will toward the young duchess, which included slights against her deceased father. Exercising her intuition, the young rogue's instincts told her something wasn't right here.

"In all honesty, Milady, we were quite interested in the letter you delivered from Stilgrave's governor, especially the part regarding the delayed return of our beloved Lord Regent," one of the older men declared, "did you happen to meet with the Regent himself and attest to his postponement directly?"

"Well ...yes, I did, and can attest that he wished to extend his stay for a short while," Nyx responded as she searched for a half-truth they might swallow.

"And was there a reason why any member from his personal guard had failed to deliver this news themselves, or declined to accompany you on our journey?" Another senior man across the table inquired with a stern look piercing through the slits of his wrinkled eyelids.

"I'm not sure," Nyx replied, "they made no request to accompany me for the return trip. I would assume that they were ordered to stay and serve in the Regent's presence."

"And, just to clarify, our Lord Regent, Sir Ryan, whom you claim to have spoken to directly, failed to provide you or your governor with any further instructions before you departed for our shores?" General Stalker appealed for her to answer.

"Well, no, nothing in particular," Nyx wavered slightly, "however, I'm merely following orders of our Governor, as is my duty," she replied, which seemed like a proper answer given the circumstances as she took another swig from her chalice.

The look on their faces changed and Nyx realized she

might have gotten herself into a fix. She put down her cup of wine and slowly inched her hand towards her hidden daggers while she sat poised in her seat. Quite suddenly, she felt unsteady as her vision began to blur in waves. The room itself started to sway, and she glanced towards her glass to realize that some type of poisonous tonic had been slipped into her wine.

"The Regent is a predictable man, Lady Kashara, and he would have never trusted anyone but one of his own men to deliver such a message; especially so without his private code noted in his letter to verify its authenticity," Shiva granted as she peered at their dazed guest, "he has many layers of security and we are quite aware that you are likely not who you say you are, and have delivered us nothing more than a lie."

With pressing regret pulsing through her like the bitter poison in her veins, Nyx tried to rise to her feet but fainted as the world around her turned dark, while the lords stood up from their seats and erupted in disturbing laughter as the young rogue lay sprawled unconscious across the dining table in her lavish gown.

Lost Souls

Interestingly enough, the lord regent's private chambers were reminiscent of Vale's study and his collection of curiosities. Though noticeably far more lavish in its accommodations, Sir Ryan's room was littered with strange artifacts in place of standard decor. I felt a creeping chill in my blood as I scanned the room and searched for anything of interest. My breath caught in my throat as I discovered a clay bowl upon his dresser which contained a mixture of ashes along with a dozen or more silver amulets embedded with human teeth.

It was clear now that the regent was not merely an accomplice of the secretive spider cult, but that his affiliation was far more involved. The brutish idols adorning the walls gazed downward with their disturbing stare as I trespassed upon his chamber. Oddest of all, a net crudely woven into the shape of a spiders' web hung above the bed itself; garnished with various bits of bone and precious stones. As tempted as I would be to cut loose a few of the raw gems for their value, strangely enough, a wave of repulsion fell over me at the thought of touching these tainted ornaments.

The stories of witchcraft I had heard when I was a child came flooding back to me. It was only my experiences of late which brought me to a new frame of mind on the subject. I was no easy fool to fall for the shenanigans of gypsy fortune tellers and carnival trickery, but those charlatans paled in comparison to the gruesome murder and bloodshed these cultists were involved in. A sinking feeling in my stomach told me that venturing to this ominous keep was a mistake.

I was getting the impression that the Lord Regent of

Blacktide was a man of wit and ambitious mind. Playing with poisons and the bones of the dead was enough of an ill omen in itself, but keeping such a secret in his own living chambers within the very heart of the castle would be troubling to any citizen of the realm. It was a time long past when such rituals of blood sacrifice and retaining trinkets from the dead were suppressed by the religious order of the Builders. Their struggle became that of the peasants and those who chose to embrace hope and forgiveness over acts of war and vengeance.

They were like two sides of a coin. The Builders revered the bones of their saints, while the spider sect collected similar souvenirs of their enemies. Either way, they both idolized effigies of death. In my eyes, either side of such a tarnished coin conveyed the same value.

A thief doesn't try to control the masses; we skim what we can from those who possess far more than they need. We don't try to sway a person's point of view or use others as unwitting slaves while taking credit for their achievements; we simply observe if something has value or not and is worth our time to acquire, which is practical enough when you think about it. Our world is one of expense or profit; which makes our choices in life far easier and with much less drama than the common man. However, those men who choose not to value another's life will never fundamentally understand that there are those who care nothing about a price tag, for we can simply steal what we may wish to possess.

With a bit of quiet rifling through the apartment, I found another chest lying at the edge of the bed. The locking mechanism was simple enough, and with a measure of practiced caution, I popped the lid. The only thing lying within was yet another scroll, identical in size to the one I found within Ryan's study. After carefully prying open the wax seal with my knife I was baffled to find it contained yet another odd arrangement of glyphs which were fairly similar in their overall design, yet in distinctly different placement than the markings on the first scroll I had secured from his office.

I had to ask myself why the regent would keep two vaguely similar scrolls of this archaic text locked away in separate chests. It didn't make much sense, but this got my curiosity churning. I took the scroll over to the window where the moonlight was streaming in and pinned the open scroll to the glass with pieces from the wax seal. I then unraveled the first scroll I had discovered in his study and placed it over the second parchment so the two would overlap. Spinning the lines inked upon the thin parchment, I finally got them to line up together ...which revealed a most curious design.

"Well now, that's interesting," I whispered to myself as I layered the two scrolls and rolled them up together.

Their secret had been revealed, and it was clear that the Regent had kept these odd scrolls parted for good reason. The question was; what did the revealed image upon it refer to? It ate away at me as I tried to remember where I had seen that pattern before, but I couldn't quite place it. There was still a piece of the puzzle missing and I needed to find it.

Searching the rest of the room proved fruitless, although I did find a few trinkets and bits of jewelry that found their way into my pockets. I could only hope that Nyx was making progress leeching equally valuable information from her royal hosts during their dinner party. Speaking of which, it was time that I checked up on her before slipping out of the castle and back to our secret room in the attic at the inn.

Making my way to the entry door, I placed my ear upon its bound wood frame and could hear that the sentry had returned to his post. Rather than trying to slip past the guard unnoticed, which would be next to impossible, I began to search the room for hidden doors or clues concealed within the walls that might reveal the placement of a passage beyond. The architecture of the entry did seem a few steps too short, so my first suspicion lay within the corner of the chamber nearest the main hall. Weaving behind the strange arrangement of totems and statues, I thoroughly searched the stone wall.

With a practiced hand and a bit of luck, I found a small wooden peg positioned behind a hung banner bearing the royal crest. A gentle press upon it was answered with a satisfying '*click*' from the device, and a portion of the column swung inward to reveal a narrow passage beyond. The direction led towards the chamber of the duchess at the end of the outer hall. Pressing my way into the tight fissure, I closed the portal behind me and tried to find my way through the darkness of the corridor.

Realizing I wouldn't get far in the thick gloom, I took out my flint and a small length of an oiled wick I had clipped from a lantern in his chambers. Keeping the flame propped on the edge of my dagger, I delved deeper into the narrow corridor.   Upon reaching the area I had assumed was adjacent to the private chambers of the young duchess, I was troubled to find several large archaic talismans painted upon the walls as if their purpose was to create a mystical ward.   Apparently, the fear of witchcraft was deeply ingrained into the history of this remote harbor city.

Any access doors or ways to view into the royal chambers had been crudely covered with boards and mortar. It was clear that this area of the secret passage had been sealed off with obvious intent. The question in my mind was that whoever had access to these private passages must have known that it was either used as a means of escape, or a way to spy on the castle's occupants. So who would place these hexes upon the inner walls where they could not be seen?

Any path to the royal chamber had been thoroughly obstructed from the secret passage, so I had no other choice but to explore deeper into the corridor to find another exit. After descending a narrow flight of stairs, I spotted another slit in the wall ahead just as the last wavering wisp of flame from my exhausted wick snuffed out to leave me enveloped in the choking darkness. The spy hole looked in from the back shelving of a pantry where a small kitchen could be seen beyond. A handful of servants could be observed within, as they were busily washing dishes and snacking on used platters of food which sat in a pile upon a heavy butcher block set in the middle of the room.

"Well, that was certainly short," one servant remarked as she took a bite of leftovers lying upon a half-eaten plate.

"One day, Milady Graystone is going to face the wrath of the Duchess if she doesn't learn to hold her tongue!" stated another maid while I eavesdropped upon their faint conversation.

"It would serve her right if she did, both her and the General need to stop chattering behind her ladyships back and learn some respect," another chubby servant noted to the others while she stood over a basin with her rolled-up sleeves as she scrubbed the dirtied plates.

Standing back from the eyehole, it dawned on me that the dinner party had already come to a close. This timing was far shorter than Nyx and I had originally assumed. Taking a moment to let my eyes adjust to the darkness again, I found another crevice through which a thin beam of light radiated into the passage a few steps ahead. Looking through the slit, I could see the far corner of a dining table that had been recently abandoned as there were several platters of partially used trays and a wide place in the middle where it looked as though something had knocked the dishes and wine glasses asunder.

If this was the dining hall which serviced the guests that I had overheard the servants mention, then they had ended the meal early and I had arrived too late. Taking a look at my surroundings, I caught a seam of dim light at the end of the tight passage. Several more strides placed me at a mechanism which revealed the hinge of a narrow door. Pulling the exposed wire on my side, triggered the switch which caused the panel to unlatch.

Slowly pushing the slat open, I found myself at the back end of a coatroom where several capes and coats hung upon hooks. What immediately caught my eye was the double-sided cloak that Nyx had worn to this evening's engagement, which was sitting untouched upon its hanger. If anything, I knew Nyx would not willingly abandon her costume cloak which housed several utility items woven within its seams. Carefully peeking outside the coat room entry, I crept my way up to the door of the dining chamber and found it had been left unlocked.

Once within, I traced its angle to see where the spy hole I used had been cleverly designed into the carved recess of a decorative sconce. Several used platters had been left scattered in disarray as it appeared that the guests of this party had departed in haste. Testing the handle at the far entry towards the kitchen, I glanced up to the rim of the door and noticed it had been bolted from the inside of the chamber; which was the reason the servants had not yet cleared the table. This left me with a sinking feeling that something terrible had happened to my apprentice.

The only other exit from the chamber had been left ajar, where I saw a cloth napkin had fallen to the floor along with a piece of silverware. This scant trail led me into the hall, beyond which appeared to have been carved from a solid block of stone. At the end of the corridor was a large iron door cast with a mass of rigid studs lining its face. Its surface was cold and heavily scarred, and appeared far older than the fixtures of the castle which decorated this section of the keep.

The scuffle marks I spied upon the floor told me this strange portal had been used recently, so I dared to explore where it led. It was my suspicion that Nyx had been secreted away into this recessed chamber, which was the concern we had shared that her invitation to this private banquet had been a trap in disguise. Taking ahold of the large ring handle, I was mildly surprised to find the thick iron door had been left unlatched. With a heave, I gave the handle a tug, and it slowly swung open.

The sharp creak it made upon its rusted hinges made me grit my teeth for having created so much noise; although it was entirely unavoidable. Realizing I may have attracted unwanted attention, I slipped inside and quietly waited for several moments to listen if a guard was forthcoming to investigate. Given my habit for precaution, I forced one of my throwing spikes into the gap at the hinge of the door so that it would not swing shut and lock behind me. Satisfied that I had covered my way of escape, I took the winding stairs down into the depths of the castle while noting that this section of the structure had been carved from the very bedrock upon which the fortress had been built.

I also didn't fail to notice the abrupt change in the architecture as I progressed deeper into the depths while several mounted lanterns guided my way. I had expected to find a torture room or dungeon of sorts at the end of the landing but was instead rewarded with an amazing sight. The bottom of the stair opened into a columned foyer which overlooked an underground city sprawling across the floor of a massive cavern. The sheer size and dimension of this hidden metropolis clearly dwarfed the sparse encampment of the spider cult hidden within the dusty mines beneath Stilgrave.

"Ah... that's just great," I whispered under my breath with

heavy sarcasm, knowing that my odds of finding Nyx among this mass of ruins had greatly diminished, while my chance of getting hopelessly lost among these remnants had greatly multiplied.

It was a stunning sight to behold an entire city below ground, with its many pins of light glowing from lanterns dappled amongst the maze of ancient buildings. In all respects, the size of this subterranean realm challenged that of the bustling city above. Though here, the air was untroubled by the sounds of trotting horses and conversations of peasants roaming the streets. In fact, I didn't see anyone moving among the winding ruins. Canvassing the entire area to locate my apprentice within this labyrinth would take far too long to uncover every route; so I did what any reasonable thief would and utilized the building heights to cover more ground from above.

The steep rises and tile rooftops of the city above were precarious enough to navigate, but here the stone structures were wet with condensation from the moisture in the air. A thin fog hung over the abandoned city, making it a challenge to gauge distances between the buildings as I leapt from tier to tier, looking for signs of life. The lights emanating from a circular complex at the center of the subterranean metropolis caught my interest as I delved deeper. Cones of yellow light flowered above the complex as the haze captured the illumination bleeding from below.

A sudden horrible shriek from beneath my perch made me pause. Concerned that it might be Nyx, I hooked my rope and slid down to the surface streets where I ventured towards the source of the commotion. The sound had come from a small house where several candles had been left in the open windows. I brushed aside the worn material draped across the entry and slid my way inside, only to find a troubling scene.

In the dim candlelight, I could see an old man lying on a

makeshift bed where a silent scream was frozen upon his face as though he had died from a terrible fright. I could find no other wound or cause for his sudden outburst and ensuing death. My hand stiffened as I reached out to cover a blanket over the man's frightful eyes, when I was drawn to the small egg placed beside him. What I found disturbing about it, was the strange black substance which had spilled from its pale cracked shell, as if something unholy had been hatched from within.

The shell itself was empty except for the vile residue which trickled out around its base, while noting that a thin trail of this dark taint led directly from where the egg lay, was traced towards his frozen carcass. A cold chill ran up my spine, and I felt uneasy touching the body further to search for clues as to who he was or why he was here. There was little within the small hovel, which had been left in such a disheveled condition as to obscure any traces that might reveal if the old man had been here for any length of time. With pause, it made me wonder if this subterranean city was a hidden sanctuary for the poor and destitute in a similar fashion to the forgotten mines beneath Stilgrave, or perhaps instead, it was a place of banishment.

It was a hypothesis which I could only guess at given the circumstance, but these were unanswered questions that could wait until I rescued my apprentice. Weaving my way through the shadows draping the labyrinth of alleys and streets, I started to stumble upon lone individuals shuffling through the ruins. They appeared to be lethargic, and moved as though they were confused and lost. It was an easy matter to slip past them, as I didn't wish to risk a direct encounter in the event these wayward souls were as unbalanced and dangerous as they appeared.

As I drew closer, I began to detect a bizarre noise emanating from the direction of the open dome located at the very center of the network. Dashing between the streets under the cover of shadows, I slipped into the outer courtyard of the circular building and made my way inside. A low but strange chatter seemed to hum through the building which amplified throughout its main hall. It wasn't until I crept through the inner arches that the source of the weird sound made itself known.

There were several dozen peasants, mostly elderly, standing still as if in a daze; however, from their mouths came a terrible noise as their jaws rattled while their teeth clicked with an eerie rhythm. I moved among them slowly, until it became clear that they did not notice my presence. It was as if they were paralyzed by some spell which held them bound. It wasn't clear how long they had been standing there, but those with exposed feet had revealed that they were bruised and swollen.

It was as if they were held captive by some unseen force as that dreadful sound droned from their lips. I had never believed in dark magic until that very moment; having seen how the minds of these unfortunate victims' had been gripped by some evil curse. Moving my way along the circumference of the yard, I came upon many more of these living statues entrapped within some wicked spell. They all stood facing the central dome, which drew me towards the source of their empty stares.

Breaching the innermost chamber, my eyes fell upon a horrific scene. Upon a large circular altar stood a pair of enormous whale ribs entwined by ropes, between them lay Nyx within their woven bonds, held there as though she were caught within a spider's web. Her hands were outstretched and laced with heavy layers of twine to the point that her arms where encased within their thick folds.

As she hung unconscious in her exotic shackles, a suited nobleman and lady in red were speaking to one another as two elderly men of the court were busy dunking sheets of cloth in a trough which contained a foul brackish liquid.

After saturating the bolts of material, they laid each section upon one of the many naked bodies of the peasants lying atop the platform; taking great care to handle the tainted cloth with long iron thongs they held in their hands. I was confused for but a moment as to their purpose, but the sections of black cloth reminded me of the same material I had found covering that cursed skull which I had swiped from Vale's apartment. It then occurred to me that that this cloth had been saturated in toxic poisons, which I had absorbed by its very touch.

Even when they were dry and appeared as nothing more than a dark material, any oils or moisture of the skin would cause them to leech into the body. Shortly after the tainted material was placed upon their exposed torso, the victims began to twitch and convulse. After several moments, these seizures lessened until the captives became as still as stone; all except for the terrible sound of their chattering teeth as their jaws continued to spasm. These poor souls were then held up and redressed while staring mindlessly before them through their dark and empty eyes.

Whoever they may have once been before this moment, was now entirely gone. The elderly men who had applied the poisonous rags helped to escort these wretches outside the chamber as they shuffled along, appearing entirely oblivious to their surroundings. As they did so, I noticed that Nyx was beginning to waver upon the central altar, as though she was fading in and out of consciousness. The tall nobleman in uniform approached her, while the woman in red followed. The baroness suddenly reached forward and grabbed her captives dress and ripped it open from the center bosom down, exposing Nyx where she hung.

"Do you like what you see, Stalker?" Shiva smirked in a crass tone towards him, "or will you turn her into one of your playthings when she joins our congregation?" the woman spat as she spun to grab a pair of long thongs and proceeded to dip a sheet of fabric into the toxic vat lying before them.

"If you do that, we won't be able to question her," the general countered, "and I have been so looking forward to taking my favor with this one while she still has a bit of fight left in her."

It was clear that Shiva had every intention of anointing Nyx with her poison-laden cloth while the girl was held captive, which would strip her of her mind. I knew the time to act was short and readied the crossbow I carried with another climbing bolt, which could anchor itself into flesh as easily as it would in stone. I didn't like making such hasty plans, for even if I mortally wounded the baroness, I would still have to face off with the military General and attempt to rescue my apprentice before she came to any harm. My only fear was that we could be swarmed and overwhelmed by these mindless drones, should they react to my attack.

As I steadied myself to take aim down the crosshairs, a sudden shout broke the tension. Looking over my shoulder to its source, I spied a small girl stomp into the inner chamber, following in her wake were several royal guards clad in black armor. Most disturbingly, my fears were realized, when to my horror, a horde of mindless drones shambled in behind her through the open columns as though these lost souls were under her control. I was dumbfounded by the verbal exchange that followed, as this small child was revealed to be none other than the young duchess herself.

"I order you to stop! What do you think you are doing, Shiva?" The tiny girl spat in a commanding tone. Lady Graystone froze in place and turned towards the duchess and her entourage of heavily armed guards, and promptly dropped the iron thongs as they clattered to the stone floor at her feet.

"Your highness ...I, I was just," Shiva stuttered as her face bleached white with fear when her eyes fell upon the small child with the painted face.

"You were going to disobey my orders and initiate our guest into the flock!" the girl declared in a sour tone as the grown woman in red was clearly unsettled by this accusation while she shuddered in fright.

"My Duchess, we had captured this spy as instructed, and were merely going to question her when she..." the general began to explain with a contrived excuse, until he too was cut short by the young girl's heated temper.

"Silence, General! I can see by her torn gown that you were up to your lecherous exploits again, you disgusting worm!" The little girl shot back with venom in her voice. Her curt response caused the warrior to right his posture while he was given a verbal dressing-down in front of the guards surrounding the royal heir.

This was a turn of events I had not foreseen, especially so since this adolescent child appeared to speak and carry herself in a way far removed from her apparent age. It was more than obvious that these nobles clearly feared her on a mortal level. The real question was, as to how she had attained this mass of mindless revenants which appeared to be under her personal restraint? As if out of a nightmare, a skeletal figure slowly floated into view out of the shadows behind the altar; its bare ivory bones and decorated skull were covered with intricate carvings of designs which I had seen before.

"You were warned not to defy my wishes," the young duchess threatened with an evil glare, "and now you will face the wrath of the Dark Shepard."

Acts of Betrayal

Nyx felt groggy and weak when her weary eyes finally opened. In her delirium, she faintly recalled something about a dinner party, but the details of it were hazy and unclear. She felt confused when she suddenly found herself upon an open dais supported by columns and high arches carved of stone; not recognizing where she was. A faint breeze blew in through an open corridor where pale shrouds fluttered in slow motion before her. The young thief struggled to stand and found her footing shaky and unsteady, which was a concerning symptom for her since she had spent her life relying on her sense of balance.

Nyx entered the great hall as she stumbled, while a dreary hum drew her down its path with a slow rhythmic beat from a tune which seemed strange and out of place, yet somehow familiar. Drawn to its source, she entered into another large room left in ruins, its walls crumbled and broken. Banks of snow filled the open cavities where they let in the bitter cold from a winter storm. Her senses seemed to be dulled, and she couldn't grasp what had happened to her.

Through the broken structure, a turbulent gale formed in the sky above where she stood; its murky eye of twisting dark clouds crackled with streaks of lightning. A faint laughter echoed from above as if to taunt her as Nyx stood defiant at first, only to press her eyes shut in pain and her hands to her ears when the cackling grew to a deafening roar as she lost her footing and crumbled to the hard floor. This cruel torment faded into the darkness while the cyclone enveloped the room around her as the countless throng of voices became one. Nyx slowly opened her eyes to a new nightmare as a shriek of evil amusement issued from the lips of a young girl standing below.

The couple standing before her spun to face Nyx as she struggled to remember their faces while her memory slowly returned. Shiva and Stalker seemed to look past her as Nyx struggled to turn her head towards the object that consumed their gaze, only to find that her arms were tightly bound in a weave of sinew that held her fast. Her captor's faces turned pale and speechless as Nyx fought with her bindings when the scene around her sharpened into full focus. The young duchess stood before a swarm of peasants whose eyes were hollow and lifeless, while their teeth snapped like a thousand rattles.

The air was damp and the sky above was muddy as the light of the surrounding torches were blurred by a thick fog. The calloused expression now cemented upon the young child's face was far different from the scared little girl she had found hiding in the coatroom an hour before. An evil grin covered her painted cheeks as she spoke with an air of authority, while the baroness and her general cowered before the taunting child. Their attention was drawn to some apparition behind her, which Nyx could not view from her bound position upon the altar.

"...What is this?" Shiva trembled as she took a step back while the general faltered beside her.

"It has been many generations since our Shepard has been lost amongst the catacombs during the wars in the time of our forefathers," the little girl answered from below, "now he has returned to lay waste upon our enemies and those traitors who oppose the nobility of the dark throne," she smiled below her sinister glare.

At this cue, the elite guards standing by the girl's side drew their swords and stepped forth in unison to defend the Duchess, but their movements went unnoticed by the baroness and her accomplice who were mesmerized by the floating specter before them.

"Forgive us your highness," Shiva blurted as she turned and collapsed upon her knees to bow before the small girl stationed at the foot of the altar, "we, we didn't mean any disrespect..." she stuttered before the duchess interrupted her appeal.

"Oh, but you did," her highness rebutted beyond the shield of her guards, "...every hour after my father died, you both grew ever more insolent and jealous of my title. I heard your whispered schemes and treacherous plans to betray the crown, and your envious designs to be rid of me so that you could take my place!"

"My Duchess, I ...we would never actually do anything to harm your highness," Stalker intervened, "we know that the people of Blacktide would never bow to anyone but you and the Regent. What you're suggesting is absurd and I..."

"Absurd?" the royal child screeched, "So you think my accusations are *lunacy* do you, General Stalker?" The duchess snapped back.

The general appeared to know he was caught in a lie, for he immediately shut his jaw, having known of the child's explosive temper from rumors he had overheard among the acting guardsmen and castle staff. He realized his folly was that he and lady Graystone had grown cocky once their Lord Regent had disappeared. In their roles, Stalker controlled the military, and Shiva held the duty of running the keep while Sir Ryan was out of the picture, with nothing but a little girl in their way from attaining total power in his absence. While they had conspired under their breath in private to be rid of the Duchess, the young girl had been listening from the tangle of secret passages woven throughout the castle.

Several generations ago, a time of harsh conflict known as the Reaver Wars, had decimated the lands as invaders from the south pushed deep into the northern territories. It wasn't until after the close of a exceptionally bloody and costly battle that a truce had been called, leaving the cities of Stilgrave and Blacktide uncomfortably close to their newly drawn borders. The tribal sects of the north had their devotion to the teachings of the Shepard while the religious factions of the south had named their Builders as divine; each side pushing their holy doctrine upon the confused and divided people of the region. When their hallowed Shepard died, he was made into a martyr; and through time and tales, this prophet was transformed into an unholy saint for those seeking solace in troubled times.

Over the years, the tales turned to legend, and those legends turned to myth as the clergy of the south took advantage of this situation and denoted the followers of the Dark Shepard as disciples of foul tidings and witchcraft. Theology can be cruel to those who oppose it, and as time passed, the folklore of the Dark Shepard faded to nothing more than trifle curses muttered in taverns and whispered as bedtime stories parents would tell their children to keep them from misbehaving. Worshipers of this forgotten prophet kept their faith alive in secret beyond the eyes of the City Watch and the smug priests of the Builders. The bony remnants of their dark saint had been kept safely hidden away by the faithful followers of the cult, and were engraved with cryptic symbols to mark them as sacred.

Existing in secrecy and living in the squalor of the tunnels beneath the city, it was no wonder that fresh tales were woven to keep their faith alive which began to embody the arachnids that dwelled within its silent shadows, and the cult of the Golden Spiders blossomed from this dark sanctuary. The tales of the forgotten city beneath the rubble of Blacktide had vanished over the years, to exist as nothing more than a passing myth among the populous as they began to rebuild after the War, and was kept as a closely guarded secret by the royal family whose castle was built upon its foundations.

Those few who accidentally stumbled upon its existence would readily disappear, as would any citizen who dared to oppose this new regime. These inmates were given elixirs made from toxic seaweed and venomous fish to keep them obedient and docile while they were imprisoned within the hidden city, and were used as forced labor to restore the vast subterranean sanctum. Those disciples of the cult preserved and perfected their varieties of these potions and exotic mixtures as they expanded the knowledge of their lethal alchemy. Over the years, these secretive cultists eventually discovered that controlled doses of these toxic concoctions could be used to sway the unwilling; giving them the tools to enact revenge upon their oppressive masters.

Only a handful of men assigned to the royal guard, who were loyal to the Duchess, were allowed passage into this underground realm; whom would personally secret away any dissidents or criminals from the streets of the city above to this dreadful domain. The General and his female accomplice had overstepped their authority, and had recently granted themselves access to this forbidden grotto when they began to suspect that their Lord Regent may never return. The two nobles cast a fearful gaze towards one another as they stood upon the steps of the altar, realizing they had gravely miscalculated the young duchess and were now held at her mercy.

"No, I don't think that, my Duchess," the general muttered as he shook his head and took a knee while lowering his head in homage to the royal successor.

"Good," the duchess snapped back, "however, you do realize that I cannot allow such transgressions to go unpunished."

"I understand, your highness," Stalker quickly muttered in reply, while the baroness remained silent out of fear.

"You've trespassed into this sacred sanctuary and had the

arrogance to accost a guest of the court without my permission, which *really* irritates me to no end," the girl pressed, "someone needs to pay the price for this offense. Which one of you will it be?" She inquired with finality.

Shiva and Stalker exchanged a confused glance with a glint of worry as to what the other might do. Just as it appeared that Stalker began to stand and start his plea, Lady Graystone jumped forward and began to shed her accusations upon the general.

"Your highness, whatever you might have heard in the past against you was contrived by your general," Shiva spat as she turned with an accusing finger towards Stalker, "he is the one who brought me to this place and planned to violate your guest, and urged me to participate in his plans to dethrone you. It is a clear abuse of his position and..."

"Liar!" The duchess interrupted her rant, and with a gesture of her hand, the skeletal specter poised above them swooped down and caught her in its frightful embrace. A look of horror flashed in Shiva's face the moment she was whisked up into the air, and they both vanished into the gloom above. Her screams were quickly muffled by the smothering darkness. Nyx had gotten a glimpse of the creature for but a second before it flashed out of sight, while the general stood paralyzed in horror to what had just transpired.

"My... my Duchess, I..." Stalker began to mumble incoherently until the little girl pushed her way past the royal guards to address him directly while she clasped her hands behind her back and shook her head in thought.

"Silence," she ordered curtly, "betrayal can be a real bitch; don't you agree, General?"

General Stalker merely nodded his chin in solemn compliance.

"You will report to the throne room come morning, along with our guest here, and if you ever speak of this place I will have your tongue cut out and fed to you; do you understand?" the little girl cautioned the man with a noted glare to make sure he was paying attention to her words.

General stalker swallowed the lump in his throat as he nodded yet again without making a sound.

"Good, I like servants of the crown who understand their place," the duchess affirmed while her General breathed a sigh of relief, realizing his life had just been spared. For all his training, position, and privilege, he now realized that his granted stature was merely a thin facade that could be revoked at any given moment.

The royal guards turned to escort the young noble on the path back to the castle, while the general stood upon the altar to wonder what twist of fate had spared him. Nyx herself, was left dumbfounded as she tried to shake off the poison coursing through her system. She had roused from a vivid hallucination, induced by the poison she was given, only to find herself cast into yet another horrific nightmare. Once the duchess departed with her guards, the mindless drones turned to exit the chamber and resumed their former placement in the darkness beyond.

"Untie me, and get me down from here!" Nyx demanded of her captor as she struggled at her bonds. This interruption to his troubled thoughts swiftly snapped Stalker back to his presence of mind.

"Apparently, the Duchess cares little for details as to what happens to you until the morn, and has left you in my care, Lady Kashara," Stalker offered with a weak grin as he tried to shake off the stress of being verbally emasculated and regained his sense of manhood from the dressing-down he had just received.

His hungry eyes fell from Nyx's livid glare down to her torn dress and exposed bosom. Nyx knew she was in a helpless position and had found herself in similar situations in the past. Whenever the drunken gutter trash of the streets or pompous nobility attempted to take advantage of her, she would play along until a critical moment to brandish a blade or bite them where, let's say, where it wouldn't go unfelt. She knew how to play men in that matter; for it was merely one of many masks she could wear to appear docile and innocent, either to lure a victim to be robbed or to delude an assailant into believing she was an easy mark. Unfortunately, she had already played her hand and was still fighting off the concoction she had been drugged with.

Stalker reached out and began to caress her breasts with his eager hands while Nyx turned her head away in contempt as he pressed forward to lick her neck; the only thing flashing through her mind at that moment was a mild consideration as to what piece of him she would cut off first once she was freed from her bonds. The general began to cackle as he fed his vulgar thoughts in anticipation of bending her to his will.

His vile sneer suddenly snapped to an expression of shock as a piercing pain shot through his leg. Looking down to its source, Stalker found the shaft of a thin iron grappling rod protruding from the high leather boot of his calf. From it, a thin cable spanned out into the gloom from beyond the flaming braziers. With a single violent snap of the cord, Stalker was yanked off his feet and landed face first onto the stone floor; knocking him unconscious.

Nyx was silenced in a moment of panic, but breathed a sigh of relief as she recognized the familiar silhouette stepping towards her from the shadows.

"My hero, yet again..." Nyx mumbled dryly in a clear but condescending tone.

"Let's try not to make this a habit, shall we," I breathed as I ascended the steps to the altar to prod the Generals limp body with my boot, to make sure he was out cold, "fill me in on what happened to you and try to explain what I just witnessed here, Nyx."

"I was drugged during the dinner party," Nyx admitted while I started to cut away at her bindings, "...and that little girl was actually the Duchess of Blacktide," she added as an afterthought.

"I thought as much," I conceded, as I recalled the caustic conversation between the fighting nobles, "...but she's not exactly what I had expected," I added while stripping one of Nyx's arms free from the arch with my blade.

"You're telling me! It seems I completely misread her," Nyx added, "but what was that thing that snatched up the Baroness?"

"I was hoping you would tell me," I conceded as I gave a nervous glance into the darkness above where it had materialized, while cutting her other arm free of its woven twine. Nyx shook herself to get the blood flowing back into her extremities while tearing off the excess bindings. Once she stepped down from the shrine, it took a moment for her to catch her balance.

"Are you going to be able to walk?" I asked with concern since I had taken the high road of the rooftops to reach this section of the cavern, which demanded a high level of dexterity. If we had to take the ground path, getting out of here would be far riskier for us both.

"I'll make do ...I hope," Nyx added as she stumbled once again, but regained her equilibrium enough to give Stalker's limp body a swift kick to his ribs. Patting her lower corset, she realized that they had removed her hidden daggers while she had been unconscious and dragged her down into this abyss, "and where the hell are we? I don't recognize this area from the map of the city."

"That's because we are directly below it," I added to meet the look of surprise flashing in her emerald eyes. Instead of questioning my statement, she held out an empty hand towards me.

"I need to borrow a blade so I can take a souvenir," Nyx granted when I hesitated before placing my spare knife into her open hand.

I had noticed her attention had been drawn directly towards the comatose body of the General lying at her feet; which made me pause for a moment before granting her wish. At that instant, a lone figure stepped back into the light of the torches from beyond the pillars, revealing himself to be one of the elder nobles which had been present during the dinner party.

"You there, stop!" he yelled aloud, but his aged voice was weaker than most to bring the attention of the royal guards who had disappeared through the maze of streets on their way back towards the cavern entrance. The elderly steward realized he was no match for the two assailants, and chose to turn and scurry up the narrow path after the duchess and her guardsmen for assistance, yelling every step of the way.

"Hmm, sorry Nyx, but we don't have time for that right now," I cautioned my apprentice before slapping the handle of the dagger into her empty palm, while dissuading Nyx from her considered butchery upon the nobleman. He might have very well deserved it, but an experienced thief knows that seconds count when you've been spotted. Any delay of flight during such a critical moment could be costly. We had to make our way out of this unfamiliar zone and back to the surface.

Nyx seemed displeased by my insistence as I turned her away from Stalker's prone body and out towards the thick gloom behind the shrine, where we could meld into the shadows. Her current form of attire wasn't exactly ideal for evasion or blending with the environment we found ourselves in. I would have to take the lead and find us an avenue out of here without putting her at further risk.

It was obvious that Nyx wasn't her usual confident self, as

she paused to catch her step several times while stumbling into the lower yard. Her physical handicap caused by the lingering poison made our situation ever more precarious if she wasn't able to maneuver and keep up with my pace. Being fleet of foot and agile was a prerequisite for our field, and any injury or hindrance could easily lead to a fatal mistake or unpleasant fall. I had noticed an open causeway directly behind the altar which marked a path between a broad maze of running channels, and pointed her towards it.

"We'll take this route to the source of the inlet," I noted to my apprentice as she faltered with her steps.

The water running in the channels had to be coming from somewhere, and since we were already deep underground, it only made sense to follow the route upstream and hope that there was a channel that led to the surface. Behind us, the clamor of feet clad in armor resounded as guardsmen poured into the courtyard of the shrine. The older man rushed to their general's aid and roused him while inspecting his injuries. The grappling hook did not penetrate too deeply into his calf, but the barbed hooks had clamped onto the leather of his shredded boot.

Ripping the bolt loose, General Stalker got to his feet; the wound to his leg only slightly hobbling his mobility.

"I will take care of this personally," Stalker snarled through gritted teeth as he snatched a spare sword from one of the soldiers. Rubbing the bruise on his head, he recalled the dark figure who had taken a shot at him from beyond the shadows before he had been yanked off his feet and knocked unconscious. Not only would it be of further embarrassment to the General if his assailant escaped, but knew that if he failed to secure Lady Kashara before his morning appointment in the throne room, as ordered by the Duchess, then he would most certainly face a fate far worse than that of the late Baroness.

Knowing there was an intruder within the sanctuary, the guards spread out among the area as Stalker noticed the echo of falling stones in the darkness when Nyx slipped while she and Ash snaked their way through the maze of channels. Grabbing a torch, the General limped after the source of the noise rising from the web of pathways weaving through the system of aqueducts.

"We have to hurry," I pressed towards Nyx who had slipped once again, while I helped her regain her footing on the wet granite of the channel barrier.

Glancing over my shoulder, I saw the distant single torchbearer heading our direction upon the rising steps of the waterway. Unfortunately, I had already dropped my crossbow in the courtyard, having used its reserve grappling bolt. The only route of escape was to climb higher among the rolling streams which cascaded down the face of the ruins rising before us. The light in this section of the cavern was dim at best, making our progress extremely precarious as we tread upon the moist stone beneath our feet.

A high ledge spotted above us gave the promise of level ground, and with it, the hope of an avenue from which we could escape. We scrambled higher while the flow of water increased in strength as several channels united near its source from a hidden inlet. Nyx took a seat to get a breather and turned to me in wonder.

"What are you doing?" she asked with heavy breath as I had taken a knee to dip my hand within the rivulet to grab a taste of the water.

"Hmm, this is fresh water..." I granted with a confused glance back at her.

"And what of it?" Nyx replied in confusion.

"I would have suspected this inlet would be sourced by seawater from the proximity of this cavern to the shore," I responded in thought.

It was known that several areas of the northern territories were riddled with caves and grottos, but this cavern was located dangerously close to the seawall. If there was untainted water pouring in from a spring above, it would be a rational conclusion that the black granite stone was providing a protective layer between the seabed and this subterranean shelter. Following that route would likely take them farther towards the source of the well water system where it emerged in the middle of the city, rather than in the direction of the harbor.

While scanning the area directly above us, Nyx noticed something which had passed my attention.

"Look up there, I can see stars!" Nyx breathed.

Turning my head upwards, I noted a glimmer of florescent clouds pass by as a patch of twinkling stars began to shine from the dark void above. Within moments, a silver lining etched along the thick clouds, and we realized that by this hour of the night, that the moon would be directly overhead. We glanced down at the lone figure bearing a torch coming directly for us, just as Nyx and I were suddenly caught in a ray of bright moonlight which pierced through the clouds above, exposing our position.

General Stalker had been hot on the trail of his prey, having gained his namesake from his ability to track his quarry and to notice trace details that went unnoticed by others. He perceived every footfall and wet handprint left behind by Lady Kashara and her accomplice. His attention was immediately drawn towards the pair when the shaft of moonlight cast upon the two rogues as they stood upon the ledge high above his position.

Knowing we had been spotted, I grabbed Nyx by the arm and sprang us towards the center of the spillway. Taking advantage of the momentary light, I scanned the surrounding area; noting an enormous carving of intricate shapes and chiseled faces lining the cavern wall, which had been previously hidden in the enveloping shadows. Towards the middle of the chamber, I also noted a strange curiosity. An odd structure attached to the roof of the cavern which had been built by a series of braces fastened among the stalactites. It appeared to be similar to a type of crane arm which I had seen before, that was used for unloading large crates from harbored ships; though I had to admit that its unusual design was quite bizarre. Hanging from the edge of the boom were several coils of hoist rope along with what appeared to be a single figure of a human body hanging lifelessly from the jib.

At first thought, I didn't know who to presume it was, if not the Baroness, but noticed Nyx was also staring at the sole carcass dangling in the darkness, far out of reach. The bright moonlight had also exposed a remarkable device composed of brass and steel embedded deep into the stonework at the center of the outlet above us, from which the water flowed beneath its perch. While trying to find a way off the ledge to escape our pursuer, I stopped to inspect this strange apparatus when I caught the glimpse of something familiar in its design. The mechanism was comprised of eight sections, slotted one above the other; each ring had boldly sculpted images upon them which combined to display the figure of a statuesque face.

Nyx struggled past me only to wonder what had captured my attention.

"Ash, what is it? That soldier is gaining ground on us!" she advised while I sifted through my pockets to remove the pair of scrolls I had recently sequestered from the Lord Regents study and his bedchamber.

I placed the thin parchments on top of one another, as I had done before, and held them up towards the moonlight, which revealed the image it held once again. Upon the exposed portrait was the likeness of a woman's face, with worn features and wriggling tentacles weaving about her like a halo. Clasping my hand upon one of the cold metal wheels, it appeared that each one of the dials would rotate. It took a moment to sink in that what I had found was a coded key to this archaic device.

The Winter Jackal

"Nyx, take this, and align these disks until *this* image appears," I motioned for my apprentice to accept the parchments I held up towards the streaming moonlight.

Nyx snatched the scrolls from my hand and began to spin each section of the sculpted rings in an effort to match the figure it revealed. With effort, she wrenched each wheel until the desired section aligned with the portrait. Below us, the lone figure had made its way up near the ledge close enough that I could now identify our pursuer as the General, who finally breached the ridge and tossed his blazing torch upon the floor between us. He took an armed stance which revealed he was no stranger to personal combat.

"Do you think this opens a passage out of here?" Nyx inquired as she spun another ring into place. It was the only clue we had at the moment, and given how the castle was riddled with secret doors and passages, I imagined this device would reveal an exit reserved for the royal members of the court as a means of escape from one of the archways lining this precarious perch.

"Let's hope so. Keep working on that lock and don't stop until you're finished," I cited over my shoulder to her as I stepped in between Nyx and our antagonist.

"Who is this friend of yours, Lady Kashara?" Stalker taunted towards Nyx, "An associate you failed to introduce ...a little rude don't you think?"

A quick eye showed that Stalker was still favoring his wounded leg as he shifted his footing when he took another step closer. The quick flash of a flying spike glinted in the light above the resting torch as it screamed its way towards his chest. Stalker had trained reflexes, and deflected the hurled weapon with the basket hilt of his sword as he sidestepped while a rain of angry sparks split the air where metal met metal.

"I should have let her gut you while you were down," I breathed aloud as I began to regret our hasty retreat. Killing a defenseless foe wasn't exactly my style and even considered cowardly in my book, but there were times when I doubted my choices; this was one of them.

"Ah, are you a gentleman or a rogue? ...By your attire, I would guess the latter," Stalker mocked as he closed the gap between us.

Having ditched my crossbow and missed my mark with my throwing spike, I was left with my dual curved daggers. Kneeling down, I placed my hands to the sides of my leather boots and pulled the blades from their hidden sheaths. Each blade curved wickedly around the front knuckle like long tusks. They were as sharp as razors and designed for use in close quarters.

However, the keen blade on my fighting daggers would do little against a long sword, and its reach gave Stalker a clear advantage. I could tell that he knew that he had the upper hand by the smirk drawn upon his lips. This man was no ordinary guard with sloppy tactics who would rely on armor to protect him, and I realized that I had to change my own defense if I was going to survive this encounter. I would have to go on the offensive and use sheer speed to wear him down.

There was nothing to use on this open ledge to shield me from his advance, but I had to keep him away from Nyx while she was working on the cryptic lock. Being a man of showmanship, the general swung his sword in wide swaths to push me back towards the ledge. My crossed daggers could only check the certain death-stroke, which stalled inches from my neck as my heel felt the rim of the bank behind me. A loud clank echoed from where Nyx had stood the moment she aligned one of the carved images upon the lock, and with a violent rattle beneath our feet, the flow of water below the ledge changed its route to another conduit.

Quite suddenly, the channel bed below me ran dry and with a look of surprise splashed upon the general's face, I dropped to the step below out of reach of his swinging blade. A scowl washed over him for a brief moment, which quickly faded as he turned his attention towards my accomplice who was still on the upper ledge. The moment he turned away, my weighted flail wrapped around his ankle, and with a sharp tug, I pulled him from the ledge. That was the second time he had fallen for that trick, and Stalker scrambled to regain his feet upon the slick floor of the empty canal.

"Wrong one, almost got it!" Nyx shouted from above as she squinted in the dim light to try to match up each of the markings on the script.

Glancing around me at the vast maze of gutters and conduits, the mechanism seemed to work by rerouting the waterway through different channels to various sections within the subterranean city below. If the apparatus merely affected separate gates to the water flow, then why would the Lord Regent have bothered to protect this illustrated-key contained upon this odd device? My distracted thoughts were soon brought back to the attention of my adversary, whose silver blade cut through the air and missed me by a hair. With the flick of my wrist, the flail retracted back into the gauntlet and I paired my blade against his to push him away.

Jumping from one channel into another dry bed, I skipped along the ledges to the far end of the outlet where the water rushed through an open channel. General Stalker had trouble gaining ground upon the slippery stone with his handicap of wearing only one boot, which allowed me to place a measure of breathing distance between us. Gaining the upper ground, I climbed my way back to the high ledge where Nyx was still busy turning the metal dials. At the bottom of the waterway I could see several more torch-bearing guards heading our direction; having given away our location during the fight.

"Hurry it up Nyx!" I called towards her.

"Almost ...got ...it," she struggled to turn the heavy ring of the final band as each layer above clicked into place.

Stalker had climbed his way back to the top of the ledge and took a glance below him to notice the guards were fast approaching our location. He turned back with a cocky smile as he dragged the tip of his blade upon the stone floor to get my attention.

"Give yourself up, there's no winning this!" Stalker offered smugly, "All I want is the girl, and I'll let you walk away..." he offered with a motion towards the cavern entrance below.

The glow of gathering torchlight was quickly upon us, and I realized that Nyx and I had only moments to spare. My first thought was that we should abandon this cryptic mechanism and make a jump for the nearest water channel, so we may ride the cascading flow to safety. If we weren't battered to death by the stone banks of the aqueducts, then we could flee towards the exit to the interior of the castle. However, that path was likely guarded by the royal sentries. We had been cornered, and it appeared as if we were caught. As I realized that this ancient device only controlled the waterway, it now seemed unlikely that the coded lock would reveal a secret exit for us to make our escape; so I lowered my guard for but an instant while contemplating our surrender.

The General took this as a sign of weakness and lunged forward, but I caught his blade as we locked hilts and came face to face. I could see it in his eyes now; he was a man with no honor or duty to anyone but himself. He was nothing more than a coward whose word had no value, and would take advantage of another whenever it presented itself. He was an opportunist, as was I, but one who was disturbed and depraved; whose tainted morals were forged from vanity.

His overconfidence led him to be standing far too close as he tried to overpower my defense, but a sharp jab of my heel directed onto the bare foot of his wounded leg caused him to buckle. A quick knee to his elbow as he dropped helped to loosen the sword from his grip, and in that instant my blade was lying squarely at his throat. A mixed look of confusion and panic crossed his face; one I had recognized in the eyes of such shallow men many times before. His lips parted as in a nervous mutter as he was about to say something to prop up his false sense of dignity, while failing to grasp how he had blundered; as such weak men always do.

A loud '*clack*' echoed from the device behind us as my apprentice connected the final sequence, and the carved portrait of a gaunt woman formed upon the strange writhing sculpture, became one. Figures of ocean waves and tentacles were carved about her head as were images of fish and crabs, and creatures of the sea. She appeared as if it were the idol of some ancient ocean goddess who once ruled the briny deep. Nyx fell back to the floor as the multiple segmented rings composing the face, suddenly collapsed upon one another and sealed themselves into one solid block.

A rumble began to shake the platform, and the soldiers below faltered while they struggled to keep their footing as they gazed up in fear at the walls of the cavern. The roar of churning water grew ever louder like an approaching hurricane, and with a deafening blast, several carved seals lining the cavern wall began to burst forth in sequence, flinging boulders and stone shards down upon the helpless guardsmen below. Icy water, reeking of salt, gushed through the cracked seals, flooding the city beneath our fragile perch. Nyx flashed a glance towards me with a look of despair, wondering what she had done.

Stalker took the opportunity to grasp for his fallen sword, but instead of my blade caressing his neck, a swift kick of my boot to his chest sent him tumbling into the cloudy water jetting below. His sword teetered on the edge of the brink for but a moment, glinting in the moonlight, only to follow him down into the murky haze. Making my way over to Nyx, I helped her to her feet. We grasped one another for support while we watched helplessly at the scene of devastation unfolding around us, as churning seawater began to overcome the walls and rooftops of the doomed city. There was no secret door to allow our escape; only the brackish water of the ocean pouring in to claim us within its cold embrace.

A flash of regret filled me as I no longer had our grappling gear and ropes at my disposal, for I had not foreseen this eventuality. The combination of my curiosity and speculation that the secret key to this mechanism hidden away by the Lord Regent might be to our benefit, would ultimately prove to be the cause of our demise. I had gravely miscalculated, and was about to pay the ultimate price for that mistake. Nyx clung to my arm in fear as we tried to steady ourselves upon the ledge while the rushing waters rose ever higher.

There was little to see in the upper reaches of the cave outside the thin cone of moonlight streaming in from above. As the torches and lanterns on the streets below were snuffed out, the entire cavern soon turned into a dark swirling abyss. As I scanned the walls for a possible way to climb our way out, Nyx tugged my arm and pointed towards the strange lattice of ropes and braces we had noted earlier secured to the roof of the grotto. There in the framework, we now saw a single ray of moonlight streaming in which had not been present before.

This could only mean that there was a way to the surface from its position, which was much lower in the cavern than the lip of the ridge open to the sky above, far beyond our reach. A glance downward showed the swirling waterline growing ever higher as the gushing torrent failed to abate in its fury. Judging the distance between our ledge and the odd framework stationed between the stalactites, reaching it would be our only chance at survival in our given circumstance. I turned towards Nyx with a tone of gravity in my voice she did not misinterpret.

"I hope you can swim," I stated firmly as I began to shed my outer gear and anything that might absorb water and weigh me down.

It took only a second for my apprentice to follow in kind as she began ripping away her ornate dress with its heavy material, which left her standing before me nearly naked as she shivered in the cold air. The rising pool of freshwater from the underground spring began to pool around us, being lighter in weight and floating upon the heavier seawater now filling the cavern. This had the effect of making the temperature we had to endure far more tolerable than the icy ocean water gushing in from the open breach. With my last strap of cord, I wrapped a security line between our waists, and we dove into the rising waters as it began to breach the ledge upon which we stood.

Nyx was still faltering in her drugged condition and was unable to give her full strength in the effort; though the shocking cold seemed to have convinced her to be more alert for the moment at hand. We swam in broad strokes towards the framework as the surrounding waterline rose towards it. We had to time this right, or we would get stuck in the surge of water and be battered along the rocky ceiling of the cave and drowned in the process. As we drew closer to the structure I could make out the form of a skeletal body covered in a dark ragged cloak, suspended loosely by several cords as it hung from the tip of a long arm attached to a wooden crane.

Being the lowest point of access, we struggled to reach this strange figurine. Suddenly noticing the line tied between us becoming ever more taught, I spun around only to find that Nyx was no longer above the surface. In her weakened condition, she had succumbed to the numbing cold and slowly began to sink. In such a dire situation, I had little choice but to grab for my serrated blade to cut the line before she dragged me down and drowned us both. Reaching for the dagger sheathed in my arm brace, I knew what I had to do.

In that moment of desperation, I realized that having a choice is still better than not having one at all, so I frantically tore off and sacrificed my wrist armor and boots for more buoyancy and began tugging upon the line secured to her limp body. Gripping her under the arm, I managed to get her head above the water where Nyx started gasping for breath and she began to stir.

"Grab the ropes, here!" I instructed as she frantically grasped for the hanging cables dangling before us as we began to climb our way over the torso of the figure they had been secured upon.

While making our way to the boom arm fixed above, we climbed over this strange effigy. Brushing aside the tattered hood on the marionette, I came face to face with the same carved skull I had swiped from Vale's apartment weeks ago. The entire framework of decorated bones had been woven into some type of ghoulish puppet operated by ropes and twine. Noting its assumed value and not wanting to come out of this empty-handed, I placed my fingers into its eye sockets and wrenched the skull free from its bindings and took it with me. Nyx had managed to make her way through the intricate structure of beams and joists towards the source of moonlight shining in from the open vent above.

Passing through to the gaping hatch, we stumbled upon an elaborate collection of gears and levers situated in a small carriage-like cockpit, which appeared to be anchored to several spindles of rope and cords leading out to the end of the crane where the skeleton was secured. This cockpit was soon enveloped by the rising tide of water as we were forced to abandon our berth of momentary relief, and we climbed our way up through the chimney by the thin ladder within the shaft. We escaped up to the surface where a secondary hatch had also been left ajar; likely by whoever had operated this strange apparatus. As the funnel filled with water, we looked around and found ourselves at the bottom of an open cauldron carved from solid bedrock, which lay hidden by a ring of walls enclosing the ancient remnants.

A makeshift ladder had been placed at the edge of the pit where we climbed our way to the plateau above. Littered around us were several more fallen ruins composed of blocks of black stone. Stepping to the windswept edge of the cliffs, I could see that we were now poised on a plateau overlooking the city; the structure from which we emerged stood unnoticed high above the level of the roadways below. Tracing our way through these ruins, we stumbled upon the open chasm which led directly into the hidden subterranean city.

Peering over the edge, by the moonlight piercing the darkness below, we could see the water had settled at sea level far beneath the rim of the chasm. If we had not made immediate flight for the escape shaft as we had, we would have drowned in this abysmal well among the broken debris swirling below. Within the cold dark waters one could make out the bodies of those wretched victims who had been tainted by the poisons of the cult's alchemists; their chattering teeth and suffering minds forever silenced. We stood there in the fading moonlight looking at one another, stripped of our clothing and gear, although quietly thankful for our lives.

Giving Nyx my undershirt, we suffered our way back to the city and into our safe-house at the Inn. It was no small feat to slip our way down the cliffside barehanded, beyond the sight of passing guards as the light of dawn began to rise. At this hour of the morning, the few drunks left within the bar were slumped in their seats. The stench of stale ale and unwashed bodies found equal challenge from the heavy snoring permeating the air as we made our way up the stair to our hidden loft.

Exhausted by the endeavor, we collapsed in the first dusty cot within reach until the frantic ringing of the bell tower woke us from our slumber midday. Feeling better after having passed the poisons from her system, Nyx jumped up and dashed to the window that overlooked the entrance to the castle.

"Hah, hah ...well, this is certainly going to complicate things," she stated with a hint of mirth as I crawled up out of bed to stand beside her while we peered out into the scene unfolding below.

Wide swaths of water recently began to pour from the castle steps and into the streets, while guards and peasants alike jumped aside in frantic chaos. Carpets and tapestries, and several articles of furniture which had decorated the inner court began washing out into view and tumbling down the wide steps into the lane. There seemed to be no end to its source as the spill began to snake its way down the avenue. Even at this distance, the shouts of the warden could be heard as fully armored soldiers appeared dumbfounded as to what they should do to stop the flood.

Although the deluge of ocean water had come to rest at sea level within the subterranean cavern, the source of the natural spring, which was originally routed through the spillway, had continued to slowly fill the cave until it finally reached the lowest point of escape. From what I had remembered of its layout, that would have been the large iron-clad doors that were located at the very center of the castle. If they had been left ajar during the alarm as the royal guards pursued us, then once the water started flowing they would have been unable to seal the bulkhead doors. It took me a moment to remember that I had jammed the hinges open with an iron spike, making it impossible to close the entry without its removal. When Nyx had completed setting the cycle on the ancient apparatus, each of the discs had locked into place. There appeared to be no alternate method for them to cut off the flow from the underground spring as its contents began to fill the ground floor of the keep.

As the layer of freshwater had been resting upon the heavier saltwater, which had turned the cavern into an enormous reservoir, this plumbing disaster would cause all types of havoc when it would eventually freeze over the streets with a layer of ice by the morrow. Inside the castle, the imperial guardsmen were frantically tripping over themselves in their heavy armor as maids and servants alike ran for their lives while they waded through the chilling water to reach higher ground. Around the inner court all sorts of articles of fancy decor to ornate works of art were torn from the tables and walls, which mingled with pots and cooking utensils and bobbing fruits from the kitchen as they coalesced within the giant pool the royal throne room had become.

Within the fortress, a mixed group of staff and sentries looked on helplessly as they tried to calm the Duchess, who stood barefoot upon her bed screaming obscenities at her servants while the lapping water rose around the furniture in her chambers. We could only imagine the discord that was unfolding inside the keep as the royal minions began to pour from the entrance to save themselves from the floodwaters. The only benefit to this situation is that we would have been presumed dead among those trapped within the cave; but the emergency of this crisis would eventually unfold into a lockdown of the entire city, so we had to take advantage of the present anarchy while we could.

Luckily, we had left our funds in our room at the Inn, and made haste in grabbing what extra clothing and gear had been left behind by the previous tenants, and we made our way out of the hidden apartment. When we reached the barroom floor there were several customers huddled at the doorway as they gazed out upon the flooded streets in wonder. The little innkeeper quickly waddled up to Nyx as he tried to get her attention, but she quickly pulled out a handful of silver coins from her purse and dropped them into his greasy hands.

"We're checking out early, and the Guild thanks you for your service," she spat curtly as we pushed our way past the group of bodies blocking the entrance.

The little man stopped in his tracks as his eyes lit up with the shine of silver tumbling from his stubby fingers, and the world outside paused as he dove to the grimy barroom floor to snatch up every piece which clattered to the ground and rolled under the tables.

We backtracked our way through the streets to the port, but were nettled to find that there was now an armored guard stationed at its entrance. Neither one of us was in the condition for a fight, nor would we wish to initiate a confrontation in broad daylight. Unfortunately, the high walls of the outer yard of the keep lined one side of the avenue while the other funneled us towards the gate.

Though we were ungroomed by this point, we obviously didn't look like sailors, and the soiled clothing we had borrowed made us appear less than noble. The guard noticed our approach and tipped out his polearm to block our passage through the iron gateway at his side.

"Halt there, no foot traffic is allowed on the docks until so ordered," he stated sternly, though he looked like a fairly young clean-cut lad who was doing his best to fit the role of a royal guardsman.

"We have to get to our ship ...over there, the ah, *the Winter Jackal*," I read the script painted on the rear of the nearest boat as I peered over his shoulder. The guard turned his head to glance at the port and back towards us.

"You mean Captain Dreher's vessel?" He asked, with slight confusion; though we were able to glean that shred of information from the lad's lack of experience, "but he only just arrived this morning; and I don't remember seeing you two disembarking from his ship."

"If you were on shift at dawn, you would have seen us unloading cargo via the private entrance," Nyx added quickly, taking the chance the young lad hadn't been on duty very long. It's usually obvious when a sentry has been at their post longer than they wish to be; as they eventually assume a sorrowful posture and bored expression after being left standing like statues for extended periods of time, which usually leaves them grouchy or falling asleep on their feet.

"Oh, well, no, I just..." the lad seemed to feel like he needed to offer a polite excuse, but quickly regained his posture of authority.

"We were delivering a 'special' shipment from *General Stalker to Lady Graystone*," Nyx put up her hand as if to whisper the secret information to the lone guard.

"Oh ...I see, the Baroness and the General, you say?" The guard asked with a bit of nervousness, knowing that their

General had a reputation of being stout with his troops. Glancing behind us, we noticed several more sentries approaching our position at the gate, and I slowly moved my hand to the dagger tucked beneath my cape; expecting the worst. The closer the patrol got, the more our options dwindled. We would have to dispatch this young soldier quickly and escape to the docks. Noticing my underhanded preparations for action, Nyx slipped a small velvet satchel out of her pocket, then reached out and gently placed it in the guard's leathered palm.

"As we said, it was a *special* shipment meant as a private gift to the Baroness; and the General paid well for its delivery," she gave him a wink as if letting him in on privileged information, "there are a hundred pieces there for your discretion, sir, and we both know the General's mood when his wishes aren't met, don't we mister...?" Nyx led on with a look of expectation in her eyes.

"Warren, third squad recruit, Warren, Ma'am," he hesitated under the shock of being handed what equated to several years worth of wages for a lowly guard, and the fear of facing the wrath of their acting General's favor should he resist his wishes. Though not so bright that he didn't realize he had just surrendered his name, as Nyx had pressed him to do so through her use of verbal trickery.

"Yes, Warren, we do..." Nyx smiled back with a nod as she made it obvious while she drew her eyes to the approaching patrol, "and if we should have to share this information with the other guards, each of them will want a cut of your bonus there, but that choice is yours."

The guard hesitated for a moment as he looked down and tested the weight of the satchel of silver in his hand, and promptly slid the pouch out of sight into his girdle. He pulled his spear back while I quietly tucked my dagger back into its sheath beyond his notice, while we swiftly stepped passed the gate and gathered our pace towards the harbor. Our boat had not yet arrived, but we would take our chances with Captain Dreher on the Winter Jackal. We quickly made our way to the outer wharf where the merchant ship was moored and crossed the gangplank to board.

We asked for the captain by name to the few crew members on the deck, while giving them the air that we were under instructions to deliver a message from the royal court. We were pointed toward the hold and found the captain below deck, who turned out to be quite a scurvy fellow himself, as we caught him sneaking a pinch of royal ale beyond the site of his crew. That made matters simpler for us, as persons with a weakness for bottled spirits made easy targets for modes of bribery.

It took little persuasion that we wouldn't expose his weakness for expensive rotgut to the city guards, which he had stolen from the royal shipment for the keep, but it turned out those minor offenses paled to the hefty bag of silver we plopped upon his table for passage back to Stilgrave. Within moments, he was blabbering orders half-drunk to the surprise of his tired crew, who had been expecting shore leave for the entire week. The extra pay and promised time of double-leave at the end of the journey eased their grumbling complaints as the sails were hoisted and the plank tugged, and we soon pulled away from the docks. Nyx and I looked out at the towering cliffs of Blacktide as the expanse of water stretched between us, knowing we had left behind in our wake a flooded castle, several people drowned, and a few lucky individuals a great deal richer for their troubles.

Trust & Treachery

It was another several days journey back to Stilgrave, where we suffered the rocking waves from harsh winter storms along the route. My apprentice and I took that time to wrap our wounds and discuss what we had learned during this arduous journey our Guild Master had set us upon. Our encounter with the young Duchess and her court left many questions unanswered, but we would have to make do with the information at hand. We had been given a small storeroom in the hold to use as a makeshift cabin since the Winter Jackal was designed as a trade ship for hauling cargo instead of lodging extra passengers.

"What would you make of this?" I asked Nyx as I removed the small bronze block from my pocket while inspecting the intricate carvings covering its surface, "I acquired this from the Regent's chambers ...any clue as to what it might be?"

Nyx took the metal block into her hands and analyzed the strange object in the lamplight. It became obvious she was lost in deep thought as she tested the texture and complex markings covering the object. After a while, she eventually placed it back upon the cloth it had been wrapped in where it sat atop a heavy barrel.

"I could swear that's the same type of metal those large rings were made from on that strange device in the cavern," she stated with a hint of curiosity, "and these designs engraved upon it are similar too. Whatever it is, it's very old. This isn't something the local smithy forged," she conceded with a frown of skepticism.

With that thought in mind, I snatched up the odd casing to evaluate the age of the metal, but was drawn by her stare back towards the rag lying on the barrel. Where the cloth had lain upon the damp surface, the weight of the metal bar had pressed through to soak the material which left a reverse design upon the rag, an image which she found perplexing.

"Hold on a minute," Nyx stated as she searched around and found a spare parchment label which she ripped from the front of a nearby container, "I need a spot of ink ...or something like it," she added as she glanced around and started to rub her fingers around the base of the oil lamp while smudging the soot over the surface of the block. She then laid the object down and carefully wrapped the bar with the paper, then gently pressed upon all four of its sides. Unraveling the paper revealed a section of detailed diagrams with several passages and markings exposed upon it.

"It's a map," I blurted with a mixture of mild surprise, and found myself impressed by her ingenuity.

"I had once stolen a few trinkets from the clergy of the Builders many years ago, where I discovered they had engraved dowels filled with designs of carved images which they utilized as giant stamps to copy identical covers for their holy manuscripts," Nyx admitted, "Grab me that candle there, would you," she asked as I snapped loose the stick from its holder sitting beside me.

Nyx opened up the lamp and lit the candle, then proceeded to carefully cover the strip of cloth with a thick layer of melted wax. Before it could harden, she quickly pressed the block into the soft wax on all four of its sides in sequence. After she was done and the wax had fully cured, we were astonished to what it displayed. Before us sat a miniature three-dimensional image of a passage route that rose and dipped at precise sections along its path. The purpose of this pattern was confusing at first until my memory jogged, and I retrieved the ancient carved skull which had been the central piece to this mystery surrounding the spider cult.

Nyx and I performed the same ritual with the soot from the lantern by smearing it across the skull and carefully pressing a strip of cloth upon it. The spherical image which the stamp from the skull displayed had left an open wedge at one point. At first, I didn't recognize what it was, but Nyx herself had once scouted the parish of the holy Builder and had seen what hidden secrets they held within their walls. With her noted mapping skills, she drew an additional outline around it to help me adapt my perspective as to what I should be seeing.

"This appears to be a map of the bishop's tower within the abbey of the Builders, which has been there a very long time," she noted.

"Yes, I heard it was originally a watchtower, which had existed when Stilgrave was just an outpost many centuries ago, and the abbey of the Builders was raised around it," I added to her assessment.

What was once a lone tower that stood nestled against the mountain, was now lost in the forest of spires that rose around the city erected by the generations that followed. An old and decrepit tower was of little interest to the nobles who kept to themselves and the pristine streets of the Ivory district. Nyx then took the hardened wax sculpture and set it into the missing wedge upon the imprint created from the skull. What it revealed was a hidden passage that penetrated into the mountainside marking the bishop's tower as its entrance.

From a close inspection of the wax imprint, it was possible to discern what level within the tower the passage entrance originated; but what it actually led to was still a mystery. After taking some time to sketch down the image of the wax sculpture from all sides upon a parchment, we destroyed the casting and hid the map. Given this vital discovery, a decision had to be made.

"We should get this into Koda's hands once we arrive; he needs to know about this," Nyx stated with earnest.

"Hmm ...let's think about that for a moment," I paused, "the Guild Master sent us to Blacktide in order to gather information about their military strength and possible plans of attack, but there is still something unsettling about all of this," I argued while handling the bronze block in thought, "patience is the mark of a good thief, and I believe we should keep the information about this secret map between you and I for the moment."

Nyx seemed a bit confused as to my proposed caution since we were sworn to protect the interests of the Thieves Guild, no matter the consequence, but she conceded and chose to respect my discretion on this matter. We had been through a great deal on our journey and we were left with more questions than answers at the end of it. My one worry was that we weren't anywhere near the end of our quest, and concern fell upon me that once we landed back in Stilgrave, our lives were about to get ever more complicated. As a thief, I had learned from experience that when you stumble across an overly 'obvious' trap, the rational conclusion is that it was placed there by design as a distraction from the far deadlier one a step beyond it, that will do you in.

There was something about this mission and the motive behind it that made me feel uneasy, and I learned to recognize bait when I saw it. This strange metal block, the hidden city, the young duchess, the spider cult and this ancient cursed skull which kept popping up time and time again; these pieces had to fit together but I couldn't see how. What I needed was a fresh perspective, so I laid in my hammock thinking about it into the long windy night until the lantern burned out while the boat rocked as it was tossed by the icy waves lapping upon the hull. At the end of it all, I was left with a vague hunch which I could no longer ignore, as a measure of intuition had saved my life through many close scrapes over the years.

Before we reached the mouth of the port, I paid a few extra coins to the Captain to let us use his skiff to reach the harbor before the break of dawn, while letting him know it would be a risk to his health if he made any mention of his uninvited guests upon this recent voyage. Nyx and I slipped into the battered dinghy and quietly rowed our way to shore in the dark hours of the morning. Though she was wondering why we were exercising such secrecy for our arrival back to our home town, her question was answered when we passed by the same ship we had sailed off in the week prior, still quietly anchored at the pier. If Koda's legitimate plan had been to pick Nyx and I up on time from our mission in Blacktide, that transport ship should have already left on its journey back to meet us at our rendezvous point at the keep.

"I suggest it would be wise for us to do a little reconnaissance before checking in with the guild," I noted to my apprentice, who agreed for the moment that I may have been right after all regarding my suspicions.

Nyx wasn't the kind of woman who expected to be coddled over minor conflicts on points of view and was bright enough to understand the color of my critical, if not objective, method of thinking. Something wasn't sitting right, and it was becoming ever more obvious to us both. We crept along the shadows of the lower district until we made our way back to my safe-house where we could get some proper gear and resupply. The thieves' guild had eyes everywhere, so we had to lie low while I left her at my refuge so that I could grab a few extra items from my old apartment. Having returned within the hour before the cold sun broke the horizon, I found Nyx fast asleep in my bed.

"As I suspected, something's amiss," I breathed as I removed my hooded cloak and laid down beside her to rest my tired bones as she began to rouse.

"What did you find?" She asked with a sleepy tone.

"My lodgings had been ransacked after we had departed for Blacktide on Koda's orders," I granted with a sigh.

"What does that mean?" Nyx inquired with a ruffle of her brow.

"It means we need to pay a private visit to our esteemed guild master on our own terms, to get some long-overdue answers," I explained while we both laid back and slept through the rest of the daylight hours to recuperate from our exhausting trip.

Of course, given my career choice, I had employed several countermeasures against unwelcome guests rifling through my private abode. My personal valuables and gear had been secured in hidden stashes, while a few cheap items were left out in view to satisfy the common burglar; but members of the Thieves Guild would not trespass onto a property which displayed our secret mark upon the door. The armored guards of the City Ward would have been far clumsier conducting such a search, but someone had gone to the extent to be quite thorough in their detailed exploration of my apartment. I could only imagine what they were looking for.

We donned our cloaks and made our way into the night as dusk fell; taking the thieves highway by the rooftops towards our goal. I was taking the chance that our guildhall was still located within the Crimson quarter, and set up surveillance on the roof above the alley so I could observe the foot traffic around the building. I noted several members slip in and out of the closed shop they were utilizing at the time, until I noted one suspect who seemed suspiciously out of place. This individual wore a lush velvet hood and polished boots with an embroidered tunic and waist belt studded with brilliant gold; which was certainly not attire characteristic for members of our lowly breed.

Nyx and I exchanged posts watching the alley entrance into the night as the fog crept through the city streets. Finally, this lavish individual I had seen before, adorned in their upscale attire, left the building but I had also noted that they practiced a measure of caution from being followed along the street. I pointed out this person to Nyx.

"That's our target," I instructed.

"Who is it?" she dared to wonder.

"He has the height and gait of a man Koda's size," I answered to her surprise.

"There's no way ...he wouldn't be caught dead wearing that getup in front of the guild," she retorted, regarding the swanky outfit our target was draped in.

I had suspected it could have merely been a costume for a job he had planned somewhere in the Ivory district among the lords and ladies, but only a fool would wear something so gaudy here in the Crimson quarter, which would make you a mark for a mugging; unless of course, that person had no fear of such reprisal. As we followed him from above, it was clear this person knew each twist and turn of the slums within this poverty-stricken quarter; which convinced me even further that this individual was our reputed Guild Master.

Nyx and I took different sides of the streets leaping from the rooftops as we tracked our prey wandering through the artery of avenues below. Stumbling upon familiar streets, I was mildly surprised to see our target pry the lock and enter Beren's old workshop. I knew my old fence had kept his shop riddled with a series of traps as wards against unwelcome trespassers, but it had been a while since Beren had disappeared into the hands of the spider cult, and there was the chance his shop could have been sequestered by the Guild to be used for some other nefarious purpose. I recalled his old smuggling tunnels which led to various parts of the city for moving stolen goods while out of sight of the city watch; and of course, the hidden vent in the back alley where I could gain unfettered access into the cellar without being seen.

Nyx took her perch on top of the spire across the road, and with a series of hand signals, I instructed my apprentice to keep her position and eyes on the entrance. Hooking a line to a nearby chimney, I quietly dropped down into a hidden niche within the alley and crept inside the basement through a covered duct. Settling into the shadows, I found the hooded man rifling through several scrolls and ledgers among Beren's work table. The voice I heard from the man as he whispered curses under his breath was all too familiar.

"Where did you hide it old man..." the intruder grunted with a calm tone colored with annoyance. Apparently, whatever he was looking for in the scattered mess of documents, it was not to be found.

"Good evening, Koda. Fancy finding you here," I breathed aloud, whereupon the guild master froze for but a moment in mild surprise as he paused with his back still turned towards me.

"*Hmm* ...Ash, my friend, I must admit, you possess impressive talents to be able to sneak up on me," Koda responded while I noticed a shift in the position of his feet, "Welcome back; I imagine you have news to report of your mission?" He mildly hinted towards the question, which I knew was designed as a distraction.

"You can take your hands off your blade and place them where I can see them both," I ordered, knowing full well he was trying to cover his movements behind his cloak, "I have a crossbow aimed at you, so I would do so slowly."

"Assaulting your Guild Master would be a punishable offense that would put a price on your head with every thief and vagabond in the city," Koda warned lightly as he placed his hands to either side of the table in full view.

"Not if the Guild already thought I was dead," I replied with disdain, "especially having noticed that the ship which was supposed to retrieve us, is still somehow anchored at port... how would you explain that, Koda?"

"Hmm," he grunted gently, while he removed his hood and slowly turned to face me, "so Nyx also made it back I assume?" he inquired in a play of words, trying to weasel additional information I wasn't about to divulge.

"You sent us into a precarious situation and left us abandoned in Blacktide; why?" I demanded curtly while keeping the small crossbow aimed at his chest.

"Clearly, your reputation precedes you, Ash; and I could imagine the day you would succeed me as the leader of our Guild," he granted, "so you can understand my dilemma of having you around as a constant threat to my authority."

"Keep going..." I urged him to continue with a motion of the crossbow aimed at his chest.

"A while ago, I became aware that your friend, Beren, had acquired a certain artifact of peculiar value to unnamed parties whom my informants apprised me existed in the underbelly of our quaint city," he began.

"Lilith, and her deranged occult," I replied.

"Yes," he admitted, "and to be honest, it might surprise you to know that I was already acquainted with their scheme to remove the city Governor, including her partnership with the Lord Regent from Blacktide. I knew what war would do to this city and its people, and of course, our way of life; so I made alternate plans to come out on top."

"So you sold out the Guild," I assumed, which was more of a confirmation than a question at this point.

"Well, maybe I manipulated them just a little," Koda conceded, "but look at how our city has fared over the years, Ash. The poverty-stricken are left starving in the streets of our slums as the wealthy lords and ladies of the Ivory district prance around in their costumed gala's while gorging themselves on lavish feasts. They care not for the working class, who are the very backbone of this city that supports their eccentric life of excess."

"So, let me guess ...you chose to become one of them," I suggested as I nodded towards his plush attire. The polished boots, his gold-encrusted belt and stitched tunic he wore, separated himself from the lower classes that made up our guild and those who struggled to survive.

"...And why not?" Koda attempted to defend his choice, proving there was no honor among thieves where wealth was concerned, "The rift between the classes grows ever wider by the day, and I would rather be on the winning side of that bet. I'm sure you can understand."

"I wasn't any real threat to you; but still, why would you want to get rid of Nyx?" I inquired as the segments of his scheme began to connect.

"Well, honestly, I sent you both off with a small fortune, and expected that one of you might choose to knife the other in their sleep to collect the full amount and disappear into the night; but I see now that was a tad presumptuous of me," Koda noted with a nonchalant grin, "...or was it?" He asked again as he tried to drag out any hint of proof that my apprentice still lived, which would only serve to endanger her further.

"I'm the one standing here before you, aren't I?" I glared as my words fell coldly to keep him off balance with the lie for him to assume that Nyx was no longer around, but I knew this verbal game of cat and mouse wasn't over and wanted to sway Koda to spill the information he was withholding. There was only one way to do that, and that was to let him believe he was still in control of this confrontation, "So, maybe it's time we negotiate a deal, don't you think?"

Koda's eyes flickered when he realized that he could bargain his way out of a bolt to the heart and buy me off. He was used to ordering pawns to do his bidding and assumed he could make a move at a later time when he held the upper hand. For now, a measure of diplomacy would spare him this mortal dilemma.

"What is it that you want? Name your price," Koda offered a little too quickly for my comfort.

"That depends on the answer to my next question," I proceeded, "What is the story behind your connection with the nobles of Blacktide to take over the city?"

Koda seemed a trifle uncomfortable to be placed under the spotlight, so to speak, which was apparent by the shuffle of his posture. I could understand his weakness for greed; and truthfully, nearly any member of our Guild would likely sell out one another on a promise of a fortune and a position of power. I remembered the many long conversations I had with Beren in this very room over the years; about how he had strived to be accepted into upper society when he was a young dashing man who wasted his youth on wine and women, but now that he had grown old and fat, that all he could do now was 'whine about women.' In reflection, my old friend Beren had a dry sense of humor that escaped most.

"Let's start with what you know about the Duchess..." I led him to answer.

"Well, that is an interesting tale," he argued.

"Answer the question and we can both walk out of here together as partners," I pushed as my bargaining chip while keeping a tight grip on the crossbow trigger. That offer seemed to be incentive enough for him to comply.

"I was once like you, as a young member of the guild in Blacktide decades ago, before getting myself in hot water and a price placed on my head by their City Ward, and ventured here to seek new fortunes," Koda explained, "The dysfunctional royal family of Blacktide was extremely secretive; exceptionally so in fact. Their oppressive king was strict and had two children which survived their mother, who had disappeared from the public eye under mysterious circumstances."

"*Two* children, you say?" I confirmed.

"Yes, one was Ryan, whom, as you know, is under the title as their current Lord Regent, and his elder sister, Erin; who went by a nickname by ...ah, Cricket," Koda recalled.

From the information that Nyx had provided to me about the nobles and from what I had witnessed, I couldn't understand how Koda's story would make any sense, unless he was just making it up to mislead me with a fabrication.

"That can't be true, their ruler had only one child, whom the Regent was to protect until she came of age," I countered to his suspected ruse.

"I spent my youth there, Ash," Koda affirmed, "and can assure you of the truth of this. Over the years, many high nobles of Blacktide fell suddenly ill, and one by one, they dropped like flies until all that was left was Ryan and his sister. From our circle of guild informants, we collected gossip and rumors from the maids and servants who served the royal family that they suspected the king's children were playing with poisonous alchemy, and were frequently ordered to clean up dead pets and other animals the royal offspring had been experimenting upon with their vile concoctions. There were even tales that they heard people being dragged off into the keep in the middle of the night, never to be seen again."

"What does that have to do with the Duchess and the Regent?" I inquired.

"There were lingering tales among the back alleys and the commoners, that the architects who had built the towering castle of Blacktide generations before, had all disappeared in a single night; likely to keep them silent from what they knew about the design and excavation of the citadel itself," Koda offered, "There were even reports by royal chambermaids in service to the king's brood that they had seen strange hexes drawn about their rooms, and that their little princess didn't age because her growth had been stunted by the putrid poisons she experimented with. Shortly thereafter, her personal handmaids had also mysteriously vanished."

"So you're saying Ryan's sister is...?" I asked before Koda confirmed my suspicion.

"The Duchess of Blacktide, herself; so the rumor goes, but they are just myths I presume. But then, it sounds like you found something of interest during your mission there?" Koda divined by my lost reaction to his words.

Now it all began to make sense. The seasoned posture of the little girl I had witnessed when I found Nyx, and the way the child had carried herself along with the level of speech for her assumed age, was notably uncommon. The subterranean city buried beneath the castle had been kept a close secret among the royal family for generations. The children of their recent king had exploited ancient texts and tonics they had discovered buried amongst the ruins, and used this knowledge to silence anyone who might oppose them. In an attempt to hide Erin's diminutive condition, which could affirm the rumors of their murderous heritage as true; after the king passed away, both brother and sister assumed new identities and terminated any witnesses with a few drops of deadly bane in their effort to protect themselves from being ousted from their royal legacy by the conspiring nobles of their court.

It was certainly a strange history which haunted that dark coastal city nestled under those high brooding cliffs. Their royalty had kept in rule by a veil of lies, and by masking their treachery within the cold shadows of the metropolis hidden beneath the castle. Under the guise of the Lord

Regent, the brother of the Duchess sought to extend his reign by overthrowing the ruling governor of Stilgrave, so that he and his sister could secretly rule twin cities under different crests without violating the strict treaties held among the other rulers of the region. It was a bold plan, but one which had run afoul several pitfalls caused by their own insatiable greed and unbridled corruption.

The Royal Duchess was no innocent herself and delved ever deeper into the practice of the mystical arts and the occult, which she helped revive through use of her position. Admittedly, it was a smart, if not ingenious tactical move to align themselves with the spider sect in opposition of the religious clergy of the Builders, who led the rival forces on their southernmost border. But here stood Koda, the wild card in this whole endeavor. The leader of our Brotherhood of Thieves, turned traitor to his own kind.

"I begin to understand now just how deep this treachery runs," I conceded with a nod towards Koda, as I relaxed my tightened grip on the crossbow; although, that was the moment he was watching for to make his move.

Koda had plans in motion with no intentions of folding to a lesser of his flock or taking a chance of revealing his carefully orchestrated plans to the other members of the guild, which would only unravel everything he had accomplished towards this scheme. He grabbed a heavy volume from the table and tossed it at my face as he vaulted away from the wavering sights of my bow. With his other hand, he tore at the hasp of his cape and flung it like a concealing blanket to distract my aim during the vital moment when the crossbow fired; knowing I would have no second chance to reload. This was a practiced move we had trained with often in the guildhall, and was quite effective against those not expecting the feint.

The bolt fired and tore through the velvet cape, striking

the Guild Master in his left forearm. This was a tactic of winging, used to block a strike while leaving one's sword arm free to attack. Had he been wearing his usual gear, the arrow might have deflected off his reinforced bracers, but Koda had forfeited his usual armor in favor of his taste to join the soft upper cream of society. He grunted in pain at the impact and retaliated with a swing of his polished sword towards my neck. Several clashes of blade against blade ensued as I ditched the crossbow and pulled my daggers to block his pressing attacks.

Splinters of wood and glass showered the room as we danced between death and a razor's edge, until Koda seemed to tire as his movements slowed. His strikes clipping a brick wall or tables edge as he began to stagger. Locking our blades together in a scissor grip, he finally gained an advantage and pressed my back against the wall where we stood face to face. It was a mark of twisted irony that the man I once looked up to as a mentor, was now so desperate to see my end.

"You could have walked away from this," I breathed as I pressed with all my strength to keep the parry locked.

"You know I couldn't do that, Ash," he glared into my eyes with a grin seeping into his features as he felt my defense begin to wane, "neither could I take the chance of you exposing my plans or using them against me as leverage; and whether it was tonight, or tomorrow, or the next ...you know that sooner or later you would have taken a knife in the back."

"You could have trusted me, Koda," I replied as we clasped the grips on our weapons, while I felt my footing begin to slide on the dusty floor as he leaned forward to unbalance my weight.

"Oh, come now, Ash, 'trust' is an empty word in our business. There is no place for men like us to exist in the upper districts among the nobles, so I took the chance of rising above this pathetic life of risking my neck for a petty coin and roaming these filthy streets," Koda snapped back with contempt in his tone. For that I could not blame him, but he had turned on his own and would sacrifice the other members of the Guild as the cost for his arrogance. Maybe there really was no honor among thieves, but at least a few of us had a shade of dignity.

In a brute move, Koda kicked my leg to make me fold under so that he could press a finishing stroke. Once I was dead, he could dump my body in the sewers to be eaten by the rats, or stash me in a crate to be dropped off the pier. There were a dozen ways for the guild to make someone disappear, but everyone thought Nyx and I were in Blacktide, so Koda could end us both and make up any story he desired regarding our demise and nobody would question it. As I glanced behind him, I saw a thin seam of light that caught my eye and quickly recalled my previous visit to Beren's shop before we had departed upon our journey.

With a heave, I pushed him to one side and reached out with the hilt of my dagger into the air beside him. Koda appeared confused by my move, not knowing what had distracted me from our engagement; but he wasn't going to waste the opportunity of his opponent's defense being left wide open. I stood there with my chest exposed, and my arm stretched out as though to allow his incoming strike, but at the last moment, I used my daggers' hilt to tug hard on a fine wire and took a sudden leap back. Two bottles of brandy resting on the rafters came swinging down from either side, smashing together from their momentum; the glass shards and liquor raining down upon Koda were he stood beside the table.

I had booby-trapped Beren's den with a web of tripwires the last time I had been to his shop, just in case any agent of the spider cult had found their way inside looking for stolen relics. My old friend was a lush for cheap wine and hard liquor, so I took advantage of his stash of booze and incorporated them into the trap itself. Koda was momentarily stunned by the downpour of glass shrapnel as he was drenched in alcohol. Koda was a hard man, but for the first time, I saw a brief flicker of fear in his eyes as I reached out upon the table and cut a lit candle from its shaft with my blade, and sent it flying towards him.

Without a word, I turned and walked away as the Guild Master of the Brotherhood of Thieves danced in the inferno which engulfed him. The way I had entered in through the alley was now blocked, and I knew the crates in the basement were stocked with combustible oils and cases of liquor. I stepped out the front door as embers flared through several vents and windows like angry fireflies in the night. It was only moments after I had dashed across the street that the shop bloomed with heat by a sudden flare, and was engulfed by flames.

I climbed the building and met with Nyx, who had kept herself hidden on the rooftops across the avenue.

"What happened down there, are you alright?" The young rogue asked as she drew close to see that I had been in a fight, revealed by the light gash upon my face.

"The Guild is without a master, and for the moment we are on our own," I replied as the local peasants began to shuffle out into the streets to address the growing flames.

A Winter Rose

From my apartment window, Nyx and I watched the spreading flames in the streets below, which had fanned throughout several of the shoddily-built shops along the poverty-stricken quarter until the fire had finally been quelled as dawn began to break. The smoky haze from the charred embers drifted amongst the morning fog as the mists rose to clear the air. Guardsmen from the Ivory district had sent a garrison down to the slums of the red quarter with a cartful of buckets to help the locals quench the blaze. This part of the city was mostly composed of brick and stone excavated from the old mines, which helped to keep the fire from advancing further for lack of fuel. However, the presence of the City Ward in the slums only served to complicate our situation.

"So, what's our next move?" Nyx asked with a hint of despair wavering in her voice.

Nyx was a young rogue who had found a sense of family in the Thieves Guild, only to find she was now held captive in something much greater than herself. With a shade of sympathy, I wondered if she was beginning to regret having been assigned as my apprentice. Not only was our leader dead, but the guild members likely thought we were deceased as well, and the Regent of Blacktide was still a viable threat if he should manage to escape their clutches. If our city authorities found and freed the visiting diplomat, the calamity overshadowing the territory could still unfold.

"We have trimmed the ladder by which Blacktide had posed its menace by cutting short a few of their rotting rungs," I conceded, "with fewer nobles leading the court and the Duchess having lost her brother and royal guardian for the moment, I would presume we have gained ourselves some time from the threat of the north, but..."

"But we still have to deal with her brother, Sir Ryan," Nyx finished my line of thought.

"Yes. No matter which side of the coast the nobles may lay, the plague of their greed still lingers," I offered as a philosophical response.

"So how do we evade tripping this political trap?" Nyx replied, "I assume if we fail to release or choose to execute the Regent outright, that the Duchess would promptly react in retaliation by invading our shores."

"Which would lead us down the same path we were trying to avoid," I added to her sense of logic, "so the only alternative I see is to buy him off."

"With what?" Nyx countered, not quite grasping how we could possibly bargain with a power-hungry nobleman seeking the prize of conquering an entire city.

"Perhaps with this," I yielded with a motion to the cursed skull I had reacquired and left sitting on the table, "he would have known that his sister, the Duchess, had recovered the relic of their prophetic 'Dark Shepard' and was using it as a scarecrow of sorts to control her fanatical subjects."

It was a strange twist of theology that the devout Builders of Stilgrave venerated the bodies of their dead saints, while the cult of the Golden Spiders used theirs as a morbid puppet as if it were some angel of death. It was all a mind game, of course, to control the population by means of their faith which was given freely, rather than demanding obedience by force. Whether one method had a distinct advantage over the other was debatable, but they were both effective means to the same end.

"Do you have a plan, Ash?" Nyx inquired with a raised brow, since I had been busy considering every angle to approach our present problem.

"Right now we have the advantage of being ghosts, and

nobody in our circle knows we are here," I led as I pulled out the pair of maps we had created with the bronze block and imprint from the skull, "we know the Duchess will want her relic back," I noted while tapping its engraved cranium, "since it is a sacred remnant of her occult; but satisfying her brother, the Regent, is another matter altogether. Ryan craves power and had been duped out of his succession by the treaties between the territories, and the game both he and his dwarfed sister had played with their subjects when they shuffled their identities to avoid persecution by their subjects," I offered as I turned the empty eyes of the skull away from me to avoid its haunted stare, "so I say we use their own game against them."

"How so?" Nyx questioned as she leaned back against the wall and began to clean her nails with the sharp tip of her throwing knife.

"Sir Ryan can't come out in public and admit that he's actually the rightful heir of Blacktide's crown, since the citizens and subjects of the realm would assume he might be attempting some elaborate coup to take the throne for himself, and we can be assured that his stunted sister would fight tooth and nail to remain the heiress and continue the web of lies she has weaved."

This only accentuated my point when Nyx bit off a jagged nail and spat it onto the floor. In the days since we had set sail in our escape from Blacktide, the flooded foundation of the castle would eventually expose the numerous bodies that would eventually come bobbing to the surface, revealing all the missing people whom the nobles had quietly poisoned and incarcerated within the subterranean city over the years. The horror of it would open the doors to a great deal of scandal and official inquiry when those victims were identified. The citizens of Blacktide and the sovereign subjects of the heiress would start to demand answers, and with a lack of nobles available in her court to take the fall, the lone Duchess would be left to her own devices at the center of the public's wrath, which would likely lead to an uprising.

Such a scandal would effectively sway Ryan from returning to Blacktide to face the consequences, since participating in the kidnapping and poisoning of their own people would likely forge the hardened defiance of an angry mob, and would likely terminate at the end of a tight noose cinched around his treasonous throat. If the Regent lost both his position and rule over his military it would become impossible for him to overtake Stilgrave. The only card he still held were the few moles in the City Ward and our Governor's office he had bribed to defect to his side. These treacherous rats would have to be exposed to guarantee his cooperation.

Unfortunately, I had likely cauterized any access to the identities of whom those traitors might be when I had set our exalted Guild Master aflame. We could, of course, present all this information to our acting Governor, like upright-standing citizens, which we weren't, and would likely end up in the stockade for our troubles. Any such move would only result in a garrison marching into the city slums to raid the Thieves Guild in order to secure the safety of the Regent. Regardless, the upper administration and master of the city ward might already be on the Regent's payroll to begin with, and that was a calculated chance we couldn't take.

We couldn't betray our fellow thieves in the Guild, who would only end up in shackles or at the sharp end of a headsman's axe; so there was only one option left as far as I could tell, and I was glad to see that Nyx and I were on the same page.

"I assume you don't actually plan on giving the Regent these maps; but instead, we should find out where they lead?" my apprentice inquired as she slipped her knife back into its sheath. She knew that one had to discover the actual value of an asset before you could properly bargain with it.

"I couldn't have said it better myself," I confessed with a slanted smile.

We would have to sneak into the abbey and make our way to the bishop's tower. Luckily, Nyx already had some experience towards that endeavor, having scored a bagful of valuables the last time she had taken a midnight trip onto the parish grounds. The ministry of the Builders was separated into two distinct sections, whereupon one area was open to the public for worship and tithing, while the other area of the temple was reserved for the clergy. Taking the opportunity to draw out a map of the chapel gardens for me to study, Nyx helped to educate me on the function of each of the buildings and their given routines.

She had taken several items from around my apartment and laid out a visual aid for me to follow to help me get my bearings when we arrived on site. There was the main shrine into which the commoners were allowed to access for paying homage to the statue of their divine Architect, where there sat a tithing box for collecting donations. More than a few petty thieves had helped themselves to the collection box over the years until the clergy chose to fit it with a heavy iron lock. The key to it, among many others around the monastery grounds, was held by the Order's bookkeeper.

Luckily for us, the accountant for their holy order was a title given to one of their most senior members; an elderly man who was slow of foot and weak of eyesight. He was considered competent enough to tally and log the funds for their treasury but did little else of use around the abbey. Generations ago, the Bishops tower was reserved for housing the highest of their order, but over the long years it had fallen into a state of ill repair and had been repurposed for use as storage. There, the various props of their trade were stockpiled, along with faded copies of their doctrines and long-forgotten scrolls written by the hands of their predecessors.

Rather than sell off or dispose of these items, their contents were kept under lock and key. Nyx claimed she had stolen a set of robes and posed as an acolyte so that she could wander freely during the time she scouted the grounds; however, in the time since she had made off with her haul of golden icons and silver candlesticks, the clergy was prompted to employ a better means of protection from being burgled. Now thick iron bars covered many of the windows, along with reinforced doors and keyed locks to thwart those sinners who might steal from the church. But Nyx, of course, only considered these new security measures as a challenge.

By the way she talked about the Order of the Builders it was clear that she didn't carry much respect for their creed, and considered those of the cloth as just another flavor of hustlers pulling a con. She had seen how their clergy would swindle even from the poorest of the destitute peasants without batting an eye, nor showing a flinch of regret while feeding those wretched souls empty promises of a joyous afterlife among the divine. The clerics would drown their parish with a river of drivel about how the meek were blessed. I had to concur with Nyx's perspective that the clergy were charlatans of the worst kind, who offered nothing for something, which was valued as an empty trade for the damned souls of their flock in exchange for their weight in silver coin.

Seasoned thieves refrained from stealing from the impoverished, for we understood their plight and been in their shoes. What these clergy did against the city's paupers was nothing short of deception and mockery, by giving hope where none existed. Some might see that as a service, but we only saw it as a scam. I had to admit, it was a good racket though, for the parish prospered off of the peoples weakness and sense of guilt.

After Nyx finished setting her elaborate stage, the floor of my apartment resembled a miniature town made of buckets and boxes and bits of wood with the paths drawn out with charcoal from the fireplace. She warned that we could pose as commoners and simply walk in to bypass the first layer of walls which separated the chapel from the upper district, but we would be left confined within the enclosed temple until we could find our way into the inner grounds of the monastery.

"Couldn't we just skip all that and scale the walls here?" I inquired while pointing towards the makeshift plank Nyx had used to signify the barrier. Though I conceded that in all these years I had never had any personal interest in doing any sightseeing of the church grounds myself.

"Those walls are whitewashed, and we would stick out like a sore thumb if we tried to scale them; besides, the crest is curved and our climbing hooks will fail to hold," Nyx shot back with a huff, "including the matter that this outer wall is married to the guard barracks for the city watch. Needless to say, this section of the retaining wall is well patrolled, even during the winter."

"Since we don't possess cleric robes to allow us to sneak into the abbey, how would you suggest we get in?" I inquired of my apprentice for her advice.

"Most every evening just before sunset, the elder bookkeeper makes his way outside the walls to tend to the trees lining the outer gate. With a little sleight of hand, we could secure the set of keys he carries and make our way past the locked gates before he knew they were missing," Nyx suggested.

It sounded simple enough, but we both knew that plans usually don't go as expected on the fly. If we failed to secure the keys we would be right back at step one. If we got caught in the act, and the elder called for help with the barracks for the whole city guard within earshot, we would be left fleeing for our lives with the Ward on high alert for the next several days to follow. In all respects, this humble monastery of the Builders was proving to be more difficult to infiltrate than the imposing fortress in Blacktide. Due to its position in the city and its unscalable walls, if our foray into the holy sanctuary wasn't pulled off smoothly we could easily find ourselves trapped like rats in a cage.

As the evening was fast approaching we couldn't afford to dally. We had lost most of our gear during our escape from the clutches of the Duchess and her minions; but shared what little supplies I had left in stock with my apprentice. Neither of us could take the chance of going to the black market of the Thieves Guild to restock; for we knew not what orders Koda may have left them about our standing. We would have to remain incognito until we settled this mystery and had something of value to bargain with against the Lord Regent.

The tunnels under the city leading away from Beren's shop had been buried during the fire; and gaining entrance to the privileged Ivory district in the upper quarter was a matter of passing through several bottlenecks of the township, each of which were under constant scrutiny of the City Watch. Even if we managed to dress in the guise of servants, with the number of recent murders in the upper quarter there was a noticeable measure of additional security spread among their patrol routes. Thieves didn't like confrontation, so what I proposed to Nyx caught her completely off guard.

"What if I posed as Koda and walked right into the Ivory quarter?" I offered, "You could slip past them while I was distracting the sentries."

"Well, it's your ass on the line," Nyx responded with an

amused chuckle as if I was crazy for even suggesting such a reckless plan, "and what am I supposed to do if you get caught?"

"Complete the mission," I answered bluntly, "you should hold onto the maps to the Bishop's tower, and if I can't make it for any reason, try to find out what is hidden in the abbey and make a deal with the Regent; then tell the members of the guild what really happened," I offered with a last note, "...and try to free me if I end up in a cell, of course."

I tried to rethink my plan, especially if I got myself arrested and if by chance Nyx discovered a boatload of treasure hidden in that secret chamber all to her lonesome – which might risk leaving me rotting in a cell while she disappeared on a lifelong vacation. Then again, Nyx had proven herself to be competent and trustworthy thus far, and she knew the consequences both the guild and the innocent people of this city would face if the Lord Regent, and the overshadowing threat he posed, wasn't completely neutralized.

Of course, it wasn't my intent to show up empty-handed, for I had remembered I still possess the letter I had appropriated from the Regents private study in Blacktide. Although our wade through the water had spoiled the ink on the parchment and bleached the contents, the royal seal was still intact; and with a little ingenuity, I forged a new letter given the materials I had on hand. With a mixture of honey, I carefully reapplied the delicate seal and ended up with a convincing counterfeit document for my troubles.

"An impressive fake," Nyx nodded with approval as she inspected the sealed document, "you have talents beyond your measure."

I handed my apprentice a set of instructions to fulfill before we made our way to the Abbey, and we agreed to an appointed time to meet and cross into the upper quarter.

On her list were a few supplies which were readily available at the port, along with a quick stop to a specified crossroads leading to the city square to fulfill her side mission. At first, Nyx was a little apprehensive about what she was supposed to do with a few dead hares and a bottle of maple sap, but I firmly discouraged her from swaying from the directions she had been given on the matter.

Nyx donned a disguise and took off early for her jaunt to the docks while I prepared by gearing up with the tools of my trade, and within the hour, we met outside one of the avenues which led to the Ivory quarter. As expected, there were more guards than usual patrolling the roads. I noticed Nyx as she arrived at the square, and she gave me a signal that the project I had sent her on had gone as planned. Without tipping off the guards that we were together, Nyx and I kept a wide distance between us as I approached the lane to the upper district.

I acted as inconspicuously as I could given my natural demeanor, and made it halfway up the street until I noticed a particular guard giving me a harsh eye as though he recognized me as we passed. I gritted my teeth when I heard him shuffle around with his armored leggings as he turned to speak to me.

"You there, with the hood," he called out.

I took a few steps and then stopped in my tracks as to innocently turn in his direction, in an effort to keep the guardsman from drawing the attention of additional sentries in the area.

"Sir, may I help you?" I answered politely but with a strong tone so that he would know he was dealing with one of the upper class. That ploy seemed to soften his hard glare for the moment.

"You look kind of familiar. What is your name and business in the Ivory district this eve?" the guardsman asked; as it took me a moment to recall his face. It was the same guard who had collected invitations at the Governor's estate during the night of his party. I cursed my luck that this particular guard would be patrolling this road, on this day, at this particular hour. Before I opened my mouth again I had a hard choice to make and took a gamble.

"My business is my own, sir; and I don't wish to be bothered," I put on the snooty accent which I had used on him before, "the Governor would not approve of his guests being accosted by the local warden without due cause!" I added with an air of authority.

"The Governor, eh?" The sentry asked with suspicion until I saw the look in his eyes as recognition set in, "You, you're that Rogue guy from ...where was it?" he snapped his fingers to his head as if that would somehow jog his memory.

"The name is Filché, Earl of Larcené from the Ro-jou' estate, off the southern coast," I added with a pompous tone. The guard then looked me up and down with a note of skepticism in his expression.

"Why are you wearing commoner's clothes, and what are you doing roaming the slums of the Crimson quarter, Sir Filch?" he motioned towards my worn attire, which was nothing ritzy as was expected among the noble class.

"These rags are merely a ruse!" I noted boldly, but then held my hand to cover what I whispered into his ear, "I do hate wearing this abominable attire, but your Governor, Lord Oren, had suggested that I attempt to dress down when visiting the impoverished districts. And actually, it does thwart these filthy wretches from begging for coin and keeps the thieving scoundrels from making one a target if you don't flaunt your status," I conceded.

"But why would a man of your stature be wandering the lower quarter in the first place?" The sentry repeated as his misgivings began to waver.

"My affairs are none of your concern," I stated again, but

softened my voice and added a look of anguish as I concluded my explanation to the nosy guard, "however, I'm not sure if you are married yourself as I am, sir, but when one finds oneself chained in the holy bonds of matrimony to a *cold shrew* who cares nothing for the pleasures required by a man of my vigor, then I am forced to find other methods of release," I added with a raised brow so that the sentry would get my meaning.

"I ...ah, I'm not sure I follow you," he responded, but in a passive tone so that I wouldn't think to question his own masculinity on the subject.

"By the grace of your Governor, he suggested that I visit a young courtesan by the name of Petunia, who only sells her services at the Rusty Raven Inn; and oh, what a fragrant flower she is my friend!" I offered with a sniff and a smile as I closed my eyes as though I was reliving the scent of a spring bouquet.

Having not hobnobbed about such personal issues with the upper class before, the guard softened his stance. Upon seeing his change of attitude, I chose that moment to pull out my forged letter and handed it to him, which he took into his gloved palm with a note of confusion as I stated it was my correspondence from the Earl. Noting the royal seal on the letter, he was reluctant to break it, since such royal documents were only meant for the eyes of the nobles. With a gruff shrug of his shoulders, he handed it back to me unopened.

"Oh, that's fine, sir ...you should get back to the upper quarter before nightfall. The Crimson district is no place to be when the miscreants crawl out of the shadows," the guard offered as advice, "...and ah, what was that wench's name again?" He added with a note of interest.

"*Petunia*," I answered while taking out a silver coin from my pocket and placing it in his hand, "at the Rusty Raven Inn. Consider this a gift from the Ro-jou' estate, and take a sip of her wine if you wish to experience a night you will never forget! She is truly a winter rose."

The guard considered my offer to take the reputed trollop for a ride, and not viewing the coinage I gave him as the bribe it was. The guard forgave my rude demeanor from the night of the Governor's party and considered my offer of discretion. With a turn of his heel and a smile of the erotic pleasures awaiting him stewing upon his wild imagination, he left me to continue on my merry way. I tried to hide the crack of the malicious smile widening upon my cheek as I pulled my hood back on and walked away, having succeeded in bluffing the poor fool twice.

I could guarantee that the nosy guardsman would be entangled in an evening he would not soon forget, for the Rusty Raven was a back-alley brothel that was notorious for its spoiled tramps and ailing harlots who sold themselves to the most desperate of paupers. Petunia was actually one of the oldest and sickly of their whores; who was as fat as a walrus and twice as ugly. If he was stupid enough to walk into that bar and flash a shiny silver ducat, there was little chance he would escape without being mobbed by every pimp and prostitute diseased with rot between their legs as he fought to reach the door.

Nyx had been watching the encounter from afar while biting her lip as our hushed conversation had pressed on, but eventually gave a sigh of relief when the insolent guard walked away with what appeared to be a smug grin stretched across his face. She made her way into the Ivory quarter through an adjoining avenue and we met once again at the crossroads outside the Abbey. Several city guards were wandering in and out of the barracks, caring more about getting off of their shift and out of the bitter cold rather than taking notice of a pair of strangers loitering outside the monastery. We weren't kept waiting very long as we observed an old man in white robes shuffle out of the abbey just as the tall shadows of the mountain fell and the sun began to sink upon the horizon.

The bald clergyman appeared exceptionally frail, as his gait was sluggish and feeble. The elder held a pruning knife and began trimming the evergreens lining the outer walls while occasionally scattering seed for the small sparrows which nested within their protective branches. As feeble as the man seemed to appear, this would make our next move all the easier. I spotted the large ring of keys hanging from his waist belt and approached to pilfer them from his person before he could notice.

Nyx made her way into the abbey entrance while waiting for my signal, where we would pass through the communal temple and into the private grounds beyond the locked gates. The elderly man moved slowly with shaky hands as he went about his work; so I stepped in to lift the keys from his belt. A quick peek over my shoulder proved that nobody was watching while I slipped beside him, and with a practiced hand, I nabbed the ring with a touch as light as a feather. With them in my grasp, I turned my footing to meet my apprentice, who was waiting inside the abbey.

"All too easy," I whispered to myself as I stepped away, only to have the bundle of iron keys in my hand meet an unexpected tug of resistance.

With a look of shock washing across my face, I turned to see an almost invisible line drawn taught, directly from my hand to the waistcoat of the Monk. A fine coil, similar to the type I used for tripwires, had been secured to the keyring itself. The elderly monk suddenly turned around and gazed directly at me, and I knew I had been caught. The seconds froze as we gawked at one another as I knew he would cry for help at any moment, and I grasped at my dagger with hesitation with my free hand while morally discouraged to take the old man's life as I looked into his tired eyes. I had stalled too long in deciding his fate, and he opened his mouth as I readied myself to bolt for cover.

"You must be Ash," he uttered with a frail voice, and the mention of my name had caught me by surprise. By his casual stance, I realized that he had the opportunity to call the guards, but had chosen otherwise.

"Do ...do I know you?" I stuttered as I was uncertain to this sudden change of circumstance.

"Alas, no, my son, but we share a common friend of yours who wished me to deliver a message," the old man replied while pulling at the thin wire at his belt," you look like the man he had described, who had also advised me to attach this cord," the cleric answered as he untied his belt and let the wire unravel. I now had the keys free from being tethered to his person, but chose to wait to see what he had to say while he slowly patted his tunic while looking inside his heavy robes for something.

"Ah, here it is," the old man finally finished his search as he yielded a small rolled note. It had my name written in script upon it across its lip, so I took it from him with a measure of uncertainty and opened it.

I raced through the lines etched therein, trying to understand how this old clergyman could have known who I was. The note was short in length but told volumes in its ability to reveal what I had been too slow to see all this time, while my eyes were drawn to the bottom signature. The letter was from my late friend, Beren.

A Proper Thief

I stumbled into the temple where Nyx had been waiting, although my troubled posture affirmed that my mind was elsewhere while I contemplated what I had learned from my encounter outside the abbey. We found but a few commoners in the shrine who were offering prayers to the large idol of the Builder that stood with his giant hammer in hand. Another priest was also present, who was busy lighting candles at the altar before he too left the chapel. Taking a step towards a nearby doorway, Nyx signaled for me to hurry.

"What took you so long ...did you get them?" My apprentice inquired to make sure I had gained possession of the keyring from the old monk; otherwise our mission that evening would have been cemented in its tracks.

I nodded my affirmation towards her for lack of words, and handed her the ring as I stood back to block direct view of the door should any curious eyes wander our way. After a moment, we were rewarded with a satisfying '*click*' as the locked portal unlatched, and we slipped into the inner courtyard. Beyond the door sat a cloister that stretched the length of the chapel alongside a line of pillared cypress trees which the local priests preferred for their landscaping. The layout of the abbey was just as Nyx had displayed by the miniature map she had assembled on the floor of my apartment. I followed in her wake as we wove our way through the monastery, ever closer to the Bishops tower looming high above the rooftops.

Having dodged several clerics finishing up their duties around the sanctuary for the evening, we managed to secret ourselves to the covered entrance of the ancient keep. This imposing spire was once the lone domicile for the original architects before Stilgrave blossomed into the vibrant city it was today. The tower itself held a belfry at its pinnacle, which was once used to toll the hour of prayer. The years had not been kind to the monolith which had fallen into a state of disrepair over the years, as additional buildings were constructed around it to house the influx of followers to their parish as the religion of the Builders grew. The exterior whitewash of the tower could not mask the numerous cracks in its mortar and missing stonework from the lack of upkeep.

"Is this tower even safe to enter?" I begged to ask while surveying the structural condition of the steeple.

"Well, it's held up over the past century; I'm sure it will stay together for one more night," Nyx offered with a tinge of sarcasm as she sifted through the available keys to use on the lock, only to end up finally settling on trying the most obvious age-worn iron key in the set.

The gear of the lock was rusted over for lack of use, verifying that any attempt at picking with my delicate set of tools would have proven pointless. Taking a second look around to make sure that no other clergy were within earshot, we forced the door open with a heave. We made our way inside and closed the door to cover our backs while Nyx acquired a lantern hanging on a peg by the entry. A few strikes of flint got it lit so that we could survey our surroundings.

The first floor was littered with chairs and large articles of furniture, caked with dust and cobwebs from being left unused and abandoned. Narrow slits of stained glass lined sections of the curved walls where we eventually found the stairwell to the second floor; an ascent which had been hidden behind the maze of desks and scribe tables stacked upon one another. Examining our archaic map, we assumed we would find the entrance into the mountain passage upon the second level where the tower was nestled into the side of the cliff, but all we found were rows upon rows of stacked shelves full of tattered scrolls and dusty tomes.

"What if all of this is just a wild goose chase and there is no treasure?" Nyx offered with a tone of disappointment while she accentuated her frustration with a shrug towards the dismal surroundings of the chamber.

Libraries with stacked shelves were usually prime places for hiding secret doors, but it was clear that the rotten planks within hid nothing behind their open-back arrangement. Tapping the embedded stones affixed to the mountainside of the tower revealed nothing unusual. There was no entrance here to be found. While Nyx unraveled our set of maps upon the counter, I removed the private note the old monk had given me and handed it to her to read for herself.

"What is this?" she asked with confusion while noticing my name scribbled across its rim.

"The old cleric gave me his set of keys willingly, along with this message," I confessed as Nyx read its contents with a measure of scrutiny and dismay.

***

Ash, I discovered that the relic you retrieved from Vale's collection contains the imprint of a map, but if you are reading this letter, I would assume you have already figured that out on your own.

I have been taken hostage by the members of the cult, and just learned that Vale had killed himself, rather than facing torture and having his mind stolen at the hands of these deranged cultists, which is a fate I now face alone.

Beware of a witch called Lilith, who poses as their high priestess. I have sabotaged her means of escape from these mines in an effort to foil her plans, for she must be stopped at all costs.

If this message gets to you in time, try to find me. If not, then I hope you will not bear me ill will for having entangled you in this scandal which put us in such grave peril. I will have my faithful street urchins deliver this letter to my contact at the Abbey, of whom you can trust.

As the blessed Builders say in their scriptures:

Keep the fires of your faith burning,
seek not a lock of iron
but a key of stone
to reveal your destiny.

~ Beren ~
***

This was certainly a lot for Nyx to take in, so I informed her that I knew that my old acquaintance was already dead by his own hand, as I had left him in the poisonous garden we had discovered deep within the mines. The rest of the note was old news, of course, except for the end where he quoted scripture; for I knew for a fact that Beren was anything but a religious man.

"I know that look, Ash; what are you thinking?" Nyx inquired as she gazed into my eyes while my thoughts were racing through Beren's written words.

"This last line has to be a coded message he meant for me to decipher," I conceded. Reading it again and referring to the maps we had made from the skull and bronze block, I realized there was a chance we may have miscalculated. "Let's climb higher," I suggested to my apprentice as we found the landing for yet another flight of stairs.

Reaching the far wall we saw that the stairwell had collapsed; though, oddly enough, the section which had failed was entirely missing from the room. The joists and supports were left broken and snapped as if someone had hastily detached them.

"Either the bracings failed and they removed the mess, or more likely, it was intentionally demolished," Nyx surmised; and by the look of the way the carpentry was pulled apart, it wasn't a professional job. Likely the clerics of the order had done this damage themselves to keep the upper floors from being accessed.

As well prepared thieves, it was a simple task to hook a rope and scale our way up to the 3rd floor repository. The room above proved to have been vacated for many untold years, which appeared to be the original Bishops chamber; long abandoned and left carpeted by a thick layer of dust. The aged floorboards creaked beneath our feet as we made our way inside while we scanned the room for clues. Another makeshift stairway continued upward from the shattered remnants below, which ascended to the narrow bell tower stationed high above. Whatever we were meant to find, it had to be in this room.

A podium stood at the center of the chamber, littered with loose notes written in scripted text. A single bed, more regal than most within the abbey, sat alone at the outer wall covered by the veil of its rotting canopy. Against the farthest end was left but a single door, but in all respects, there was nothing of value that we could find. I peered through the mottled panes of the window set beside the bed, only to realize there was something odd about the layout of the chamber.

"Keep the fires of your faith burning, seek not a lock of iron but a key of stone to reveal your destiny," I repeated softly as I reread the last lines of Beren's note.

"Ah, this must be what we're looking for," Nyx jumped over to the heavy oak door bound in iron as she fiddled with the ring of keys, and promptly attempted to open the lock. Using the same old key she had used to open the door to the tower, she set it within the latch.

"Nyx, don't!" I called as I turned my gaze up from Beren's note to see what she was doing, knowing I had no time to spare in stopping her. In an instant, my dagger flew through the air and pinned the keyring in place before she could finish turning the lock. Jumping back, Nyx unsheathed her fighting dagger in alarm as she glared back at me in anger. The edge of my blade had sliced her hand, and I saw the flare of distrust bloom in her eyes.

"So you want the treasure all for yourself, is that the way it's going to be, Ash?" she stepped aside to take a defensive stance as a pair of throwing blades slipped into her palm.

Nyx had mistaken my intent and I regretted having injured her, but my honed reaction was automatic. By the look in her eyes, I could see that the young rogue was a moment away from pressing an attack to regain her initiative, and I was fully aware that Nyx could handle herself in a fight. One false move could leave me mortally wounded and left bleeding out on the floor, and she had proven to possess a deadly aim with her throwing knives. There was little I could do but to drop my defense, but knowing that it would be a fatal mistake should she decide it was an act of trickery.

"I didn't mean to hurt you, Nyx," I began to apologize, but she held up her bleeding hand with its long red gash from my blade as proof to the contradiction of my words. Her eyes became cold as ice as they slowly began to flood with a blend of hatred and confusion; which was a deadly mix for anyone who stood upon the receiving end of her volatile temper.

"Is this some trick... did you just use me to get into the abbey and decide you would be better off walking out of here without having to split our shares?" She accused with disdain creeping into her voice, "You've made it quite clear that you're a lone wolf, Ash, and I've just been an inconvenience to you all this time."

Her reaction was far more defensive than I could have predicted, which caused me to consider if she might have been a covert agent assigned by our late Guild Master, all along; whose covert mission was not actually to assist me as an apprentice, but to spy on me and my contacts. Maybe that was why Koda had been so insistent about knowing her whereabouts before our heated duel in Beren's shop. There was always the chance Nyx had been on Koda's payroll and had been working undercover all this time as a ruse. I couldn't dismiss the thought that Nyx may have been his backup plan; and even though Koda was now out of the picture, she was still pursuing his agenda as ordered.

Instead of lowering my guard, I pulled out my sparring blade tucked within my forearm cuff, and began to recall my aching suspicions which kept nagging at me as to how Nyx had walked straight into the heart of the spider cult without meeting any resistance. Perhaps she had been in league with Koda's plans to cooperate with the Lord Regent of Blacktide and his dastardly plan to overthrow the city. It began to make sense now, realizing that she had been pretending all this time to be my associate just so that she could gather information towards their objectives. The night of the Governor's party, Koda had sent the guild into the manor to protect his confidential asset, Nyx; and also the reason our esteemed Guild Master had sent me in alone to accost their priestess, Lilith, to meet my end.

Had the witch priestess killed me, I would have been conveniently out of the way; which Koda admitted had been his plan all along. I also had to consider that Nyx had also been far too eager to report back to Koda the moment we arrived back in Stilgrave, and I now saw that she had only played along with my plans so as not to raise any suspicions. She had left me to face Koda alone as we fought in the cellar and acted so surprised when I had returned the victor of our confrontation. Little did she know that I had retained one of the poison samples we had found in the sewers and coated the arrowhead of my crossbow with its contents, which was why Koda had lost his strength halfway through the fight, and saved me from a sticky end.

Had I been such an arrogant fool to have been duped all along by a pretty face who had acted so eager to be my apprentice? I had to admit, Nyx had played her part well.

"Put down your blades, and tell me if you've been working for Koda all this time," I demanded coldly; although Nyx seemed baffled by my question.

"Of course I was working for the Guild Master, by his direct orders," she admitted without hesitation, but her tone was still perplexed.

"So, you admit that your assignment was to spy on me and gather information for Koda, to help him on his scheme to overthrow the city Governor," I implicated her as a participant in Koda's strategy to see what she might reveal. However, she tried to deny the glaring facts set before her.

"What in the seven hells are you talking about, Ash?" She blurted with a sideways glance which I found hard to read. Nyx seemed genuinely confused by my accusation.

I could usually see through a false denial, but it took me a nervous moment to consider if I had overestimated my position. Nyx and I had been through a great deal of stress these past few weeks, and we had faced death several times over while covering each others' backs; yet here we were, ready to spill each other's blood. It didn't make sense; perhaps I was wrong in my suspicions, having over-processed the scenario and mislabeled the actors in this unfolding conspiracy. I had fallen victim to the poison of paranoia and had reached the point of not knowing whom to trust.

I let my long blade fall to the floor, where its tip pierced into the rotted wood. Having seen me drop my guard and the flash of turmoil filling my eyes in the seconds to follow, Nyx took the initiative and stepped forward with her blade raised. I realized my mistake too late and withdrew with a lurch in reverse until my back was flat against the stone wall. Nyx was a skilled fighter and had her sharp blade against my throat in an instant; leaving me to await the cruel stroke that would finally end this desperate struggle my life had been.

She stared into my eyes with the warm blood from her wounded hand dripping from her wrist. However, rather than uttering spiteful words before ending my life, she instead, pressed forward and kissed me. In all honesty, that was the last thing I had expected. Her sharpened blade left resting under my chin convinced me to comply, although I felt surprised by my own willingness to embrace her affection. It was an enlightening moment to discover I had misread her far longer than I had thought.

"There now ...you see, Ash, I'm not here to spy on you or engaged on Koda's behalf; I look after myself!" Nyx pressed with a soft tone that clearly illustrated her intentions, "I've grown to care about you, but you attacked me ...and I need to know why," she demanded while her blade did not waiver from my neck.

"I would need to show you," I offered as I gently pushed her dagger away from my throat while she leaned back. Handing her Beren's note, I pointed out the last line he had written within, "of all the things I thought I had taught you, Nyx, was that you need to practice a measure of patience, but you were too eager to press onward," I scolded as we approached the door wrapped in iron, where I dislodged my dagger and carefully removed the key from the lock.

After a moment of tracing a seam along the door, I noted a false edging set within the frame, which ran directly upward into the ceiling. A measured ration of scraping at the plaster revealed a concealed wire threaded through a covered channel hidden beneath the stonework.

"What is that?" Nyx asked as she wrapped her wounded hand while I referred to the cryptic note my old friend had left for me to decipher.

Beren had done a great deal of research on the Spider Cult and the Order of the Builders; and when he phrased *'seek not a lock of iron'* within the text, he was trying to warn me of a trap, which wouldn't be immediately obvious to anyone else who may have read his letter. Tracing the hidden cable upstairs all the way to the belfry, we found that it had been rigged to the giant bell by a simple dead-release mechanism which would have sent it crashing through the rotted floors and crushing anything in its path. Having pointed this danger out to her, Nyx finally put away her blade, having realized that my brash actions had saved us both.

"So he left you a clue?" Nyx ceded to the fact that her wild recklessness could have cut our evening short in a most catastrophic manner.

Retreating back into the bishop's quarters, we came across a small hearth tucked into the wall, which we thought was strangely placed since its flue would have had to be inset into the side of the cliff.

"*Keep the fires burning,*" I repeated again, noting the empty hearth. Grabbing some bits of paper and decayed furniture, I snapped them into shards and stuffed the splintered wood inside the small fireplace.

With a little help from my flint, I was able to get the tinder to light. As the fire burned for several moments, we patiently waited for some secret door or mechanism to activate with quiet expectation; but alas, no such portal materialized.

"What does this last line mean?" Nyx questioned with

confusion, "...*but a key of stone, to reveal your destiny*," she read aloud, "I don't see any stone keys lying around."

We had thoroughly searched the room, including the pile of ash in the hearth, wondering what we had missed, but it wasn't until Nyx had repeated the quote that I almost hit myself for being so naive.

"It wasn't an actual key fashioned out of rock, but this!" I pointed at the arch of masonry over the small fireplace, where at its crest lay the central keystone.

Testing it with delicate fingers, I felt the central brick give way as it pressed inward. A series of clicks could be heard echoing from beyond the wall while Nyx and I stood back as a crack formed in the mortar around the hearth. We watched with quiet patience as the frame of the fireplace slowly withdrew into the darkness lying beyond.

"And, as a reminder... let's not rush this, shall we?" I warned my apprentice with a cautious smile, lest any more traps should await us within the hidden passage.

As the hearth fully receded, its central pit unlocked and dropped into a depository bowl. It took but a moment for the dwindling embers to ignite the contents set within. Though dried by age, the waxed wick lining the wall began to flare and its illumination raced down the passage which bore deep into the side of the mountain. Nyx and I gave each other a wary glance mixed with a dose of elation as we crept inside, wondering what we might find.

It was prudent at this point for us to refer to the drawing of the map we had acquired from the metal block, as it was our only clue to the path we should follow within. It wasn't long before the main passage branched off into several avenues, each splitting in different directions. Deciphering the safest route to reach the central chamber displayed on our graph was proving to be far more problematic than we had first anticipated. Where passages were shown to intersect on our diagram, none actually existed herein;

which left my accomplice and I at a loss.

Taking the small lantern we had obtained from the tower entry, we made our way down the main hall when a glint caught my eye hanging high upon the wall.   Upon inspection, I found it was another spider emblem embossed with gold leaf which had caught the light.   The question was; what was it doing here in the secret depths of the holy abbey?   The Order of the Builders and the sect of the Golden Spiders were opposing religions, and its presence here made no rational sense.

Backtracking to check the adjacent passages, they proved to be free of any such secret markers.   As perplexing as it was, we could only conclude that the map sculpted from the bronze block must possess a secondary purpose. Further along, we crossed several more passages, and yet again a single spider emblem hidden in the masonry guided our way.

"This architecture looks ancient, similar to the style that was used in the underground city back in Blacktide," Nyx mentioned as she perceived a notable change in the decorative design of the masonry.

We followed the narrow hall as we delved deeper; the interlocking passages creating a virtual maze through many rising and descending corridors until the tiny golden markers eventually led us to the exterior portal to the central chamber shown upon our map. We were so lost in the labyrinth by this point that the diagram we had drawn from the wax sculpture would have been nearly useless without the spider emblems to help steer our way.   Now standing before us was a circular door with a diamond-shaped keyhole at its center, accompanied by several more combination rings stationed above it.

"Well, I think you were right about this place being identical to that ancient architecture under the Regents castle," I conceded to Nyx as she withdrew the brass block from her leather pouch.

As she had suspected, it fit within the device perfectly; although once it was inserted, there was no apparent way to remove it as it fell flush into the mechanism. The dials set above it were familiar, for each facet displayed the engraving of a different face depending on which of the dials were matched. Each ring was separated, which spun the forehead, eyes, nose, cheeks, and chin; of which all of these separate designs were uniquely adorned in their own style of artistry.

"Well, this is certainly familiar; but are you sure you want to do this?" Nyx inquired, as we both knew what happened the last time we fiddled with an ancient lock of this variety.

If these tunnels suddenly flooded by some underground spring, there was simply no way we could reach the exit in time; but trap or not, we were pressed to discover what might lie in the chamber beyond. Nyx began to slowly turn each ring on the sculpture, while I noticed that there were eight figures represented on the dials; akin to the legs of a spider. Referring again at our map, I drew out the extensions of the passages we had passed, which fanned out from this central chamber, and within this drafted image, it revealed the iconic symbol of a spider's web. Recalling the facial image from the pair of scrolls she had replicated before, Nyx lined up the dials accordingly; and we stood there nervously while each of the appropriate rings set into place as bronze pins locked within the metal bar inserted at its center.

Quite suddenly, the ground beneath our feet quaked as securing bolts were released and the giant door receded as one solid piece that slowly sank into the floor before us. We cautiously stepped into the antechamber as countless specs of light reflected from the ceiling above. Peering upwards revealed that the roof of the chamber was covered with thousands of the spider emblems, each gilded in brilliant gold. The round chamber was lined with several stone sarcophagi, with but a single short pedestal standing within the center of the room.

Nyx let out a sigh of disappointment, as she had been hoping to find a long-forgotten treasure trove hoarded away by the clerics over the centuries. I too, had my own anticipation towards that end, but one thing that I had learned over the years was to keep my expectations low; especially so when exploring mysterious crypts. Each of the eight tombs present were sealed and appeared to be of an exquisite quality that was usually reserved for royalty. Nyx made her way to the pedestal upon which sat a single bound tome.

"Ash, look at this," she called after I had stepped away to inspect the lids of the curious vaults.

Walking back over to where she stood, we could see its hard leather cover was embossed with the emblem of the Builders hammer, which oddly enough, also bore the familiar stamp of the spider cult upon the image of the gavel. Flipping the dusty volume open, we found names of the royal families from the surrounding region tracing back several generations; although noting that all of them were of women. Nyx shook her head in confusion, trying to understand what it all meant. I held up the lamp and pointed out another matter of interest.

"That image of the female face adorned with the ocean waves and tentacles is sculpted upon every one of the graves in this mausoleum," I mention while motioning her over to see the carvings for herself.

"These coffins are of all the sovereign queens who had ruled over the lands for the past several centuries," Nyx yielded, having recognized many of their titles, "...but there are no kings buried here."

It was an odd discovery, especially when we delved deeper into the scripted text. The passages within revealed that the theology of the original Architects and their disciples had believed in caring for the poor, while their own clergy had lived humble lives; and at one time there existed an equal sharing of wealth among its citizens. Drawn within its pages was the familiar figure of their female deity whose bounty came from the sea, and noted that the women of each royal family had once held the honor of representing their goddess as a living icon of generosity and abundance during lavish ceremonies held as a blessing to the inhabitants of these coastal regions.

These affluent figures in their social order assembled to speak their hearts and strived to create a better society for the common people, and thus, encouraged acts of charity so that their newfound kingdoms could prosper. They saw that equality of wealth and education supported the overall health of their society, which greatly reduced the disparity and suffering amongst its populace. Before the time of the Reaver Wars, their men busied themselves as they toiled in the mines and quarried stone to build their keeps. In their roles, the women and homemakers gathered throughout the region and preached a philosophy of kindness, and the obligations of their rulers towards the welfare of their subjects. This ideology was soon adopted by the women of nobility who entered into a pact among themselves to create a culture of prosperity for all.

However, such a covenant did not sit well for the kings, their dukes, or lords and noblemen, whose blackened souls were enshrouded by greed, and they sought to quell these 'covens' as they were known. They conspired to condemn these public figures and assemblies as dissidents to their entitled rule. It was a battle Ash knew all too well, in this ugly duel between the impoverished and those who leech far more than they could ever need.

Nyx and I looked through the elaborate illustrations of their goddess, shown sitting upon a rocky shore before a turbulent sea as she wove fishing nets for her followers. However, the following pages revealed a much darker series of events which had led these high born women to be entombed within this hidden grave. It appeared that the worship of a benevolent female goddess did not sit well with the kings and royal monarchs who became wary of their queens possessing a power greater than their own in the eyes of the people. In their envy, they had feared that the admiration of their subject's leaned towards their royal wives, instead of themselves; so in an act of jealousy, the kings of the territory conspired to persecute their ancient traditions of devotion to a female deity, and replaced such piety with a far more militant form of rule.

From that point onward, women in their era were no longer treated as equals to men, and thus, condemned to be faced with prejudice and suppression. Their queens were stripped of their titles and silenced in all matters of rule from the royal courts, for fear that they would resurrect the charitable ways of the past that might sabotage the iron grip their tyrannical Kings now held against their subjects. Their social order suffered while men were ordained to hold supremacy and privilege, where women did not. Furthermore, lesser affluent families were stripped of their wealth, leaving their offspring destitute to beg in the streets. Once they had attained power of one gender over another, the arrogance of their leaders became ever more oppressive, for fear their realms would slip again towards the influence of empathy and compassion once held by the ruling class. Their system of tradition had been utterly shattered, although we found it curious to discover that the core faith of both the Holy Builders and the elusive Spider Cult had been one in the same.

"As recorded here, the women of the royal households buried in this tomb were once known as The Weavers," Nyx conceded as she read on in fascination of the words next to the image of a maiden braiding a fisherman's net.

"And were eventually demonized through propaganda to be titled as witches who wove dark magics, and over time their old ritualistic practices were twisted by wild tales. Members of the spider cult came to resent the split factions, who had taken advantage of the poverty and destitution created by their military rule during the era of hardship and regional wars; which ultimately splintered the borders across the northern territories," I reflected while finishing the text.

Both spiders and hammers were ancient symbols of builders; icons that had evolved into very different meanings over the ages. Apparently, these crumbling catacombs had existed long before the days of our neighboring coastal cities; by which many had been built upon the ancient ruins of these forgotten realms. Over time, the hammer became a holy symbol of the architects and miners who quarried rock, while the golden spiders became the icon of those undesirables who were forced into the dark recesses of society. For all our efforts, the only item of value within this vault was this bound tome and the historical secrets it held within.

Likely there were gemstones and riches buried within these graves, but even a pair of thieves would not desecrate the place of rest to those who had suffered for the sake of others. It was now clear that the history of this region had been rewritten by the militant rulers in order to conceal their sins, which they hid away in this forgotten crypt. In their struggle for domination and power they had sacrificed those who sought peace, and chose to bury their shameful deeds. In doing so, their descendants had been robbed of their legacy, and left behind to wallow in the shadow of those who would rule them.

Nyx placed the volume in her bag and we navigated our way out through the ancient labyrinth, and back to the tower. It was clear by now that the line of ordained bishops and priests of the abbey had been keeping this dark secret hidden for untold generations. Royal warmongers and totalitarian rule had thoroughly stripped any sense of equality among the inhabitants of these lands, which had led to an unjust distribution of wealth during their pursuits of conflict and social disparity. Our forgotten history had been diluted into tales of myth and folklore, where the commoners became stuck in their station in life, which was denoted by their gender or status. Within our cities, there were those who struggled, and those who did not; by which cruel circumstances had molded their lives was nothing more than their anointment at birth.

It was a cold and misty night as we made our way back through the fog to the Crimson quarter under the cover of darkness. Tired and exhausted, Nyx and I strode into the Thieves Guild side by side. With proof of our tall tale in hand, we addressed our fellow rogues and conferred over recent events which had led to Koda's death and exposed his intentions of selling out the guild. The fact that Koda had already informed the members that my apprentice and I had met our fate in Blacktide was reason enough to question his candor, and only helped to further expose his deceit. When their questions were addressed and fully satisfied, we turned to the issue of Sir Ryan, the Lord Protector and Regent, whom the guild had kept captive during this period.

Many members of the guild wanted to slay him and send his body back to the Duchess in pieces, but we warned them that such a savage deed would only act as a catalyst for war. Inciting such a situation would not only bring down the wrath of Blacktide and its legions, but also the vengeance of the City Watch against our Guild. After our argument was heard, I was finally able to convince them that the Lord Regent should be released so that he may return to his territory in the north. Both Nyx and I met with the Regent in his holding cell, and in short words, we warned him of what had transpired in Blacktide and the full tapestry of the political plot we had unveiled; both of his conspiracy to overthrow Stilgrave, and of the corruption of their royal rule. After our one-sided conversation with the nobleman, I had a fellow member of the guild retrieve the same spirited horse I had used the night of the party when the Regent and I had first met; where it was left waiting outside the guildhall. Afterward, I sent a courier to the Governor's mansion to let him know where they could receive their missing diplomat, whom they could find at the city square that morning.

At the break of dawn, the Regent of Blacktide was to be released from his confinement and led to his awaiting steed, and was provided a route of the city streets so he could make his way to the harbor where a ship waited to return him home. I knew it was a risk to let the Lord Regent go free, for he and his traitorous accomplices might still try to betray the Governor, regardless of the leverage we held against him. Nyx, herself, was not alone in this concern, which she voiced as we left the guildhall and made our way back to my private apartment that overlooked the city square. Soon the light of the morning sun rose over Stilgrave as the gallop of hooves upon the cobblestone echoed through the city slums while the Regent made his hasty escape from his captors on the borrowed steed. Governor Oren had already arrived at the square with a troop of city guardsmen to await the appearance of the visiting Regent, who had mysteriously disappeared the week prior. Nyx sat beside me on the sill as we gazed down from the open window of my flat upon the scene which unfolded below.

It wasn't until that moment that Nyx finally recognized the narrow section of road where I had instructed her to place the carcasses of the wild rabbits within puddles of the sticky tree sap the previous eve. From our vantage point, we saw the Regents horse racing through the twisting alleys along the route he was provided; but upon reaching the route fork, instead of turning towards the docks, he reined his mount towards the Ivory district. As the Regent reached the lip of the city square, his horse suddenly reared when it turned the blind corner and a flock of hungry crows were startled from their feeding on the remains of the dead hares Nyx had adhered to the cobblestones. The governor and his band of guards waiting at the crossroads watched in alarm as the Lord Regent was violently thrown from his horse and came crashing down upon the hard cobblestones, breaking his neck. Several sentries rushed forward to the Regent's aid through the brood of cackling crows, only to find his body broken and twisted by the fatal fall.

Nyx spun her puzzled gaze towards me with a curious expression in her eyes as I turned from the window to sit in my armchair, and casually poured myself a drink from the last spot of brandy my old friend Beren had left behind. Considering the unfortunate circumstances, our Governor now possessed legitimate reason for sending an envoy to the Duchess of Blacktide, to inform them of the most unfortunate accident they publicly witnessed, which had taken the Regents life, along with a forged letter they would eventually find along with a volume of evidence stuffed within his saddlebags, revealing that her Royal Steward had been indulging himself with cheap wine and the many disreputable talents of the local whorehouses in the Red district over the previous days.

By my hand, another letter would eventually reach the head priest of the abbey to inform them that the secrets of their hidden past had been revealed; and that it would be in their best interest to persuade the Governor and nobles of the upper districts to consider the consequences if such sacred testaments were disclosed to the local commoners. Inclusive, was a stern warning against the Ward's continued abuse against the impoverished and underprivileged peasants of the city, and enticed them to resume the old traditions of charity and kindness to the weary people of the lower quarter who had bled to build the gilded walls in which the highborn now reside. It was a choice they would have to make, or face the repercussions should their current hierarchy of the city become exposed to the populous to the length of their treachery and corruption. Since both Koda and the Lord Regent were now out of the picture, there was little risk that their fellow conspirators here would dare to expose themselves and were destined to quietly slither back under the rock from which they had crawled.

"I'm confused ...how did you know that the Regent would be killed?" Nyx inquired with a genuine look of dismay glowing upon her face, but the answer she received was all too familiar.

"I didn't, actually," I confessed, "but I knew that those of royal blood aren't exactly known for their measure of patience. The Regent could have headed straight for the docks and escaped, but instead, he decided to race like a madman through those narrow alleys; which I presume, was in his desperation to alert his accomplices in the city and rally them before the Governor got word of the plot."

Nyx and I had been through much together, and although we didn't find a treasure trove of priceless artifacts or a king's ransom buried within the ancient crypts; we also didn't come out empty-handed. I sat up and placed the hefty bag of coin which Koda had awarded us for our mission to Blacktide, and plopped it down on the table next to the carved skull, a relic which I had repurposed into a convenient candle holder. Several hundred silver ducats would allow us to live comfortably for quite some time. Nyx and I were both birds of a feather and we weren't about to misspend our capital on excessive extravagance meant solely to impress the snobs and shallow socialites of the upper classes. It wasn't our style.

Nyx moved towards me with the grace of a cat and placed her knee between my legs where I sat; pressing her face towards mine as I leaned back, feeling caught like a mouse in a trap.

"You know, the members of our Order were talking about electing you as their new Guild Master," Nyx mentioned with a curious smile as she lowered my hood to brush my hair aside, "What do you say to that?"

"I imagine it might be a challenge to manage that band of misfits; yourself included," I countered with a dash of humor.

"Well, now that all of that unpleasant business is out of the way, let's talk about what happened in the Bishops tower, shall we?" she inquired softly with a hungry look in her eyes.

"Oh, *hmm,* you mean," I began to stutter with a shade of embarrassment when Nyx referred to the brief moment of intimacy we had shared in that heated moment, "...I was meaning to ask why you did that?"

"Well, it takes a proper thief to steal a kiss, don't you agree?" Nyx smiled as she leaned in to pilfer yet another, though this time, I was a willing victim of her warm embrace. That evening, our shadows moved as one in the dancing candlelight, and from that night on, and for many more to follow, there were two less thieves prowling through the dark streets of the city.

About the Author

Michel Savage has been devoted to writing throughout his career. If one reads between the lines, they will find his novels revolve around the reminder that we are only borrowing our small place on this planet but for a brief period of time, and to take responsibility for the environment, for one another, and all other living creatures with which we share this world. And in doing so, hopefully planting a seed in our conscience of the importance to preserve what is left of the wilds, our untainted woodlands, and ever-dwindling rain forests.

He has had the blessing of sharing his stories and artwork around the globe, which is a gift in itself, and would encourage others not to waste too much of their lives chasing someone else's dreams, but to follow their own.

One of the most valuable lessons he has learned in his years is that there are far more important things in life than power and money, such as kindness, compassion, and consideration towards others.

...share that thought if you will.

Also by
Michel Savage

Shadoworld
Shadow of the Sun

On a distant, slowly rotating world, Bronze Age tribes must migrate thought their lives to avoid the long cold death of nightfall. As of late, strange events have been deeply troubling the tribal elders; revealing evidence perhaps, that something is lurking on the dark side.

As for a pair of young misfits, the ancient mystery is about to unfold; to reveal their peoples forgotten past, buried deep within the underworld, shrouded in the shadow of the sun.

Shadoworld
Shadows Gate

Asra found himself alone in the middle of the barren sands, unable to remember who he was or how he had gotten there. Saved by a caravan of traveling gypsies, he entered into an exotic world of dancing acrobats, fortune tellers, and mystics who performed their skills for cheering crowds across the desert empires.

However, his destiny would change the day he stumbled upon a forbidden shrine to find a mythical creature entombed beneath its shattered ruins. Promises were whispered and a dark pact was made with the ancient demon; a bond of magic that would lead him on a perilous journey to reveal his forgotten past.

Outlaws of Europa

The 2nd moon of Jupiter has been turned into a prison planet where for several generations, robot drone ships have been dumping the scum of the universe and are patrolled by a ring of advanced security satellites that would destroy any vessel attempting to land. After a century of research, old core samples from the ice revealed that the frozen oceans of Europa held the base element of an immortality drug that can extend the human lifespan several-fold. Now greedy military corporations race for this new fountain of youth, only to discover they can't disable the orbiting sentry that was programmed to protect itself at all costs.

It appears the Confederation has a problem. How do they get past a self-evolving AI that has appointed itself as Warden, and furthermore, retake a planet roaming with Earth's worst criminals who might well be immortal themselves.

Rebels of Alpha Prime

For the past century, the military has exercised its control over the citizens of Earth, having deceived the public of their true intentions for generations while the 2nd moon of Jupiter had been transformed into a prison planet. In a desperate attempt to cover their illicit operations, the Confederation Council sent a group of recruits on a secret mission to the forsaken wastelands of Europa to retake the penal colony, who discovered they had been used as expendable puppets while marked as registered convicts left abandoned upon the frozen moon.

Having thwarted the plans of the Confederation while avoiding certain death by the bloodied hands of the local inmates, they evade the clutches of the corrupt military operatives and escape with their lives. Now they must save Earth's interstellar colonists on a distant world and fend off the rogue Confederate troops that appear hell-bent on seeking revenge.

Hellbot
Battle Planet

Tranquility was one of those out of the way planets in a system far out of reach from the normal space lanes.   Loners, dreamers ...whoever they were, chose to colonize this world. Thirty cycles ago something went terribly wrong.   It was rumored their terraformer reactor went critical, and few escaped the chain reaction that clouded the atmosphere with a planet-wide sand storm. A decade of hard labor evaporated overnight. What wasn't buried under the ocean of sand was left to fry under the twin suns.

Human explorers began to wander back into the forgotten zone. No one knew of the machines that had evolved, or the war that raged beyond the edge of the universe ...where mankind did not belong.

A Couple of Zeros

 Jacob was an autistic young man with a child-like mind, cared for by his sickly mother who stayed with him in their tiny rundown apartment. Mia was a kind and spirited girl who lived across the way. They were a couple of nobodies from a small Southern town, living at the outer edge of the suburbs in a decaying housing complex. Their neighbors were the frail and forgotten, the elderly and lost families who were all too familiar with the strife and struggle of keeping food on the table and trying to make ends meet.

Jacob's mother lay dying, and nobody knew what might happen to him when she passed away. One evening, a shiny black car rolled up their dirt driveway and the boy heard a sharp knock at his door. Little did Jacob know that fate had come calling and would turn his small world upside down.

Forgotten Future

At the edge of the world an impossible relic from the fables of antiquity has risen from the frozen wastelands of Antarctica. Professor Logan and his exploration team rush to investigate this historic find, but this unique discovery puts their lives in peril when they unearth the remnants of a long forgotten civilization left buried beneath the ice.

Within the twisting labyrinths below the melting glaciers they uncover an ancient culture which had perished from a mysterious cataclysm. They soon realize that a polar shift had triggered the destruction which now threatens a global disaster that could sling our modern world back into the Dark Ages.

Broken Mirror
Apophis 2029

Hurtling through space was an enormous tumbling rock known as MN4 our astronomers affectionately named after an ancient Egyptian god of destruction. Asteroid Apophis was the talk of the year that every scientific community on Earth was aware of, though its flyby in April 2029 was to be nothing more than a spectacular celestial event; but as warring nations were locked in global conflict, our civilization was unprepared for the devastation that followed in its wake.

Several years after governments fell and society dissolved a ragged pack of survivors stumble upon the buried truth, revealing what circumstances had led to the aftermath that ensued; leaving them to question their struggle to salvage what few splintered shards were left of our world that would forever define our bitter legacy.

Project EVE

In the late 1940s after the 2nd World War, a classified government program was created in order to explore the military use of psychics to gain an advantage for their soldiers during armed conflict. At a remote laboratory in the mountains, a secret compound comprised of several hundred test subjects were trained to enhance their abilities with the goal of achieving the skills of telepathy and mind control.

Assigned to investigate this covert project, Walter Grant found himself entangled in a web of conspiracy and deceit when he discovered that the residents of the colony were being held captive by the scientists who had hidden the ugly truth behind their dangerous experiments.

At the heart of the project was a girl named Eve, whose extraordinary mind held the key, a child who would prove to them why humanity could not handle such power.

Witchwood
The Harvesting

Every day around the world hundreds of people go missing without a trace. Year after year their numbers add up to millions of lost souls who are never to be seen again; and their numbers keep climbing ...this is where many of them went.

7 - The Fall

A strange and unexplained phenomenon led to the fall of civilization. It began on an evening like any other. The Sun had set on another day, but by the next morning, humanity realized that there were no more stars in the sky. Somehow, overnight, mankind had become alone in the universe and only an AI program knew why.

The Faerylands Trilogy

Faerylands I
The Grey Forest

Long, long ago the Faerie had roamed free, but for countless centuries now the fey themselves have remained unseen; hidden and withdrawn, shrouded within the boundaries of the Evermore. But just how they became imprisoned there was a mystery their own elders had forgotten or refused to speak of, and a subject of taboo among the ancients.

The Elvenborn had become a dying race, and now a strange and dreadful blight was encroaching upon their sanctuary. Ivy knew there was something terribly wrong with her world, something unspeakable her kind were hiding from. The Faerylands were vanishing, and she had to find out why.

Faerylands II
Soulstorm Keep

Many centuries after the passing of mankind, the blight known as the Craven still lingered, lurking within the shadows; a dark hunger awaiting its chance to consume what little was left of their fragile world. Only one among the Elves knew the true face of their enemy, with the knowledge to awaken the Undying and save the Faerylands before the living veil of the Evermore was forever lost.

Ivy Elvenborn was presented with an impossible quest - one that would take her on a distant journey to the Tower of Madness to seek the guidance of an ancient relic guarded within, but it would lead her to trespass beyond the gates of a forgotten castle; a ghostly fortress of despair where no living Faerie had ever tread. If she failed in her task, the entire race of Fey would be the last of their kind.

Faerylands III
Sorrowblade

Untold ages ago the race of Elves were cast to the four winds, forced to dwell in the underworld within the veil of the Evermore to protect the Tree of Life. Split into separate clans, their dying race withdrew to the far reaches of the world. There also existed a darker faction of Elves which had burrowed deep into the depths of the earth, evolving into the seven houses of the Drow. From the seed of the Elders came the children of the Faerie with a dire legacy to fulfill; a generation of Elvenborn whose destiny was to save the Faerylands.

Almost forgotten among the Fey were the whispered legends of a warrior priestess from the Sisterhood of Blood; a young outcast trained in the forbidden sorcery of an accursed cult known as the Obsidian Order. These maidens skilled in both spell and blade were charged with battling the dark and terrible blight known as the Craven which infested their world. This is their saga, for without their noble sacrifice all hope was lost.

Faerylands Special Edition
Ivory
the Dreamkeepers

The Elvenborn were bestowed the task of healing their realm, a land left in chaos by the hands of men.

Limerick was but a simple bard who stumbled into an epic quest that would test his courage and take him beyond the edges of the Faerylands. High in the mountains sat the ruins of Aldana, where the spirits of the forest gathered to bring balance to the world and end the dreadful blight of the Craven.

Along this journey, the young bard would learn that everything is not as it seems, and that dreams are but a shadow of something real.

Artwork from the Faerylands series available online
Enter the Grey Forest

www.**GreyForest**.com